First Part

THAT SUMMER

A SENSE OF THE BEGINNING

Norbert Gstrein

A SENSE OF
THE BEGINNING

Translated from the German by Julian Evans

MACLEHOSE PRESS
QUERCUS · LONDON

First published in the German language as *Eine Ahnung vom Anfang*
by Hanser Verlag, München, in 2013

First published in Great Britain in 2016 by
MacLehose Press
An imprint of Quercus Publishing Ltd
Carmelite House
50 Victoria Embankment
London EC4Y 0DZ

An Hachette UK company

This translation was supported by the
Austrian Federal Ministry of Education, Arts and Culture.

ISBN (TPB) 978 0 85705 358 9
ISBN (Ebook) 978 1 78429 036 8

2 4 6 8 10 9 7 5 3 1

Designed and typeset in 12¼/16¼ Roos by Patty Rennie
Printed and bound in Great Britain by Clays Ltd, St Ives plc

The LORD shall fight for you,
and ye shall hold your peace.
Exodus 14:14

1

THE SUMMER I WANT TO TELL YOU ABOUT, ALONG WITH EVERY-
thing that came before and after it, is ten years ago now, but even
though I must have forgotten a good deal of it, I feel I can still
trust my memory. For a long time afterwards I didn't go out to
the house by the river which I associate so vividly with Daniel and
those weeks we spent there as if no other world existed. It's my
house, but to call it that is something of a euphemism. The truth
is that it's just the remains of an old watermill that had belonged
to my extended family for generations – a ruin, no more, that I
acquired in a flight of sentimentality because suddenly, one day, it
was offered to me and otherwise would have been auctioned off.
Despite the fact that I'm still paying off the loan, it was, with the
land that came with it, practically a gift, as the saying goes, albeit
one of very modest proportions – remote from any built-up area,
a long way from town, and far enough too from the nearest village, not far upstream, which started encroaching on the Au with
its new housing estate a long while ago, that when you sit out on
the veranda on a summer's day, let your mind wander and picture
a steamer panting upstream against the current, coming into view
around the bend downriver and slipping past you like a ghost ship,
with its passengers standing waving at the rail, you do feel you're
in a different world, or at least on a different continent.

I thought I would never use the building, or even get as far
as restoring it so that, though not actually habitable, it could at

least offer me a roof over my head, and it went against the grain with me to buy anything just for the sake of acquiring it; but the thought that it might fall into someone else's hands clinched it. I wanted it, and my justification was that all I was doing was "holding things together", although when I thought about what lay hidden behind those "things", the only "thing" I felt clear about was that they might mean anything, and not just material things. About the place itself I had hardly any memories, except for one: I had been there once as a child when the hay was brought in and had sat high up and proudly with my cousins on top of the hay cart's load, looking out over the wide fields jolting sluggishly beneath me as the cow pulled it home. Apart from that there was very little that connected me to the place, even though it's the part of the country my mother's side of the family comes from. From the house it's a short walk to the spot where, before I was born, my grandfather was hit by a motorcycle and killed, and further down the river, accessible through the gorge when the water level drops, is the cavern where Robert, my brother, took his own life, and also, although no-one knows exactly where it might have been, where my uncle walked into the river. If I climb the low, forested slope behind the house I can also see the meadows which once belonged to my family and where, in the second to last year of the war, an American bomber that had been shot down crash-landed in flames. As soon as I glimpse them I have my mother's story about the event in my head again. She was eight years old and had run with the other school-children to the place where the plane had gone down. They had seen it on fire, circling the mountain over to the east — a natural navigation point — and the teacher hadn't been able to keep them in the classroom: they had all dashed out together as the bomber came gliding in, its engines droning, low over the ground. I have a clear image of my mother as a girl, although there are hardly any photos of her from that time and it's only since she died that I have developed an obsession with looking for her in every image that could possibly date from the thirties and forties of the last century. The other weird thing is that I always see myself in those pictures, as if I were the same age as her, still a small boy, and somehow at her side in the summer of 1944, perhaps even unwillingly holding her hand and pulling her along, stumbling behind me.

Since the last stretch of the autobahn opened I have taken to driving out occasionally to the service area, which was built at almost exactly the spot where the plane must have come to a stop when it crash-landed. The autobahn disappears into the mountain directly behind it, so that the village is spared the traffic noise; you can watch endlessly how the tunnel swallows up car after car like some great mouth. I sit there and drink a beer or two at the bar before setting out for home, a drive that I cannot make last longer than a quarter of an hour without the greatest difficulty, which is why the same idea occurs to me every time – why don't I take a room at the motel there and stay the night? I've even got to the point of thinking up an answer, if anyone were ever to ask me why I was staying, but as I make my way to the front desk my courage always deserts me. Nearly everyone who works at the services is from the village, most of them so young they hardly know who I am, but because I don't want to be noticed I tread carefully. One week I'll drive out there on a Monday, the following week on a Thursday, and I'll make sure that one time it's before the evening shift finishes and the next time after, so I can hope with some certainty that I won't come face to face with the same people too often. It's no more than a couple of kilometres from the service area to the place where I leave my car when I want to go out to the house by the river – I don't even have to get back onto the autobahn, there's a separate exit – but in normal circumstances I might only once every six months or so have the thought that I should stop by to check everything is O.K., or simply to sit outside the front door for half an hour and watch the river flow by.

Which is to say that not having had much to do with the house and everything for a very long time was probably partly why I thought I had seen Daniel's picture in the newspaper. I had gone to dinner at Bruckner's, as I did every Tuesday and Friday in term time, and unusually for me had flicked through the papers that were left out there; I'm certain it was only my casualness that made me think it might be him. There must be some research that explains this "recognition by cursory glance" so I don't need to worry that I can't say why, on closer inspection, I did think so. A particular inclination of the neck? Something in his eyes? The slightly open mouth? The truth is, I don't know. It was a very grainy photo, probably taken by C.C.T.V., his head picked out in a crowd of other people by being circled and brightened. He looked unshaven and was wearing a hoodie too, as though he didn't want to be identified, which would turn out to be one of the reasons why the investigation had put him under scrutiny from the outset.

Three days earlier there had been a bomb threat at the station, and the person in the photograph, the caption said, was being sought in connection with it. The tense atmosphere in the town had already subsided; I couldn't get over how quickly people's lives had returned to normal. A few hours in which a sense of a state of emergency had taken hold, a brief blip of excitement after the first news in the newspaper, then the old lethargy had returned again, the conviction that things – good and bad – did not happen in our town but somewhere else. I was left staring at the newspaper image with a persistent feeling of unreality. It was him, I said to myself, and yet the next second I could have sworn that I was making it up. After an anonymous phone call had been received and an unattended bag discovered in one of the toilets, the whole building, ticket offices, waiting room and all, had been sealed off for hours, with train services brought to a standstill. In the event the bag contained only a dented car battery with a jumble of wiring, which looked far more menacing than it was in reality. Next to the bag there had also been found a piece of paper with cut-out letters of different sizes glued to it, saying, "Repent!", "First and final warning!" and "Next time it will be for real!", followed by an indecipherable scrawl as some sort of would-be signature.

I waited till Agata came to my table. When she did, I asked her to have a look at the photo, because I thought she was the person most likely to understand my suspicions. After all, she had been working at Bruckner's — it would have been her first or second season at the pub — when Daniel had spent every weekend of his last year at school there playing cards.

She put the tray of empty glasses that she was holding down on the next table and sat facing me, leaning on her elbows. Her boss did not like her fraternising excessively with the customers, and in exchange for the privilege of her making an exception for me, I let her treat me like a child when she felt like it. From the way she was sitting I expected as much this time and waited as she reached for the paper. I hardly needed to look at her expression as she peered at me over the top of it: I could picture that mixture of mockery and irritation that enabled her to suffer even the most pathetic show-off in his own parallel universe for a moment or two, before she was called away or decided she had had enough. She was from a small village in Hungary, just across the Burgenland border, and derived a paradoxical pride in being, as a result of that fact, so wholly ready for everything life threw at her subsequently that nothing could surprise her. She tolerated the most extreme oddities in her regular customers, and perhaps it was having to listen to the clientele of single men who turned up at her bar night after night that caused her to develop this particular way of looking at you. It was a look that conveyed a wordless request to get a grip on yourself when you had definitely had a beer too many and were threatening to get abusive, or when your pearls of wisdom started to get on her nerves, or when you decided to tell her the story of your failed marriage one more time, taking out as you did so some crumpled snapshots dating from happier days and assuring her how terrific your kids had turned out to be. She had this absent-minded way of pulling a cigarette out of the pack and lighting it as if she was unaware she was doing it, which was somehow, at the same time, an expression of the most intense concentration. I watched her as she once more accomplished this with one hand and, after her first drag, stared at the photograph again.

"You're not seriously asking me to tell you who that is," she said, narrowing her eyes comically and making a vertical line appear at the bridge of her nose which she then pressed with her thumb as if to smooth it away. "I wouldn't recognise my own brother in such an awful photograph."

She stifled a yawn when I asked her if she wanted me to give her a clue. Then she nodded. I hesitated and she started to get up and go, and simultaneously I saw a trace of amazement and fright pass across her face and knew she had understood.

"You don't even think that yourself."

She was clearly, out of sheer superstition, not going to say the name, and I gave her time to get used to the shock while I thought back to how much she had liked having Daniel around, how she used to become unusually flustered when he came into the pub and how she sometimes sat down with the card players at closing time and let them play their last hands without hassling them, just to be close to him. He had not had to make any effort at all to attract her and she was by no means the only one to be attracted to him. I had stayed the night with her twice, and both times I had spent half the night talking about him, which had seemed quite normal to me then but now, and not just because of her defensiveness, felt like a particularly weird thing to have done.

"If you ask me, you're seeing ghosts," she said, having glanced around as if she was afraid that someone might hear us. "You should get out more."

This was her usual recommendation when a situation became too uncomfortable for her, when she wanted to put some distance between you or remind you that she was in charge. But merely because her accent had become more pronounced – when usually it didn't occur to anyone that she had an accent – I sensed how hyper she was. Something in our conversation had got under her skin, and she made no effort to hide her displeasure.

"So when was he last here?"

"I don't know," I said, even though I knew precisely when, and looked past her at the big tear-off calendar next to the counter, which showed a Sunday in April but was inevitably a couple of days out of date because the staff never took the trouble to tear off each day as it happened. "It's definitely been a while."

"If I'm not wrong, it must be nearly two years," she said. "Wasn't it at Judith's wedding?"

I didn't answer, and she laughed.

"I know you don't want to remember it, but I happen to like imagining him there."

She said it had been a gruesome occasion. I made no comment, although I could barely stop myself from telling her to keep it to herself.

"He was even supposed to be a witness, wasn't he? But he bailed out at the last minute," she said. "And he still came to the reception."

It was an old story, but it still fascinated her. We had often discussed it, and it came as no surprise that she still had a bee in her bonnet about it. It also didn't matter whether I told her she was wrong or not, it ended, as always, with her complaining about it.

"A witness at the wedding of the woman he'd made a fool of himself over for so long. Just the thought of it is in bad taste! The whole town had seen him running after her like an over-excited puppy. With all due respect to his fantasies, I need someone to explain that part to me. He just didn't need something like that. And my God, a boy like him. If he'd been just a tiny bit smarter, he could have had three women dangling off each finger."

Again, there was nothing for me to say. I decided to say nothing, also, about the brief visit he had paid me almost six months before: our last actual encounter. It had been in early November, evening and already dark outside, when he had appeared at the door out of the blue. He couldn't be persuaded to come in at first but ended up staying the night. I was not surprised – he had turned up at my place like that plenty of times in the years after he left school, at first pretty often and then less frequently. Nor did the fact that he had asked me to lend him some money, no questions asked, particularly bother me. I asked him how much, and when he said everything I had there, I looked at him in surprise but went into the bedroom and fetched it. It was not a big sum, but not small either – 2,500 euros that I kept casually tucked under a few shirts along with the passport I had reported as stolen, to maintain the romantic idea I had of being able to disappear at any moment – and he took the bills, all in hundreds, folded them with a wary glance and put them in his trouser pocket. He had borrowed money from me before and repaid it, without explanation and without me having to remind him. So it didn't occur to me then that he might be in trouble, and in fact the thing that most irritated me was when we sat down together at the kitchen table later and he asked about my house and whether I still sometimes drove out to the river. He started talking about it during a lull in the conversation, out of a sudden sense of awkwardness, and I couldn't shake off the feeling that he was only saying it for my sake, offering me some precisely measured dose of sentiment in return for my kindness. His words sounded like a consolation, although for what I couldn't have said, except that time had passed and I was still sitting there as his former teacher while he was moving up and onwards and hadn't been my pupil for a long time.

My having kept this secret from Agata, and still keeping it secret, was unlike me. I felt she had genuinely cared about Daniel over the years. She regularly enquired whether I had heard anything from him, and he had become, quite deliberately, a constant in our conversations whenever I walked into Bruckner's. She'd sit down with me and ask about him with a dreamy "Where's Daniel these days?" or a skittish "What's Daniel up to these days then?" She was curious for herself, but it had not escaped her notice that they were questions that preoccupied me too, and so we wondered together when he started not showing up as often as he had in the months after he finished school. We wondered if he was still in Bosnia, where he had gone after dropping out of university to help rebuild a war-damaged village, if it was true that he was crewing on a cargo ship, or if he had actually won a Green Card in the annual lottery and gone to try his luck in America, or – one of the last possibilities – there was always Israel, because he had been there once when he was still at school and had raved about it ever since. Then again, he was also said to have been seen working as a labourer on a village construction site twenty kilometres downstream; he was working December to March or April in one of the valleys as a ski instructor and somehow making ends meet for the rest of the year; he was driving for a trucking company, shipping new cars from Germany to Turkey or even Iran or Iraq, or living hand to mouth when he couldn't find anything else or didn't feel like working.

I had described him to Agata more than once as one of my best students, and that was what I said again now. I think "most promising" were the words I used, adding "smartest and most talented", and then I felt cross with myself for my nostalgia. I had not considered what course the conversation might take if I was not careful, and when I saw how she immediately sat up and took notice I realised that with those words I had taken it in the direction I was least comfortable with.

"You're a fine one, Anton," she said, laughing, although the heaviness in her voice could not be ignored. "If you keep this up, you're going to find yourself retiring and still missing him."

Apart from Agata, there was no-one among my friends who addressed me by my name, and I preferred them not to. With her it was something different: it wasn't a warning, a formal instruction kindly to be the person I'd always been up till then, but astonishment at what I might come out with next, and right at that moment that resonated with me. I watched as she ran her tongue from one corner of her lips to the other, and while I thought about how to extricate myself, she sucked her breath in sharply between her teeth and cleared her throat.

"A teacher who can't say goodbye to his students."

"You can talk," I said. "What is it with you?"

I had never quite understood her attachment to Daniel. I could not imagine that she had had anything other than brief conversations with him on any more than a few occasions during the months when he had regularly gone to Bruckner's, and in the years that followed she could not have seen him very often. I didn't want to ask her, but I expressed my astonishment by reminding her of her persistence.

"'Where's Daniel these days?' Remember, Agata? If you asked me once, you must have asked me a thousand times. 'What's Daniel up to these days then?'"

As I said it I regretted having talked to her at all. I watched her, in the silence that followed, pick up the newspaper again and look as though she was studying the picture more closely. Something hard had come into her face, and as she turned back to me it seemed to affect her voice too.

"It's weird how we've all let ourselves get a bit carried away by him. I'm not saying it because of the photo, but strictly speaking he never once came across as good-looking. And no-one could say he was sociable. It must have been something else about him that hypnotised us."

I said it was because of his manner, his utterly earnest way of taking things, but she just retorted that a bit more friendliness wouldn't have done him any harm. Then suddenly she seemed to remember what we were actually talking about.

"Shouldn't you be jumping up and going to the police to give them a statement if you really think you recognise him and believe he's the one they want?"

I didn't say anything but was relieved that someone called her over just then. I don't know if I would have told her that I wouldn't be going to the police, but it was pretty clear in any case, and the ironic look she gave me as she got to her feet was intended to make it clear that she had understood. There was no complicity in the look, just a slightly assumed amazement at the game I was playing, and when she looked over her shoulder at me as she walked away

I knew I could trust her not to give anything away, if only because she didn't take any of it seriously. She was wearing the work clothes she had been wearing all these years, black skirt, white blouse, and I thought, idiotically, that they gave her a reliable quality. I wondered though whether I should specifically ask her to forget the conversation, and then when she came back a few minutes later with faintly flushed cheeks I felt reassured that she wanted to pick up the conversation exactly where we had left off.

"Your best pupil, then," she said, as if to sum everything up in a word. "Shouldn't he have done something with it in the end?"

There was a sudden sarcasm in her voice that was never usually there when she talked about him, and then, as I remember it, out of nowhere, she asked me about the house.

"Do you still drive out there sometimes?"

I shook my head and she said something about a "retreat", saying that Daniel had once described it as his real home.

"He used to go on and on about the days you spent by the river. He called you the most important person in his life. You must have been very close to each other."

I couldn't think that she meant anything by it, but I looked at her with alarm. Back then the whole town had gossiped, and the first hikers who had heard that a teacher was spending whole days out in the wilds with two of his students quickly found their way to us. They would venture as far as the boundary of the property, greet us officiously and make small talk while they looked discreetly around them. She must have known about the gossip, but whatever her motive was in bringing it up, a frivolousness in her wilful way of reminding me of it made me distrust her.

"You know the story," I said. "If you like I'll happily tell it to you all over again, but it won't change a thing."

When another customer called her, I took advantage of the

interruption to say my goodbye. I had not wanted to say anything else about the photo but I ended up doing just that, even though I was merely underlining my concern. I asked Agata if I could take the cutting with me and she looked at me with a smile and said I was welcome to go over it with a magnifying glass quietly at home but it wouldn't tell me any more because it was all in my head. She walked off and I gazed after her before I too got to my feet. She was still young, not yet thirty, and in some ways still the mysterious stranger who comes from afar and hears everything but says nothing. She could almost never be persuaded to reveal anything of the life she led when she went back home for a few weeks every spring and autumn. I had asked her about it more than once but she always ducked the question, saying that she could tell me everything about herself but at the end of it I still wouldn't understand anything about her world. I didn't press her because I was very careful in those days not to let myself feel rejected, but now I felt I knew what she was talking about. It wasn't just about her, and it wasn't just about me. What she had wanted to say was simply that no-one knows anything about anybody when it comes down to it, and I couldn't fault her on that.

2

BACK THEN, I HAD BEEN GOING OUT TO THE RIVER ALMOST EVERY day, despite its still being the last week of school, to sit myself down in the sun with a book. There was nothing more specific behind it than a desire to escape from the world of teaching as quickly as possible, nor any plan when increasingly often I began to put my book aside and clean up the property, which until then I had left just as it had been when I took it over. I made a start on clearing the meadow of the stones that lay there, gathering them all together and wondering if I should take them down to the river bed, or to the gravel bar directly in front of the house, but then piling them next to the mill's walls or rather the ruins of its remaining walls. Perhaps I had already subliminally had the idea of using them as building material, but I had not thought of it consciously, and the reality was that after months in the classroom I was so happy to be working outdoors, with all its pointlessness and apparent futility, that I felt for the first time that I'd grasped why people imagined Sisyphus to be the happiest of men because I caught myself wishing that someone would come along after me and undo everything I'd done so that I could start all over again, or perhaps extend my stone-collecting and weeding beyond the boundaries of my property and into the surrounding fields and the Au and then move gradually up to the village and beyond it. I had already carried out the less pleasant tasks, had cleared the inside of the mill of beer and cola bottles, broken glass, tin foil, an old shoe, a couple of broken badminton rackets without strings and the excrement in the corners – human excrement or animal excrement, I didn't know. I had carried the half-charred tree stumps from an apparently well-used fireplace down to the water, thrown them in and watched as they drifted, swinging sluggishly, and got caught in a whirlpool before being picked up and snatched away by the strong current in the middle of the river. I spent half an afternoon trying to roll away the last stump, which lay there like a boulder, but having heaved with all my might and, panting and sweating, rotated it around its centre of gravity, I gave up after the first three revolutions and left it barely three metres from its starting point, where for a while it left an exposed oval of fresh, damp earth glistening in the sun.

It was around the end of the second week of the holidays, just after I had started to build a boundary wall out of the collected stones, that Daniel and his friend Christoph turned up. I had heard the clatter of a moped approaching along the river bank, but hadn't taken a great deal of notice because it wasn't the first time and there were several days when I had heard the noise of engines coming from the direction of the sports ground, which wasn't far from my property. I hadn't bargained on anyone coming to visit, and they must have been standing there for a while before I noticed them because suddenly all other sounds seemed to fall silent, and the rushing of the river underlined the stillness. I straightened up and they were there, a few metres away, looking at me. They had got off their moped and were waiting for me to go over to them, and it only struck me later that, with the thick branch I was holding and my tight-lipped demeanor, I can't have looked particularly welcoming. We exchanged no more than a few words before they went off again, and it was only when they appeared the next day holding a bottle of wine and asked if they could sit with me that the story which later grew in people's minds into some sort of monstrosity started.

It had been only two years before that I had bought the mill and its piece of land, and two years before that that I had come back from Istanbul where I had been teaching for two years – another two years – at the Austrian School. Two plus two plus two, six years in total, since Robert had gone down to the river on a Sunday morning and put the barrel of the rifle (he must have smuggled it out of the gun club with him) in his mouth and pulled the trigger. I'm telling you this because the two of them asked me about it and because in all those six years they were the first who had dared, or possibly even the first to think of daring.

At first I was surprised that they had come back at all. I thought I had made it quite clear that I wanted to be on my own and set no store by the company of others, and this time I prepared myself to confront them from the moment I heard the sound of their moped in the distance. There is a peculiar thing about the acoustics at the river; sometimes you hear what the laws of physics say you can't hear – voices that are carried on the wind as if they come from another world, the murmur of a religious procession, or the sound of cow-bells from a herd grazing in the Au tinkling like heavenly chimes. Generally I let myself be as little upset by these sounds as I was by the sound of engines, but this time I was on my guard as I watched the two of them approach, weaving slowly along the moss-covered forest path as though avoiding potholes or rain puddles and trying to stay upright and not flip out. I had not asked them the previous day whether they had stumbled on me by chance or whether they had heard that I was staying by the river and so had intentionally headed that way, but the question became somehow superfluous when, realising that I had seen them, they waved, and I, without reflection, waved back.

I put down the shears I had been using to prune, somewhat ineffectively, a bush that was growing in all directions, pulled off my gloves and took a couple of steps towards them. In recent months they had frequently come to my flat on their famous Saturday afternoon rounds – appearing at the home of one teacher one week, another the next, standing at the door and waiting to be invited in – so I was surprised now by how much like strangers they seemed. It must have had something to do with the surroundings, with the remoteness of the place, or perhaps it was just that they stood there with their crash helmets in their hands and made no move to come any closer. I didn't feel threatened in any way but – despite having no grounds for thinking so – it occurred to me briefly that they might have come with ill intent, that there might be some score to be settled, a reckoning they had been adding up against me over the years without my knowledge and for which they had now come to exact payment.

They made an unlikely couple. I don't mean because of what they were like at school, and definitely not because they were good or bad students, though there was a world of difference between Daniel's application and Christoph's slacking, which had been most noticeable in the sixth form but was probably there long before that. I don't mean the boyishness, or maybe even girlishness, of the one, and the heavy build of the other, who seemed to have been born that way and sometimes had the loud mouth to match. Nothing like that, and nothing that their origins or home lives might have influenced either. No, I'm talking about what really should have divided them, but didn't; what, instead, bonded them more closely and made them practically inseparable in their last year at school. In a word, Judith, or, in two, their love, or, in three, four or five words, their unrequited love for her. The previous year I had watched the two of them falling for her almost simultaneously and seen how their friendship was based on the fact that neither of them had a chance and on how both, after their first rebuffs, took on the role of ironic admirer. It was as if they had each decided, quite independently, that instead of yearning for her they would make fun of their own yearning, even before it had properly set in and so they pranced around their beloved in ever more inventive twists and turns, shadowing her puppyishly, bowing and scraping and throwing themselves at her feet in the most extravagant outbursts of enthusiasm. You could see the three of them going down to the school yard to smoke, strolling arm in arm together at lunchtime, the girl in the middle, tall, blonde, her chest pushed forward but still almost without breasts, and to her left and right, her two beaux, each trying to outdo the other in their banter, sometimes turning and taking a few steps backwards in front of her, hoping for a smile, a glance, the slightest remark from her.

That doubtless also explains their restlessness on Saturdays, their endless riding around on the moped, the way they lay in wait for her when she was going to be collected by her boyfriend. He was a couple of years older than her, already at university, and only came home at weekends, and I remember many times when the two of them tried to talk her into standing him up, into not going to him when they saw his car in the car park outside the school. She would grant them five minutes, ten minutes, go along with their jokes about the boy waiting for her, even when he could be heard hooting, then suddenly drop the pair of them mid-sentence. I don't know how they managed it, watching her disbelievingly as she strode away, turning back towards them several times, swinging her bag, laughing as she paused at the top of the stairs before stepping down them sideways like a woman in high heels, without another backward glance.

I recalled all this as I walked over and told them that I wanted to know what had brought them out to see me again. They had not put the moped on its stand and neither of them answered, just stood there with their crash helmets, as though at the slightest hint that they were not welcome they would instantly make themselves scarce. It was a picture-book summer's day, more than thirty degrees in the shade, a heat haze hanging over the meadows, crickets chirping, and I didn't yet know that Judith, with whom they had spent almost every afternoon of the last weeks of term at the swimming baths, had gone to Italy with her boyfriend.

They spent the whole day with me by the river, and it wasn't Daniel but Christoph who first asked me about my brother. At first we sat on the stone steps leading up to the mill and drank the wine out of the paper cups they had brought with them. For a long time no-one said anything, we just listened to the rushing of the river and the sound of the trains on the far bank, where the line runs up along a slight embankment. Then we went down past the puddles and stagnant pools left by the last flood and the yellow flood warning signs, all the way out to the gravel bar, where you get a feeling for the amazing expanse of the river bed. I can't remember whether Christoph had given any sort of hint about what he was going to say, but as soon as he asked me whether it had happened somewhere around here, I knew what he was talking about and just said, yes. We immediately fell silent again, looking out over the water until I had the impression that I only needed to stare for long enough at one place for it to start rippling at that spot merely from the effect of my gaze.

It was all so unspectacular, just as it sounds, yet something must have happened that day, possibly because of the question and my answer, something that made them feel responsible for me from that moment on, or in any case made them seek out my company.

They came back the next day, and by the fourth day I found myself listening out for the clatter of their moped, and then, after a few more idle days, when we just sat in the sun reading and talking and occasionally walking down to the river to paddle or even swim a few strokes, the water ice-cold even in midsummer, they suggested renovating the mill to make it habitable. It was just a whim – there was no electricity, no running water, let alone any proper building consent – but they refused to listen to my reservations and started work immediately, and I let them. They borrowed a pickup truck from Christoph's father, drove it as close as they could, and used a wheelbarrow to ferry the construction materials they had "organised" from the grounds of his timber yard. I watched as they piled up boards, unloaded bags of cement, stood rolls of roofing felt next to each other against a tree, and then one day there was suddenly a veranda, with the view I mentioned, there were repaired walls, makeshift windows had been put in, one looking towards the river, one next to the door, with leather loops for hinges, and out of bare boards they had rustled up a roof and made it wind- and weatherproof. It was not much more than a kids' hidey-hole in the woods, and you obviously could not have called it a house, although we did, but it had at least been turned into a place where you could keep dry when it rained. Their finishing touch was to hang a paraffin lamp in one of the two rooms, and afterwards they talked incessantly about what such a hideaway could be good for.

I don't know whether, to begin with, the passing hikers simply wondered at our industriousness or whether, right from the start, they talked about the strange trio we made. Further up the river there was a swimming area, but I was aware that we stood out when we lay on the gravel bar in our shorts in the afternoons, or played three-way catch or sat around a fire and waited till the meat we'd speared on sharpened twigs and held over the flames was tender.

Nor can I say when I became aware that the seemingly random passers-by in our vicinity were possibly not so random after all, but one day, when a few boys came down from the sports ground – ten- or twelve-year-olds in grass-green sweatpants and white vests – and stopped a short distance away and one of them stepped forward and shouted something unintelligible at us, making the rest of them laugh, I knew we had become a talking point. They were not actually aggressive, but before they disappeared again one of them picked up a stone, held it up against the sun as if he wanted us to see it clearly, and threw it in our direction. It was not a targeted throw, more a gesture that we could interpret as playful but it nonetheless left a threat hanging in the air that did not dissipate as the band vanished amid laughter.

This was confirmed to me shortly afterwards by my headteacher at the *Gymnasium*, who phoned me one evening, wanting to know if everything was all right. It was the holidays and I had no desire to talk to him, but he was the one who had helped me get the job in Istanbul after I told him it was probably best if I went away for a while; he was the one who had offered to have me back immediately if ever I had the slightest feeling that I might have made the wrong decision; and I was still touched when I remembered how he had come to visit me with a small delegation of colleagues the first autumn I was there, and unobtrusively kept an eye on me while I gamely led them from one sight to another, inspecting the Hagia Sophia, the Blue Mosque and the Topkapi Palace with them while trying to conceal the fact that, apart from the route to work from my flat, I knew almost nothing of the city. He had held out a sheltering hand to me ever since, and when, every few months, I was invited to dinner at his house, his kind and protective manner was not lost on me. I used to wonder whether one of the other teachers had told him that I was beginning to withdraw again, whether he had heard that I had been seen a bit too much in Bruckner's recently, or whether there was no alarm signal needed and it was just a routine check on my welfare. Admittedly in the long run it became somewhat wearisome, yet off I went each time with a bottle of wine and flowers for his wife. I liked him. I liked how he welcomed me, a bit stiffly but always with a pat on the shoulder, half man-to-man but half as if he thought of me as a boy too, and I liked his wife, who told him to let me come in first, instead of immediately engaging me in conversation; I liked the warmth of her scolding and the way she called him Karl, because Karl was a child's name to me, one that instilled an absurd, and if I think about it for a second, entirely unjustified, feeling of trust – a name from a world where nothing bad could happen or, if something bad did happen, everything could be made all right again.

Obviously I did not call him Karl, because to me, despite his familiarity, he had always been Herr Aschberner and always would be. Even though he called me "*du*" and I managed with circumlocutions not to have to do the same back to him.

"If what I've heard is true, you're spending a lot of time down at the river," he said, and his voice sounded anxious. "You will let me know if I can do anything for you, won't you?"

He had known my father: perhaps that was it. Or perhaps it was because he had lost a son whom he never spoke about. Then again, perhaps he did not need any deeper motive to feel he ought to be concerned about me.

"Weren't you going to go away this summer?"

On the last day of school he had asked me to go and see him and had asked me what plans I had for the holidays, and I had told him that I didn't know where yet but I was going to go away, even though I had already started my pilgrimages out to the river by then and had no intention of thinking about spending my days any other way for the foreseeable future.

"I thought about it. I've changed my mind," I said. "In any case it's not much more than four weeks now till the new term starts."

There was a reluctant muttering at the other end of the phone and I had an image of his wife standing behind him, tapping him on the shoulder and whispering something in his ear.

"What about the two boys?"

"What about them?"

"You know what people are like."

He was a circumspect man, and I was relying on him to change the subject at the appropriate moment, but he carried on.

"Rumours are flying," he said. "I know they're not your pupils anymore, but it's not a good idea to make yourself vulnerable like this."

I had not considered it from this perspective at all but now I visualised what he meant, two boys by the river with a man, and it was a picture in which I really couldn't imagine myself the way he had formulated it – that the man could be me, or even what his role in some kind of tellable story could possibly be. I saw again in my mind's eye how Daniel had once run, squealing like a child, into the shallow water by the bank and then directly along the water-line upriver, rowing with his arms or, more accurately, flapping, looking as if he was on the point of taking off, throwing up his legs right and left, and with me right behind him. I had thought it was an invitation, and had run after him for as long as it took me to catch him and then, in a sudden surrender, I had thrown my arms around him and held him tight for a moment, maybe a bit longer than a moment, yes, much longer in my memory. And he had sud-denly stood there quite still, slightly bent forward, and I had placed my hand on his boyish breast and had had exactly that phrase in

· 25 ·

mind – I had placed my hand on his breast and thought "boyish breast" and how cool his skin was from the water that had splashed him and felt beneath it the pounding of his heart. Nothing else, not even that he might have experienced the situation as special, in the way that I had. He had walked back with me, not saying a word about it but not in any kind of meaningful silence either, the way you might think; he was the same as before. It did not occur to him to make any comment on what had happened or to talk dismissively about it to cover his embarrassment, and it was absurd for me to be preoccupied now with whether anyone had seen us, a hiker or one of the peeping Toms who were supposed to hang around in the undergrowth near the swimming area but who, whenever I heard about them, always seemed like figures from a fairytale.

"Vulnerable?"

The head cleared his throat.

"Well, no, not vulnerable exactly."

He paused for a long time before saying the word, as if it needed to be carefully seasoned before he uttered it, and then seemed more relaxed about defending his use of it.

"We never find the perfect expression, do we? So we don't need to argue about that. But you understand," he said. "I would just like to ask you to be a bit more careful."

I didn't know how I was supposed to do what he asked, but the effect of his words was that from then on I started to look at things a little more clearly. I didn't say anything about it to the boys, but if Daniel lay in the sun to read and used my thigh as a headrest, I pulled back, keeping my distance, and whenever Christoph stretched out naked after swimming, on the flat part of the gravel bar that jutted out a way into the water, I would throw him a towel. I told them they should put shirts on when they went off upriver to the swimming area only wearing their trunks, but of course they laughed and asked me if I thought we were still at school, or why I was appointing myself the keeper of public morals. I eyed the hikers the way they eyed us when they came too close to the property, and then, when I started getting ideas about what people might see from the trains passing on the far bank, which at that time sometimes trundled past irritatingly slowly, their carriages seeming to flit backwards and forwards behind the trees on the embankment like a surrealist painting, I knew that it was all madness and I stopped. I watched the rafters, who had a camp further up the river, past the swimming area, as they bounced down river in their big inflatables with ten, twelve or more aboard, always in party mood, laughing as they waved hello and still laughing as they disappeared again, an invasion of cheerful conquerors in their helmets and lifejackets. They brandished their paddles in greeting as they reached our part of the bank, and it might be three minutes before they plunged into the gorge and its rapids, all of them working flat out to stay on course and not capsize. I've never been down there, even though it can't be more than half an hour's walk along the bank when the water level is low, but I knew that friends still laid flowers at the place from time to time and that there would be a candle burning there too for days afterwards that could probably be seen at night, flickering in the middle of the river.

3

WHAT DO YOU WISH AS A TEACHER FOR YOUR STUDENTS, WHAT can you wish for them? And does it have the slightest impact on what they eventually become? So many years I've been a teacher, already twenty, so many cohorts of pupils. At some point I have asked every one of them the question of what they themselves would like for their lives; at some point I have asked every one of them, in their last school year or earlier, what they want to be, or study, or if not study, what they want to do with their future. I assume that the more recent classes have already heard from their predecessors that they will have to face the question one day and so I am used to the agonised and scornful looks – you have to expect them when you're a teacher and you show your human side too much and forget that you can never abolish the distance between you and them. I asked them about their conceptions of luck, how they defined it, and when they said this or that, starting with the usual things – family, success in their careers, you know the kind of stuff I mean, even if they called it something else – I borrowed a formula from the mathematicians and wanted to know whether they considered it to be only a necessary condition or also a sufficient one. People are always saying that students are more willing to adapt these days, that they have clear ideas and clear objectives that they want to reach in the quickest way possible, that they imbibe the credo early on that there isn't a place in the sun for everyone and that therefore only the fastest, most skilled and maybe most callous will secure a spot and everyone else will have to put up with what they can get, but I don't believe it. They are still so young, and if anything there's still, behind the assumed masks, a kind of trembling, a sense that something in the eternal promises about the next stage in life being always the one to long for doesn't add up. After nursery school you look forward to school, after school to studying, after studying to a profession and after a profession to retirement and a nice spot in the cemetery or a handful of ashes, scattered on the wind.

The truth, obviously, is that I only get to hear about what happens to a very small number of my students. Most walk out of school on their last day and when, after the holidays, the new school year starts, they aren't missed by anyone. Yes, now and again there will be a little epilogue carried on in conversations with your colleagues, when so and so has particularly stood out, perhaps for being a particular star at natural sciences or for scribbling the Latin mistress a coded but easily decryptable love letter in their exercise book or something of the sort, but the idea that you would mourn them is a myth, just like the related cliché that bears no deeper scrutiny, that you, the teacher, feel left behind when they leave, that every time you experience the feelings of abandonment that parents feel when their children have just left home. You sometimes see one of them in the street, remember their name or don't remember it, ask a question or two, receive an answer or two, and it's already over, in the past, without sentiment or nostalgia, and often enough it's as if it never happened. You hear that one has joined the board of an international company in Vienna, another has started studying in New York, or a third is to be appointed press officer to the provincial governor, and you try vainly to remember their faces. An astonishing number come back to the town, whether they planned it that way from the start or whether something went wrong with their attempt to launch themselves on the wider world, and ultimately a lot more than you would imagine complete the circle and come back to teach at their old school, and suddenly you see them again, as your colleague, after having told them six or seven years earlier that if they don't pull their finger out a bit more they'll be in for a shock in their working life later.

I don't want to say that the dead are the best remembered, but somehow you do think of those who died young – the ones who could have gone on living – with greater intensity, as if there's more room for them in your memory because of the time they didn't claim from life. I don't know whether it's a lot in terms of the annual student numbers, but there are four in total, four of my former pupils who are no longer alive. Two had an accident, one of those Saturday night stories you read about in the newspaper after the weekend, driving from one nightclub to another, three cars racing each other, the drivers all drunk; in fact the valleys around here are full of roadside crosses, there's one every second or third bend marking the location of an accident. One boy collapsed during a football game and died instantly, an overlooked heart defect he had had since birth, and another had cancer, struggled through his final exams and died less than two months later, as if to pour scorn on all the striving to prepare him for life. The one that I think about most often, however, is a girl who did not go to my school but who for a few weeks came to my house on Sunday afternoons to get some coaching. She came from one of the villages and had that reserved manner of a child from a poor family in the past, the sort you basically don't see anymore. I was supposed to practise essay writing with her, and generally she sat mutely opposite me, always a bit pale-cheeked, always with her over-large eyes and questioning, puzzled expression, and what especially distressed me about her is that I only got to hear of her death more than two years after it happened and somehow felt that my long period of ignorance meant I had failed her, because she had not been in my thoughts at all, not even once in a while, just as if by that omission I had deserted her all that time in a way that could not be repaired. She died not long after I went to Istanbul, and either because people did not want to burden me with the news so soon after my brother's death, or just because no-one thought of it, the first I knew about it was a few weeks after I got back, when I went to the cemetery. I wanted to visit my grandparents' graves, and when I was wandering among the other graves afterwards I found her gravestone with her photo. She had had a pulmonary embolism after a routine operation for a broken leg after a bike accident, and I knelt down and wanted to ask for her forgiveness that I had not saved her from it.

When I think about it, I suppose Agata is the only one who understands why I have always loved Daniel. Perhaps "understands" is going too far. Anyway, she is sympathetic. Other people do not usually express their reservations about him, although of course I sense them, and I notice their surprise or, if that's naïve of me, their disapproval. They feel they know he has disappointed me, and some have made pointed remarks to that effect, to which I have never reacted. I've tended to behave as though I have no idea what they were talking about, have asked them how they could be so sure, shrugged it off as a misunderstanding when they have backtracked. I could also have told them that before every ending there was also a beginning, and that perhaps that justified everything else, or at least explained it.

I was thinking about all this as I left Bruckner's the night I thought I had recognised Daniel in the photograph. I put the page of the newspaper in my pocket and stepped outside into the drizzle. It had last snowed only two weeks earlier, and even now there could still be another cold snap in store, but I decided all the same to leave the car there and walk home, to give myself time to think. I could not get the photograph out of my head, but even more than the photograph, the words bothered me – the words found in the bag at the station. They were not exactly conclusive, yet that "Repent!" had its place in Daniel's thinking, and he was no stranger to biblical attitudes either.

Walking down the high street at night always gave me the creeps. So many businesses had closed down; there is something ghostly about strolling past the empty premises, and sometimes a light burning unexpectedly on a floor above only intensifies the ghostliness. The windows of the other shops looked unchanged, as they had for years, a flickering neon tube here, a flashing light there, and that night a single car was weaving around the flower planters that had paradoxically been placed there as traffic-calming measures. Apart from me there seemed to be no-one on the street, and not just because of the weather but because it was like that every day, except perhaps on Saturdays; three or four years earlier it would have been reason enough for me to think about whether I shouldn't go away again, maybe abroad somewhere or at least to Vienna. But three or four years can be a long time.

That night was obviously not the first time when I had thought about what sort of influence I might have had on Daniel, but now the subject resurfaced with full force. He had been my pupil for four years, from the first year of upper school till his final exams, and when I envisaged going to the police and having to help them with their enquiries it was clear to me that a couple of remarks, plus the suspicion that it could be him in the picture, would be all it took to make everything certain. I would only have to tell them that once in winter, of all seasons, he had lived for two months on his own in the house by the river, and there would probably be a police unit immediately dispatched to fan out and surround the property and call him on a loud-hailer to come out, even though it had happened five years earlier. Back then I had finally started to think that there was something not right about him, that the weirdnesses and abnormalities he openly displayed could no longer be made light of, as I had done till then. It had happened after he dropped out of university; he had not been studying properly for the whole of the previous semester and one day he turned up unannounced at my flat to ask me whether he could have the house "for a few days", though he said nothing about living there as long as he eventually did. My first reaction was to look at him uncomprehendingly but when he said it was just a try-out, I didn't need to worry about it, I said yes and so afterwards he came over two or three times a week to have a shower at the flat, going back the whole way on foot or stopping a car and getting a lift. He bought food and would spend a few hours in a café or at the library, always taking more books out than he could have got anywhere near finishing, and otherwise led the life of a recluse. In theory he had already prepared for the whole scenario that summer by the river, but I never thought he would do it for real, and not at the coldest time of the year. I remembered how, when it had been especially cold, I had sometimes, even late at night, gone out to check up on him, but each time he had refused my offer to come back with me. He would have a fire burning in the fireplace – that was something he had been particularly keen on when they were renovating the mill – and I would find him sitting swaddled in his sleeping bag in front of it, reading with a torch, or already asleep, and my footsteps would wake him. There was snow on the ground nearly the whole time, and you could hear it crunching a long way off in the crisp darkness. Twice it was snowing in earnest, and one of those times he plodded towards me under the trees and said that if I didn't envy him his life in the wild, it was my hard luck.

It is frightening how logically you can chart the path that took him there, but it would be just as logical if he had not landed up in the house by the river and subsequently adopted that vagabond life of which I only knew the outermost contours, but had instead become a professor with a chair at a provincial university somewhere, or at least a teacher like me. A lone wolf, fair enough, a bibliomane, a model student whose favourite subjects were maths and, as if for good measure and to illustrate the absurdity of it all, religious studies, a harmless fantasist whose nickname at school was Jesus and whom the girls looked at as if he was from Mars – well, it was a gift, a template for anyone who wanted to assemble a life out of two or three bits of data. I had always teased him for what I called his double love of infinity that found its fulfilment both in numbers and in heaven, after Dr Prager rhapsodised about him being able to recite the first hundred digits of pi from memory and Herr Bleichert prophesied that here was a boy who would take up the Cross and follow in the footsteps of the Lord, just because he ministered at school mass when he was fourteen or chose the Bible as his favourite book. It's easy to laugh about it, yet it was actually their enthusiasm that made me pay attention to him in the first place. They were very competitive about him, and whenever they discussed him in the staffroom the same themes recurred, how on the one hand they thought the world of him, and on the other what fears they entertained for his future if no-one took him by the hand and succeeded in leading him away from his tendency to ruminate and dream and lose himself in unreal worlds.

I have often asked myself why he, of all people, stood out. There were always students who for some reason had a special status, but in all my years as a teacher he aroused people's passions the most. I won't waste my breath on the stories that circulated about him and quickly developed a life of their own but which, if you looked closely, were no more than the silly excitements of a small town. There is perhaps just one that is representative: that while I was away in Istanbul he was supposed to have had a bodyguard to protect him from the others, a proper bodyguard, a boy who never moved from his side but then had to leave before upper school. The point being that in everything that was said about him there seemed to be something defining, even though I found him rather unforthcoming in person. For instance, it was said of him that he was never at a loss for words, but that was quite different from how I felt I knew him. What was certainly true, however, was that he drove a series of my colleagues to desperation because he felt he needed to explain their subject to them, with the result that they did not like him, although they at least conceded that he was no waffler and had something to contribute to the most esoteric of topics.

Obviously none of this constituted any sort of proof, but I knew that it would be dragged up when people started looking for the beginning of the story that ended with the picture in the newspaper, just as my relationship with him would inevitably serve as an explanation. From the first year that he had been one of my students I had lent him books, and of course you could find among them titles that were calculated to make him unfit for a normal life, but then hundreds, thousands of people have read the same books and know how to cope with them without feeling compelled to sabotage their life in the way he did. I can still remember precisely how he asked me one day what he ought to read, because it was the same question that Robert had always asked at his age, and ultimately – after I had tried at length not to give them to him – it was Robert's books that I gave him. For a long time I cold-shouldered him, not wanting to acquire the reputation of a nerdy teacher who scurries around one of his star pupils, until one Saturday at the end of lessons he buttonholed me and it all started.

I was busy packing things into my briefcase when he suddenly materialised in front of me, a boy like many others of his age, still reserved and shy one minute and assertive the next, to cover up his shyness.

"You don't like me."

It was a simple statement, in which the accusatory tone that usually accompanies such a declaration was quite absent. I looked at him wearily as I suppressed the impulse simply to agree with him.

"Why wouldn't I like you?"

Of course I should have responded more energetically, but, beguiled by the big eyes behind the thick glasses, by the severely parted hair or some other aspect of his appearance, I let myself be drawn into the encounter. I put a hand on his shoulder.

"How do you work that out?"

"Well," he said, "I don't think we need to talk about that."

He now looked awkward.

"I can live fine with you not liking me, but even so I'd like to know whether there's anything that can change it."

He held my gaze and would not look away.

"Perhaps you can just tell me what I should read."

In my memory that phrase has always had something rather devastating about it, and as I walked down the high street I whispered it quietly to myself. I had arrived at the football ground, and at the police station at the far end there was still a light on. It was one of my usual routes when I went for a walk at night, and whenever I got near to the ground I always imagined that the floodlights might be switched on with a loud *clack!* and light up two teams, ready to play at the centre spot, waiting for the whistle, and the packed stands would explain why the town was so dead at this time of day. After my return from Istanbul I had trained the youth team for a few months, and because I still went to the home games, every inch of the ground was familiar to me. Behind the goalmouths the wind seemed to be lifting the wire mesh in the moonlight with a soft, whistling rustle that I could not be sure if I was hearing or just imagining, and it made me think of bats. It was like an undulation behind them, as if you were looking from underwater or through the shimmer of heat on a summer's day, though in fact it was making me shiver more than anything else. I walked across the car park, where two mobile homes were parked, and in one of them there were voices, the flickering of a television and, as I stood in front of it, everything was momentarily still so that I could follow the soundless movement of the picture through the slats of the blind.

I know Inspector Hule says that I went to see him that evening, but it is not true; he was standing outside the station as I walked up to it; I did not see him and was surprised when he spoke to me out of the darkness. He was divorced, which made him a candidate for Bruckner's, and in fact you could find him there from time to time, and sometimes when I walked past his office late at night and saw that he was on duty I used to ring the bell and he would happily let himself be interrupted in whatever desk-work he was doing, but on this occasion I neither did so nor had it in mind to do so. It was pure chance that he had just come outside for a smoke, and it was only when he moved that I saw the glow of the cigarette he was holding in his dangling hand.

"Still out so late," he said. "Fancy a coffee?"

I said no, but he brushed my answer aside and asked me to come in with him. It was a cool evening, and as he walked up the four steps to the entrance I saw that he was in shirtsleeves. He was broad-shouldered, not large, and in the light a bald patch shimmered through the hair on the back of his head; from behind, his narrow hips gave no sign of his substantial stomach, which gave him an intimidating but simultaneously comfortable look. His son was in my class, and I had enjoyed his trust since he had once come to my consultation hour and I had done everything I could to allay his discomfort as he sat opposite me, almost unrecognisable off-duty and smelling strongly of hair gel, with his stubble showing through, like a junior officer. He offered me a seat in the little ante-room, where there were a couple of plastic chairs, a small table and a leathery rubber plant, and walked out, his soles squeaking on the lino floor. The light was flickering here too, and while I wondered whether it might not be intentional I looked alternately at the rough bare concrete walls and the counter, behind the glass of which all I could make out were silhouettes, until he returned with two steaming cups.

"Something on your mind?"

I was used to his way of talking, although I always wondered where it came from. His swallowed mumbling through clenched teeth seemed not to let any verbs through or somehow to force every sentence to be garbled. But whether he had seen too many detective movies or cultivated it himself, I knew that the correct response for someone addressed this way was to leave a significant pause before answering. So I said nothing for a while, before saying no and that I had just been passing by chance – which with hindsight I would have preferred to have kept to myself – but it is correct to say that after a further hesitation I started talking about the bomb threat and that he played it down when I asked him what people should make of it.

"Probably just a kid's prank."

He said that it was always the papers wanting to make a story out of things, whereas in most cases the best thing was to pass over them without comment.

"Whoever it was, it's not even certain that he's actually capable of building something that can be effectively detonated. Anyone can fill a bag with a bunch of metal scrap and make a phone call. It's always happening, and experience shows that the best thing you can do is not give crazies like that any publicity."

He had loosened his belt and was sprawled on the other chair as if he wanted to show me that it was not worth wasting any more energy on.

"If you knew the reasons why people do something like that, you'd shake your head in disbelief," he said. "It's all the same stuff that sends them off the rails in other ways too − boredom, heartbreak − or, to put it another way, just normal life."

I was as surprised by his talkativeness as I was by him suddenly speaking in complete sentences, and then he came out with something really unexpected. He blew on his coffee and said how difficult it was to live when you didn't have anything you could imagine dying for, and yet that was precisely the experience a lot of people had of life nowadays, and that some of them just couldn't cope with. It was like something Daniel might have said, that summer by the river when we talked about what he would do after his final exams, or even more so in those two winter months he spent back at the house, when it was already fairly clear that everything he had lined up was not offering him a way forward and probably not even a way out. He, Daniel, had said then that living just in order to live was as absurd as living in order to die − he had a fondness for such sayings, a penchant for paradoxes or anything to do with a play on words and apparent philosophical profundity. I recalled that I completed his version with the missing variant – dying in order to live – and he stared at me and told me it wasn't my subject, I should leave all that to Herr Bleichert, but yes, if you were a believer then that was the best outcome. Sure, it was because of his age, and the idealism and defeatism of youth, except that in his case it did not change as he got older. While others looked back and laughed at their flights of existentialism and were happy that they were what they were and had what they had, he became increasingly hung up on it. I suddenly remembered the lists he had compiled with ever-renewed eagerness, his "Important–Unimportant" lists and his "Still to do" lists, in the last version of which I had found the entry "Love a person".

Thinking about all this irritated me. I was unprepared for such a conversation, or not with Inspector Hule in any case, and I started to think how I could steer it in another direction. Not saying anything would probably have been enough, but I had already picked up what Hule had said and quoted it back at him ironically.

"Oh right, normal life," I said, as if something hopelessly inflationary had been added to the notion. "Since when has that been part of the police's job?"

I felt I had said something very ordinary, but having been faintly bored by the conversation, Inspector Hule now looked at me with new interest.

"We deal with nothing else," he said, and there was an unmistakably reproving tone in his voice. "That's exactly why we're here."

I had walked straight into that, and as he stood up and stretched I wasn't sure whether I should take it as an invitation to go, but I stayed where I was and watched him as he started to pace up and down in front of me. A phone rang behind the glass screen, and what I had sensed as a silhouette earlier turned out to be the inspector's young female colleague, who had been sitting there inconspicuously the whole time, listening to us. She picked up the receiver, and after yes and no put it straight back down again, while the inspector was silent and I looked up at the clock that hung over the counter. It only now struck me how dim the light was, as its flickering stabilised, and that it possessed a sharpness that gave the objects in the room a thick outline, as if they had been drawn with a charcoal pencil. It made the inspector look pale and I knew how pale I must look too, as pale and unflattering as a police mugshot in which you wouldn't dare to blink, because you knew that one moment with your eyes closed, a second or a fraction of a second, and it could be the snapshot of a corpse.

Up till that point I had held back from mentioning the picture in the paper. When I enquired whether the police had had any reactions to it yet, it seemed to amuse the inspector.

"Shall I tell you how many calls we've had?"

He stopped in mid-stride, laughing, and turned to his colleague as if he wanted to show what a waste of resources it was when someone with his years of service and his experience was required to follow up something of this kind seriously.

"Dorothea, would you like to tell our friend?"

She seemed to realise it was a rhetorical question and made no move to answer.

"We could print a caricature of a chimpanzee baring its teeth and scratching its armpits and we'd have the same deluge of responses," he said. "The country's heaving with informers. If you'd like to join in the speculation and give us a tip too, just say the word."

I was outside in the street again before I asked myself whether it was chance or whether he had guessed what was worrying me and what thoughts I was thinking. I walked with an uneasy feeling back across the car park, where there was no light coming from the second mobile home now, although voices could still be heard through the slightly open window. I stopped in front of it again for a moment, but just as the light inside the police station had turned me into a potential felon, where I was standing was the classic wrong place at the wrong time and so I walked quickly away and back home.

At the flat I made myself a cup of tea and went to the shelf where Robert's books were. They stood apart from my other books, in their own space, and I paused in front of them, as if they might now provide me with an answer that they had failed to provide before. I had read or reread them all in Istanbul, the many dozens of novels I had recommended to him over the years, that I had bought for him or that he had got for himself. For me they represented the closest part of him that was left to me, the most personal thing, and the thing I felt I could cling on to and that I then obviously could not cling on to.

I again remembered the reluctance with which I had allowed Daniel to share them in the beginning – the jealousy – at the same time as I was unable to do otherwise, and later how eager I had been for him to read every last one of Robert's books. I never told him that I suggested the same titles to him that I had suggested to my brother, but I have no doubt that at a certain moment he must have sensed it. It all began fairly accidentally; the first time he asked me what he ought to read, I mentioned book titles as they came into my head and that seemed to me to have a good chance of keeping him occupied for a while, and then later it was an easy consolation, beguiling him with the same worlds that Robert had let himself be beguiled by. It sounds like an experiment, like some soft form of brainwashing, but I can promise you that there was nothing dogmatic about it, and I was more motivated by sentimentality than by the belief that I could implant something from one young man's brain into another's, a breath of his soul, something living from what he'd been before he had decided to die.

Books, if I can put it like this, had also been the last sign of life Robert had shown, two weeks after his death. It was after the summer holidays – he had spent the last school year in the United States, in a suburb of Saint Louis – when a postbag of books was delivered that he had posted himself. This linen bag, all the way from America, with a "US Mail" label, had something frighteningly pathetic about it. It had been on its way for more than three months, and because our mother refused even to touch it, so sinister did it seem to her, it fell to me to open it, and I admit that even I hesitated at the well-tied bundle and was torn. Robert had left nothing behind, no note and absolutely no explanation, and suddenly here was this canvas sack from America, like a bequest and an explanation from the other side.

I hadn't held the books in my hands for a long time, novels like Walter Percy's *The Moviegoer*, F. Scott Fitzgerald's *The Great Gatsby* and Paul Bowles' *The Sheltering Sky*, and as I took a few of them off the shelf at random I remembered Daniel reading them that summer by the river. He had lain on a towel with a straw mat under him, right at the farthest tip of the gravel bar, and had only come back to the house occasionally, to point out something he had read or to get himself something to drink, while Christoph carried out the last of the renovation work all on his own. Together they had got as far as installing the flue that for a long time had lain next to the veranda, they had laid the roofing felt and finally, on a whim, hoisted a fantasy flag, but no sooner had Daniel started reading than it was all over for him. He withdrew into himself for hours at a time, and then one day said that it had gradually dawned on him exactly why I had bought the old mill. I didn't ask him what he meant but whenever I thought back to those weeks later, everything shifted in me again just as it had shifted in me at the time. The river immediately became wider, vast in its expanse, the distance from the town greater, the mountains retreated, and I saw us on an open plain on which die-straight roads intersected and at the edges of which you could fall off the earth, beneath a sky revolving like a planetarium across which clouds drifted, world without end. It was not the first time I had experienced such a shift in the relative magnitude of things, but what bothered me more than anything else was the light. It reminded me of the light I had drawn as a child, in which there was an eye of God together with the obligatory triangle and very bright beams arrowing out of it that were supposed to show a fatherly gaze keeping watch over everyone.

I had a message on my answering machine. The head was asking me to go and see him the following morning at break. Unusual as it seemed, it gave no hint, even on the second and third hearing, to suggest that it had anything to do with the bomb threat or Daniel or the picture in the newspaper. He just said he would be happy if I could arrange to drop in on him at his office, and although he never usually operated that way – normally he talked to me in the corridor when he wanted to see me – there was no reason to suspect anything. I deleted the message, turned off all the lights in the flat and went, as I always did, to stand by the window in the bedroom and look out at the street before getting into bed.

I had seen Daniel standing there one day, after he had spoken to me in school. I never asked him about it, but I am certain it was him. He stood in the entrance porch of the building opposite, in front of which the children had built a snowman, and the light from the nearest streetlamp fell short of his face but there was no doubt it was him, looking up at me. He had not been put off after our conversation in the classroom and had walked home with me (against my will), even taking it on himself to carry my bag, and something of the tension he radiated that day, something of the paradoxical combination of aggression and devotion, if not sub-servience, also seemed to be present in the form down there in the dark. I thought about opening the window and shouting across to him or about going downstairs and giving him a fright, but in the end I just put the T.V. on and sat down where he would see me and waited to find out what would happen. It was a quarter of an hour before he left, and if I'm right he purposely took his time about it and made no attempt at all to stay in the shadows, as if he was perfectly happy being recognised.

4

SINCE THEN I HAVE THOUGHT ABOUT HIS GHOSTLY APPARITION
as often as I have about our conversation of the previous day and
its extravagance, and about how uncomfortable I always felt when
anyone came too close to me in the way Daniel presumed to do.
Maybe I have exaggerated the exchange a little, and made his confrontation about my not liking him sound even more wooden and
unreal than it was at the time, but the way I have written it down
brings back the mood of that December day which finished with
Daniel jogging along beside me through the town. I remember that
it started to snow as soon as we left the school, and by the time
we arrived at my building it was falling in thick flakes and he stood
there as if he literally wanted to hand himself over to me and – just
as literally – be shaped by me. I had not asked him before why he
was suddenly so anxious about the right books to read, but I did
then and he said that I had once said that you are what you read,
and he had always wanted to be someone else or, if he couldn't be
that, at least totally himself.

His scorn was unmistakable, but I recommended three books
anyway, among them Stifter's *Indian Summer*, because I had discovered that it was a decisive test and either turned a person off
reading once and for all, or finally made them a reader. As I said, I
was careful at the outset not to include any of Robert's books, and
perhaps what most surprised me was that nothing else happened,
at least not for the time being. I was worried about the first lesson

the following Tuesday, because I expected his presumptuousness to continue and thought he might have a go at me in front of the whole class the way he had the previous Saturday, but he sat at his desk as if the discussion between us had not happened. Yes, he stared at me, and I was nervous, I hardly dared turn my back on him and watched every word and phrase I said for how it would sound, but towards the end of the lesson I asked him a question and he answered me without irony, without any presumption of intimacy or anything else that might have compromised me. As soon as the bell rang I hurried to get out of the classroom as fast as I could so that he couldn't accost me again, but the next lesson I didn't bother and all that happened was that from then on he would ask me for new book recommendations every week or two. He had read the first books I gave him, or claimed he had – he didn't say whether he'd liked them, so I couldn't tell. I also didn't know where he was getting the books from: they were all to be found in the school library, but he might have been in a position to buy them for himself. The time when he started borrowing them from me was yet to come.

I can't say that there was anything striking about his written work at that time. If I were to say there was, it would only be with hindsight, so as to make things seem more logical. Well written, yes, well, at least no spelling mistakes, properly punctuated and occasionally even an unexpected thought, an unusual way of expressing himself, but I don't kid myself: the naked unguarded idealism that they contained goes with the age as a rule and is sometimes just the easiest way to make the teacher happy, or what students think will make the teacher happy. Basically it's a system of mutual deception, not a world problem for which there would be no suggested solutions outside the classroom, with a fancy structure divided into introduction, body and conclusion, and woe betide you if you have nothing else to say apart from the fact that the subject is more complicated in reality and depends on making the right compromises; woe betide you if you give the impression that you don't believe in goodness in the world, don't believe in the possibilities in people, their pursuit of happiness, and the right to a beautiful life before death.

Which is not to digress particularly, only to indicate why the article Daniel wrote the following spring for the local paper about his two weeks in Israel was, in one sense, a surprise to me but then, in another sense, no surprise at all. He had been one of two pupils selected to accompany Herr Bleichert on a trip to the Holy Land that my colleague wanted to make over Easter with a group of pilgrims, and the consequences had packed a punch. The paper was a free sheet delivered with the mail, a fantastical mixture of adverts and regional news, which I throw straight in the recycling, so that the first I was aware of it was when the head called me in and enquired whether I knew anything about it. Herr Bleichert had a day off, so it was from me instead of him that the head had requested more information. It was nine o'clock and he had already taken three calls asking him what outrageous mischief was being spread in connection with the school, the reason being that the article was not only signed with Daniel's name but readers were also informed that he was a student in the *Gymnasium*'s upper school and would be taking his *Matura* in two years' time.

"Have a look at this," the head said when I walked into his office, handing me the open newspaper. "If I'm not very much mistaken, we have a problem."

He offered me a seat and stood by the window while I scanned the article. The headline was "The Land of Israel" and underneath it "Impressions of a Pilgrim in the Holy Land". At the end the paper announced that this was the first in a series that would be continued in three further articles in the coming weeks. After a quick first glance I began to read more attentively. All the time I was reading, the head seemed to be shuffling from one leg to the other. Chewing on a pencil, he alternately stared at the chestnut tree outside his window and then turned expectantly back towards me.

"Pretty muddled stuff," I said, looking at him. "How on earth did it get into the paper?"

"You're asking me," he said. "As if you didn't know who the owner of this rag is? You've only got to see the old hypocrite in church on Sundays. He was on the trip with them, and this sort of bigotry is exactly his idea of telling it like it is."

"But what's Daniel got to do with it?"

"That's what I'd like you to tell me."

He looked at me as if he wanted to make doubly sure that I wasn't hiding anything from him.

"You're very close to him."

I would not have put it like that, but I did not contradict him, merely pointing out that he would do better to get Herr Bleichert's response, and at the mention of the chaplain's name the head came alive. He called to his secretary and asked her if she had managed to reach him, and when she said no reacted with a frown of disappointment that I felt was disproportionate and reminded me of his wife and the warmth she displayed towards me every time I visited them. Then he turned back to me and added that it had been Herr Bleichert who had brought this on him, and God help him when he finally got his hands on him.

"Ultimately he talked the lad into this trip *and* paid for it out of his own pocket," he said. "Who really goes on this sort of trip, apart from the usual bigots and a few ageing altar-boys?"

I had asked myself the same question. It had been announced as a once-in-a-lifetime opportunity to get to know the places in

Jesus' life, and had almost been called off at the last minute after a Jewish settler had fired into the crowd at the Ibrahimi Mosque in Hebron at Friday prayers and killed more than two dozen worshippers and wounded many more. There could hardly have been a worse moment for a trip to Israel than so soon after this attack, which later became notorious as the Cave of the Patriarchs massacre or the Machpela Cave massacre, because more people had died in the rioting that took place in the days that followed and an uprising had been expected in the occupied territories; it was hardly possible to imagine how the pilgrims had got around the country in their rented bus. It had been supposed to be a journey "of peace and reconciliation", and Daniel told me later that this was what Herr Bleichert had said each time to the armed soldiers at the roadblocks where they were stopped and checked and then either waved through or turned back without explanation. Laughably, on such occasions they had parked the bus at the roadblock and held an open-air mass, inviting the soldiers to pray with them – as laughable as when they had visited Bethlehem and driven out to "Shepherds' Fields" to sing "Silent Night" in the church there and then collected together a few Palestinian children and broken bread with them in sight of the settlements of east Jerusalem before giving them some coins and pictures of the Mother and Child as a reward for their co-operation.

Actually, you hardly knew whether to laugh or cry, so unconnected to reality was it, and the head was right to be het up.

"Just what everyone's been waiting for, obviously. A sixteen-year-old to explain to them how a hundred-year-old conflict between Israelis and Palestinians, with all its wars, can be solved. The love of Jesus as a universal panacea."

Only a day after their flight back home, nine people had lost their lives in the Palestinian suicide bombing of a bus in a town not far from Nazareth. It had been an act of revenge at the end of the forty days' mourning for the dead of Hebron, and exactly a week later there had been another attack, with six dead. Since then not a week had gone by without a new attack, and an article like Daniel's, which made no mention of such events, was obviously a scandal if he insisted on treating his trip to Israel solely as a journey to a biblical land that had no present, just a past in a pastoral setting whose idyll was menaced only by the wrath of God.

"Perhaps we shouldn't take it too seriously," I said. "It's just his youthful idealism. He'll soon come round to seeing that it takes more than a little goodwill. In any case, he's certainly not the only one who thinks the way he does."

It was a half-hearted attempt to come to Daniel's defence, but the head looked at me as if he hadn't heard me properly and said that if that were the case, then they were all crazy and he had no interest in them, as long as they didn't go to his school. He took the newspaper out of my hand and quoted – without looking at it – that the God of Abraham, Isaac and Jacob was as much a god of war as the God of Mohammed. It was there in black and white, and so were the words he barked out next, again without glancing at the paper. He said that Daniel had described it as a call to genocide which the Lord had addressed to His people, but in which the boy had committed the error of taking Him literally when He ordered the Israelites to strike the Amalekites or the Canaanites.

"Do you know what that means?"

I said no.

"To overcome them with the edge of the sword, to stamp them out and blot out the memory of them from under heaven. Just look at the exact words. 'Devote to destruction man and woman, and infant, ox and sheep, camel and donkey.'"

"Where on earth did he get that from?"

"It's in the Bible, and obviously he's also quoted the verse in which Joshua asks the Lord to hold back the sun so that night will come later and the killing can continue in daylight."

"That's in the Bible?" I said. "It's ghastly."

"It's the word of God," he said. "It's what the boy's made out of it that's ghastly. Even though recent events have been completely ignored in his article, people are going to make a connection. No student can be so naïve that he can't see that, or if he is so naïve he ought to stay at home and not travel blindly through a country in a state of emergency."

The head had talked himself into a highly excited state, with which I sympathised. He then said that it seemed to him even less appropriate than usual in this situation to set the genocidal God of the Jews against another god who was a child and made of nothing but love.

"You could just as easily reduce the whole cult of the Nazarene to him having supposedly said that he had come, not to bring peace, but the sword."

I watched him as the phone rang and he walked to his desk, shaking his head, and picked up the receiver. He gave little sign but I couldn't miss the fact that it was yet another caller about the article. When he put the receiver down he complained that the ripples had already reached Vienna: it had been an official representative of the Jewish religious community, who had demanded that he make Daniel withdraw this nonsense and that an explanation of how the article had been allowed to appear should be published in the next edition of the newspaper.

"That's all I need," he said. "The first thing I have to do is call up Herr Frischmann and ask him to halt publication of the series."

Frischmann was the paper's owner, whom the head described as a 99 per cent reasonable man with whom there were nevertheless certain subjects you couldn't talk about because the remaining 1 per cent was Catholic zealot, which was frequently enough to make him a loose cannon.

"For that reason alone it's by no means certain how he'll react. He'll only have to get a whiff of who's behind the protest for him to dig his heels in and refuse point-blank to take orders from anyone. Then there'll be no talking to him at all."

He looked at me, but I had the feeling that he was looking through me and would have preferred not to have let me in on the story at all. Suddenly he seemed to be in a hurry.

"Come and see us again soon," he said with an absent-mindedness that was unlike him. "My wife keeps asking after you, saying that we never hear from you."

With his hand on my shoulder he guided me to the door, naturally not without enquiring if everything was all right with me but, in complete contrast to the attentiveness and concern he usually showed towards me, he did not wait for the answer but told his secretary she could show the boy in, as though I already wasn't there. I went out while Daniel, who must have been waiting in the corridor, went in. There was a moment when we passed each other and he looked at me as if he not only knew what it was all about but also as if I had been in on it from the start, or that what he had done, he had done with me in mind or at least under the assumption that I would approve. I could have been mistaken, but there was both agitation and satisfaction in his look, and something else. The look was actually the look of someone who has a close relationship with someone else – yes, just the way the head had put it – and he seemed positively determined that the secretary should not miss it, and to enjoy it when he saw her looking back and forth between us in confusion.

It was much later when I found out how Daniel's conversation with the head had gone, basically not till that summer by the river, when the subject came up and I asked him about it again.

"How do you think it went?" he answered. "He walked up and down in front of me and wanted to know if I could imagine what I had done to the school's reputation."

Although he had carried on pacing all the time he was talking, the head had seemed to want to stay calm, but in the end he had erupted.

"You're not fooling me. Everything you wrote is secondhand rubbish you've been fed by the chaplain. I don't accept that you yourself believe one single word of what you wrote."

"Yes I do," Daniel said. "I do."

"All that pathetic Jesus-drivel."

"I'm sorry to contradict you, sir," he said. "But I must tell you that I do believe it."

He was away for more than an hour, and when he came back into class it was my lesson, but he didn't let anything show and sat still on his bench. He may have watched me more attentively than usual but he didn't say anything to me at breaktime, which I was expecting him to do. The three subsequent articles did not appear; instead there was a short editorial that carried Herr Frischmann's initials in which, in honeyed phrases, he stated that certain circles in Vienna might take exception to the fact that Israel was also the land of Jesus, and so the paper was waiving its continuation of the travelogue but reserved the right to return to it at an appropriate time. For a time Herr Bleichert's bass voice no longer dominated conversations in the staffroom, from which I gathered that he had been properly slapped down, and what could have blown up into a scandal subsided into whispers and silence. I didn't think any more about it until, a few days after the commotion, one of the head's invitations summoned me to dinner at his house, and his wife suddenly started to wax lyrical about Daniel.

"From what I've heard, he seems to be a remarkable boy," she said, after mentioning that she herself had thought for a time that she would go on the trip. "I think it's a pity that no-one encourages him in his thinking."

She had been a believer since before her son had died, but it had never been something that had played any part in my visits and I was worried there was about to be a full-on confession. I looked at her: she seemed to have aged noticeably since the last time, or perhaps it was the head's concerned expression that made her suddenly look older – a fortysomething woman who found it visibly more difficult to maintain her poise. She had, as always, got herself ready as if she were going out, applied lipstick and put her hair up, and did not seem to notice how he was staring at her. In fact he did not let her out of his sight, and it was obvious there were things he did not want to hear from her, in a way that made it one of those moments that provide a profound insight into the tangled web of a couple's life, whether you like it or not, and I did not. A fraction of a second was enough for a man and a woman to be no longer the same people, and I could imagine how they would suddenly change towards each other when I left, and it saddened me. I feared what the head also seemed to fear, which was that she would talk about their son, or perhaps that that was what she had been doing all the time when she talked about Daniel.

"Tell me what he's like," she said, with an eagerness that made her lips tremble and also seemed to be responsible for making the dampness of her skin visible on her cheeks. "He's your favourite pupil, after all."

This was after dinner, during which she had again declined any wine so firmly that I thought she might have a drink problem. The empty plates were still on the table and the head stood up without speaking and started to clear them away. I stared at him, looking for support as he opened another bottle, and seconds crawled by before I finally answered.

"I'd say he's far in advance of his years in some ways, and in others a long way behind," I said, and I wasn't saying it for the sake of it, it was what I thought, even if I had never really articulated it to myself. "He asks me to recommend books that he should read and reads them as though each one is a revelation."

"He apparently still goes to school mass regularly."

"Yes," I said. "The chaplain is thrilled to have him."

"And he must write good essays."

"Yes," I said again. "A bit precocious perhaps."

"Has he got a girl?"

It was striking that she didn't say girlfriend, and I tried not to let my irritation show. Her son had not been twenty when he died, and that seemed to resonate with her question. I'd have preferred not to answer her at all, because for some reason I suddenly felt that she was getting too close to me too, but I couldn't ignore her.

"I don't think girls interest him," I said, not caring at all whether she would misunderstand me. "At least I've never seen him with one."

It could have gone on like this if the head hadn't interrupted us. His hands resting on the back of her chair, he stood behind her as though ready to grab hold of her at any moment. He said that he had told her all this already and he didn't understand why she wanted to hear it from me all over again, let alone what meaning these trivial details had for her. He didn't seem irritated, but when she started speaking again it was plain that he was hiding something under his show of calm.

"All I'm saying is that you shouldn't have stopped the articles just because some people in Vienna were threatening to cause a scandal if you didn't."

"It's not 'some people in Vienna'," he said. "It was the Jewish religious community, and no-one was threatening to cause a scandal."

"All the more reason why you shouldn't let yourselves be dictated to."

"No-one was dictating to us, dearest."

"That's not what you said to me last time," she said. "As soon as it's about Israel, everyone starts shitting themselves and for fear of saying anything wrong no-one says anything right either."

"Oh darling, do you really think it's as simple as that?"

"I didn't claim it was simple," she said, and the more he resorted to his game of indulgent contradiction to try to disarm her, the more stubborn she seemed to become. "And stop calling me darling."

No, it was apparently not the first time they had had this conversation, and I could sense how uneasy he felt as his wife's excitement turned to scorn at the threat to world peace presented by a sixteen-year-old schoolboy.

"What he wrote might be a bit obsessive but perhaps that's no bad thing, given the one-sided reporting we otherwise have to put up with about Israel."

He had stopped correcting her, and I made no response either. Neither he nor she had ever spoken to me about how their son had died, and I only knew the story told around school. If it was true, drugs had been involved, and ever since, people said, she had lost faith in reality and become receptive to all sorts of sectarianism, all sorts of threadbare "evidence" that things were not how they seemed at first glance. This had never struck me on my visits before; I had thought of her as a gentle, introverted woman who preferred meekly to accept things for what they were rather than set herself up in any kind of opposition, but now it did strike me. I had always been surprised at people who spent their time proving that Shakespeare wasn't Shakespeare, whatever that meant, or that two or three hundred years of our calendar had never existed, and I felt that here too there must be some personal need hovering in the background – behind the increasingly bizarre statements she wrapped herself in. Perhaps it was her determination to undermine everything that made the fragility of her own existence more bearable to her: breaking things down, I sensed, was the only way she could ultimately accept that things did indeed stand on solid ground.

I left them late that evening. The head came out with me and I thought he was going to say something by way of explanation. Instead he just pressed my hand and shook his head. I waited till the door had closed behind him and hurried away through the darkness. It was after midnight when I got home and I can still see myself standing in front of the bookshelf with Robert's books on, deciding which one to take to bed with me. At the time this was still a nightly ritual for me, and although I've left it behind me now, I remember the conflict it represented for me. Even today I can't say whether Robert read himself out of the world or whether it was the exact opposite, a vain attempt to keep himself in the world by reading. As so often, I took down one volume after another and then put them back without opening them or after leafing quickly through them. Then I turned off the lights and stood for a while without moving in the dark.

5

THE MORNING AFTER THE SURPRISE AT BRUCKNER'S, I WOKE UP
feeling I had escaped from a nightmare. I still didn't know what I
should make of it, and when I pulled out the newspaper cutting
again and looked at the photo I couldn't make up my mind. I
thought about my conversation with Agata and about Inspector
Hule's reassurances and could not work out how I had once again
managed to fantasise my way into such a dark place on such slender
grounds. There had been a bomb threat that not even the police
seemed to take seriously, and here I was blowing it out of all pro-
portion; but the kind of state I was in only came home to me when
I thought about calling, of all the people in all the world, Barbara,
even though it was also not the right time of day *and* I hadn't been
in touch for a very long time *and* she would ask me about the
incident and was obviously the last person I could discuss it with.
She had always advised me, when the subject arose, to break off
my connection with Daniel: he had no future, because he wanted
to be exactly like that, and he would take me down with him into
the abyss. She had in fact made a huge fuss about it, and sometimes
when he turned up and she was visiting me, had gone to stay in a
hotel, until after a particularly violent clash she had made it clear
once and for all that she would not spend another night under
the same roof with him and I had to decide: him or her. This was
after his winter months staying at the house by the river, and his
stay in Bosnia, at a time when I still thought he would end up

settling in the town somehow and I had tried to get him a job at the library or in the municipal administration, when he'd turn up at my place and ask if he could stay for a couple of days, seeming embarrassed when I asked him what he was up to, embarrassed and quick-tempered too, saying he would soon be on his feet and didn't need my help. Whenever I offered him a few schilling (or, later, euros) – or slipped them into his trouser pocket without saying anything – he was pleased, but he always refused to talk about how he got by otherwise. I heard scraps here and there, on the street and in the pub, and when I wanted to know whether it was true that he was working on a construction site, or delivering beer for the brewery further upstream, he didn't answer because to me he wanted to preserve the appearance of being destined for great things. He sketched out plans about how he would get rich overnight, and if he were to do it by robbing a bank, then of course it would be so elegantly executed that he would become an instant legend; he talked about picking up his studies again in the autumn and one day, in all seriousness, boasted that he was going to write a novel about our summer that would make him world-famous and rich and a hit with women.

I had got to know Barbara in Istanbul years before, when she was still studying, or to be more precise not in Istanbul but on a trip from Istanbul to Adana, in the far southeast of Turkey. She had dashed onto the platform at Haydarpaşa with her friend and they had boarded the train at the last minute, two young women with rucksacks packed over their heads who had sat down opposite me as the train rolled out of the station and started to talk to each other in a strikingly self-conscious way. They were from Vienna, and for a day and night we shared the compartment with a Turkish family, mother, father and two children, on the famous Baghdad Railway. We went on talking in whispers after the others had gone to sleep, and at the end of the journey I had Barbara's phone number in my hand, which she'd handed over to me with a look of curiosity, as if she wanted to know what I would do with it. It took, as they say, for ever for anything to occur between us; months often went by when we didn't see each other, then we'd meet for three or four weekends in a row, but I always longed for the time "before" when there was nothing going on. In my head I kept that picture of her that I had preserved from our first meeting, her categorical way of engaging in conversation, of changing the subject when it got too personal, the clarity of her thinking which was mirrored in the clarity of her movements and – as I thought much later when, in a hotel room in Vienna, she pulled her dress over her head without fuss and stood in front of me, naked – her body.

About Daniel: I am convinced that she didn't like him from the word go, and that was much more to do with her work than with our little exchange in which she asked me what kind of relationship I had with him and I answered her question with another question and said, how did she mean? It was a touchy reaction, I admit, because she was not the first to want an explanation from me, but as I say, I don't think that was the reason for her reserve towards him. It started straight after I had introduced them, she had already qualified as a lawyer at the time, defending mostly young offenders, and perhaps I'm being unfair but I couldn't get rid of a feeling that from the moment she met him she couldn't help seeing him as a potential client. Whether that was clear-sightedness or professional blindness, it did not escape me that on the weekends when she came to stay, his mere presence made her feel attacked in every part of her existence. She avoided being alone with him, and accused him of not respecting her wishes and intentionally bringing about encounters when I was not there. I didn't know what was true and what merely an expression of her feeling cramped at living in such a small space with him. If I was to believe her, she only needed to go into town and he would pop up on the other side of the street within seconds of her leaving the flat and follow her, which came across as all the more obvious because he would turn away as soon as she looked towards him. She would collect the bike from the basement and he would meet her on the stairs, as if by chance. She would go running in the forest and see him sitting in every tree, and of course I remember very clearly her suppressed panic when she woke me one night just as it was getting light and said that she was sure he had just been in our room. I sat up and listened, and although I could not read anything into her face I felt her tension and let myself be persuaded to go and see him.

Directly after this we had that conversation that changed everything. It's so easy to say, but when I came back to our room and saw her sitting bolt upright in bed I knew straight away that something was fundamentally wrong. No sooner had I said that she must have been mistaken than she jumped down my throat. I had never seen her in such a state, simultaneously distraught and composed, and it seems clear to me now that I had been underestimating her feelings for a long while. I had relied on her quickly appreciating how harmless Daniel was, that he was a confused young man who, given time, would definitely get back on his feet; but the opposite happened and she was adamant that it was not a game, that she had the impression that he wanted to test exactly how far he could go and how much she could take. He was hard to get the measure of in those days, she was right about that, beginning with how he looked: he could turn up at my flat looking as scruffy and rumpled as if he had been sleeping rough, and a couple of weeks later he could appear all spruced up, even if his shirt and trousers were too big and his pullover too small, and he'd topped them off extravagantly with a slouch hat or his favourite cap with earmuffs. Along with his tendency suddenly to start quoting from the Old Testament or to cross himself, as if to bring himself back to his senses, it was enough to make her anxious.

"I'm still not clear why you let that weirdo into your home," she said. "I find it pathetic, the way you cling onto him."

I had already explained to her several times that I couldn't leave him in the lurch in his situation, and did so again.

"He relies on me. It's not as if you don't know exactly why he's here. I can't just show him the door."

I could hear the pleading in my voice, which I hadn't intended, hear how unconvincing it sounded, and how she laughed when I asked her to give me a bit more time.

"You see him as your creation," she said. "That story about the books you give him to read is sick." She seemed to hesitate, then went on vehemently, "Just what is it that fascinates you so much?"

They were the same reproaches as always, accompanied by an exaggerated weariness at having to get involved with the subject all over again, and I could have said anything I liked, I still wouldn't have got through to her. She had tilted the window open and the rain was audible, a regular hissing that had started the evening before, and now it was early morning and it was still raining or had started again. The light on the table on her side of the bed was on, casting a pale, milky light, and I could see her face clearly and it was neither hostile nor expressionless: I recognised with a shock that it was the face of a stranger.

"I'd very much like to know what you feel you have to apologise for," she said. "For months you've been promising me, 'Just a few days more and it'll all be different,' but you don't want anything to be different. You want it all to stay exactly as it is. I'll say it again, it's pathetic."

I had feared nothing more than this conversation. Crouching on the floor by the bed, I let the first storm wash over me, and my only resistance was to try to hold her hand, to which she responded by moving away from me. It would be another hour until day broke properly and I clung to the thought that if I could hold out till then I would be saved from everything that was happening, because it would all reveal itself to be a nightmarish episode.

"I've told you, he was my best pupil. At the very moment when he's in difficulty, should I behave as if I've forgotten that? Surely you understand that I feel responsible for him?"

"Whatever," she said. "It's just sentimental crap."

Her voice suddenly sounded resigned.

"The truth is, you're probably also proud of him lying around in a darkened room all day watching T.V. or reading the holy books you give him and that are supposed to bring him enlightenment."

It wasn't long since she had read his report about his journey to Israel, and I had been careless enough to tell her that he was also secretly working on a novel. Now she started to attack that too. She had picked up the habit of referring to him scornfully as "Mr Artist", and said it was the old story: that he could do whatever he pleased, because he was a chosen one, that he had the right to be obnoxious because he thought himself exempt from the rules that applied to ordinary mortals. I had heard it all before and never really taken it seriously because I could not imagine her being capable of that kind of resentment, but now I was learning differently. She complained for the umpteenth time that he would grab himself between his legs whenever she met him in the corridor, and that he left the bathroom door unlocked and she had to see him sitting in all his splendour and glory on the throne if she wasn't careful to make sure in advance whereabouts in the flat he was at any given moment.

"But why should I be pissed off? He's Mr Artist, so of course he can do that. Everything serves as inspiration for him, and who am I to deny him that?"

She had pulled even further away from me and looked as if she might fall out of the other side of the bed. I had stopped touching her, but her movements were still defensive and I knew that whatever I did would feel false and trigger the same reaction in her and drive her further away. Outside there was the sound of a car approaching, and seeing her listening to it I hoped that the sound of ordinary life would make her conscious of the absurdity, but no sooner had the sound of the engine faded into the distance than she started again.

"That's what you get for your homilies. 'You've failed as a teacher if you work hard for years and all you produce are useful members of society.' You should hear yourself talk sometimes."

"Am I supposed to have said that?"

"Don't behave as if that's no longer what you think," she said. "Do you want another sample of your wisdom?"

I would happily have gone without, but she needed to get it out.

"'Anything's better than a normal life, anything's better than to become one of the clowns that keep the whole nonsense going, one of the tie-wearers who never realise that they put the rope that's choking them around their own necks.'"

It sounded terrible, and even if I couldn't deny that I might actually have said it, I refused to accept the picture of a secondary-school teacher gone wild that went with it.

"Nothing but clichés," I said. "Spare me that."

The way she laughed still rings in my ears.

"They're your own exact words, and you couldn't have said them with more contempt. You probably have to be unsackable and entitled to a thirteenth and fourteenth month's salary to be able to make speeches like that and not realise how hypocritical they are. I'd like to call it romantic but actually it's just pathetic and stupid and I don't know how you have the nerve to put yourself above everyone else."

"But I'm not."

"Oh no?" she said. "Just look at you. Where do you get your certainty that you're better than the rest of us? Just try applying your theories to yourself."

She was sitting with her back to me, on the edge of the bed now, her feet on the floor. She had bent over to put some shoes on and her hair had fallen forward over both her shoulders. She went on talking, and it sounded as if she was just going over things for her own benefit, things didn't need any more words.

"Still, after all your years of hard work you've at last got your perfect candidate, a student who's so utterly different from every-one else that you can place your very highest hopes in him," she said. "With a gentleman artist of his calibre, no-one need ever worry that he'll be a useful member of society."

She went further, saying that she would rather be locked in a room with the worst delinquents she had to represent in court than go out for an evening with Daniel and then, just as I thought she had finished, she came out with the prediction that I haven't been able to get out of my head since.

"It'll probably be less than three years before he gets involved with the police and the way I see it, that's exactly how you want things to turn out too, deep down."

Yes, the conversation was everything I had feared. In fact it was not the first time she had had a go at me, but after the first out-burst she had never come so close to breaking off our relationship and speaking, not obliquely, as she usually did, but directly about Robert. I had begged her to leave him out of the equation when one day she asked me why I didn't move away from the town, why I didn't want to come to her in Vienna and not only preferred to go to the dogs in this backwater but even took a sort of ghastly pleasure in doing so, so self-regarding infatuated with loss was I. Certainly it didn't take much to conclude that I was punishing myself, that I had imposed a penance on myself for some intangible offence. All of this was as obvious as it was false and as far-fetched as it was right, but I didn't want to hear it put so baldly, and particularly not from her. That time I simply replied that it was beneath her dignity, and ever since she had not said another word about it, but I wasn't under any illusion: next time, or the time after that, there was no guarantee that I would be spared.

As soon as she got up she drove away, and I don't know if I'm over-analysing the situation, but when I sat down to breakfast with Daniel I did feel I detected something triumphant in his behaviour. When I had gone through to him he had been lying in bed, his eyes open, and had put a finger to his lips, and now he seemed buoyed up by the awareness of an unspoken understanding and spread butter on his roll in a relaxed way that was totally unlike his usual habit of slopping a few drops of milk over a bowl of cornflakes and hurriedly gulping them down by the fridge. He had fetched the newspaper and made coffee and was waiting for me, freshly showered, combed and outwardly as baby-faced as a confirmation candidate. He sat down where Barbara would have sat and beamed at me, as if he already knew what would only become clear to me over the following few weeks, namely that she would carry out her threat and never come back.

Four or five months later I saw her on T.V., and it was Daniel who drew my attention to her appearance. There are often televised discussions relating to her work in which, since that first time, she is called to take part, but this was her first appearance and I hated sitting with Daniel and watching her make her point, hated that he could look at her the same way I could; I really hated him that day, I can't say it any other way, and not just because I knew he was envious of her, because he refused to acknowledge how cleverly she argued and how young and fresh and concise she appeared to be, among all the other long-winded speakers. Just then I remembered how she had once said that she didn't know what other problems he had but he certainly had a problem with women, and although she was wearing a suit, as I sat next to him I couldn't escape the feeling that he was staring at her in an unpleasantly appraising way. I hadn't said anything when he had stood over our bed in the middle of the night and Barbara had lain at the mercy of his stare, but I could have strangled him at that moment. I wanted to switch to another channel, but I stayed sitting in front of the screen as if paralysed, literally pierced to the heart by her sudden presence and the equally sudden awareness of her absence, and could only watch her, open-mouthed with amazement that it was the same woman, the same smile, the same eyes, the same way of tilting her head to the side when she listened. Her husky breathing when she paused had always been a totally private quirk of hers for me, but now it sounded like a signature that she had cultivated for her public self and I peered across at Daniel to see whether he had heard it too. I saw her roll her eyes at the stupidity of one of her interlocutors and I loathed him seeing her face the way I had seen it, with her pupils rolled upwards, dead and empty like a mask.

The programme's title escapes me now, but it was about increasing criminality among today's youth, and it was significant that Daniel kept up his aggressive attitude throughout, making it clear whenever she said something that in his opinion she didn't know anything about. I found it hard to follow the discussion and I didn't know whether I should believe him when he claimed at the end that she had really been talking about him, him and me. What she had actually said was that there were too many teachers for whom the image of the good, obedient student had fallen into disrepute, but I don't suppose she needed me as a model, much as it might sound like a continuation of the discussion that night. I let Daniel go on talking, although it pained me and I knew that when he imitated her, explaining in her voice that the classic virtues were being denigrated, saying in her voice that there was a problem when people encouraged every kind of deviant behaviour and thus lost sight of what was actually going on, he was directing it at me. Then he went off into a high-pitched voice, saying the words pride, and decency, and honesty, and then with a long pause after each saying "nil", rounding off his performance with a neighing laugh.

On that occasion I had wanted to get in touch with her first thing next morning, but it was only a momentary impulse and at the idea of actually talking to her I had instantly dismissed the idea. Her unexpected proximity on my T.V. screen had finally distanced her from me. The time that had passed since then would have made my calling her now seem even more bizarre. I would have had to say I was calling about Daniel and listen to questions about whether he was in difficulty and whether I remembered what she had prophesied for him when I had told her about my fears, and that on its own was enough to put me off. Perhaps she would choose that moment to tell me that as I had chosen him, I would have to work out for myself where I stood with him, and my telling her that she was wrong, or reminding her that she had left the flat without saying goodbye and before I was up and had had any chance to make my mind up, would not make any difference.

I went to particular trouble getting dressed that morning, choosing one of the two suits I had had made for myself in Istanbul and that Barbara, using her favourite adjective, had described as pathetic. She had begged me not to wear them in her presence because she could not decide whether I was taking myself too seriously by dressing in such an old-fashioned way or whether, on the contrary, I was trying for some incomprehensible reason to make myself a laughing stock. I said, both, refusing to make any further comment, and now, remembering what I had said, I felt it was a comfortable sort of attitude, if I could only keep it up.

It had been just before Christmas of the first year in Istanbul when I had resolved to change my outward appearance, and little as I had gone out till then, I started extending the radius of my walks around my flat in Cihangir and the Austrian School in Galata, even once going along the Golden Horn to Eyüp and then beyond, until night fell. For all my adult life I had dressed at best carelessly and would probably never have given it another thought if a coffee-table book of moody photographs of Istanbul at the turn of the century hadn't alerted me to the city's fashionable extravagance. In fact, I had felt connected less to the men pictured in the photographs, all dressed in the style of the day, than to the past and places that no longer existed. Nonetheless, the same day I went to a tailor near Taksim Square and ordered a light summer suit and a three-piece for winter, as though that was all that was needed to wander through the streets like one of those lost figures, to lean against a lamp post with an obligatory cigarette in the corner of my mouth or walk side by side with a woman into a future that had already turned into the past long before. I can still remember the half-darkness at the back of the shop in which my metamorphosis began, a darkness where a few discarded dummies stood clustered together and old patterns gathered dust on a table under a naked bulb, and out of this darkness the ageless tailor just seemed to materialise to take my measurements. There was nothing hurried about him, it was more something unstoppably compulsive; he tried to avoid all contact, floating his hand at minimal distance and with long flowing gestures over the outline of my body, as if conjuring, before he applied his tape measure. He restricted his speech to the minimum too, after I had made myself understood and selected the cloth, and when I came back ten days later and kept the three-piece on, he nodded approvingly, as if he knew the reason why I had dressed myself in his tailor's shop and wanted to confide to me that I was not the first, and in truth there was a whole legion of men whom he had not only fitted out with new jackets and trousers, but with new lives too. I've worn both suits so much since I bought them that they have gone baggy at the knees and elbows and have shiny places, but have not lost their function; on the contrary, they perform it all the better, the older and shabbier they become. They transport me in a twinkling into a parallel world, making me visible in a way that is sometimes very close to invisibility, the sort that you can only get from a magic cape.

6

THE HEAD DEMOLISHED ALL MY ILLUSIONS AS SOON AS I ENTERED his office. He started talking about Daniel straight away, saying that he had not thought we would ever have to have another conversation about the lad; his mere use of that word immediately brought back the situation from twelve years earlier and the commotion that had gone on for days about his report from Israel. All that was missing was him starting on about my "close relationship with Daniel" all over again, but that he did not do. He sat at his desk, not bothering to get up or greet me but instead continuing to sign papers in a folder, and there was something pointedly perfunctory about the way he jerked his chin to indicate the chair facing him.

"Apparently there are some people connecting him with the bomb threat," he said without looking at me. "I'd be interested to know what you think."

He was sixty-two or sixty-three now, his hair thick and snow-white, on good days still an imposing presence, as people say, while on less good days his weariness left a grey patina over his face, as though dust was imperceptibly trickling from the lines around his mouth. It was common knowledge that Frau Pfeifer, the new biology teacher, was his elixir of youth and very much responsible for whether it was a good day or not. Over the last two years his wife had gone into dry dock — as her unambiguously and hatefully named stays at the sanatorium were called — twice for a period of several weeks, and the last time they had invited me to dinner I had formed the impression that their solicitude was getting a bit tired, and they had enough to deal with themselves.

"How long have you worked here?"

I was so surprised by his question that at first I thought it had to be a misunderstanding, as he put down his fountain pen and gave me a searching stare. I was used to him not always expecting an answer to his questions, but I obediently worked it out and told him and he responded that that was a long time and that my early upsets were a long way behind me now. It was supposedly idle chit-chat, and I had to be careful not to fall into the trap when he then switched to generalities, saying that he did not know a single teacher who had not doubted the value of what they did at some point, but the important thing was how you dealt with it, the important thing was whether you went on, despite your doubts, when things all suddenly seemed meaningless, or whether you just threw in the towel and sought your salvation in flight.

"I don't want to offend you, but if you need a time-out, just make a sign," he said. "Maybe another stay in Istanbul would do you good, or at least a semester off teaching duties or a year doing admin, to give yourself some space."

He took his watch off his wrist and placed it in front of him on his desk, and his look now was that typical teacher's look to which none of us is immune, with its mixture of benevolence and retribution.

"You know I've always spoken up for you."

This was unmistakably a reference to my long-standing dispute with the Parents' Association, which from time to time would get agitated about my reading recommendations and a couple of months earlier had got extremely hot under the collar about a couple of sentences I had uttered in a lesson, so I had an idea about what he was alluding to.

I had said, here's the thing about democracy, which is that all that really matters is the precedence of the physical over the spiritual, because it's not about the head count in an election, and absolutely not about the quality of the heads either, but the fist count. I had said that the majority were nearly always wrong about things, you only needed to look around to find examples everywhere, and the fact that they carried the day notwithstanding had less to do with the triumph of reason than with the threat of force and was, as with any playground brawl, merely due to the fact that the smaller group caved in more promptly because it didn't want to be beaten up by the bigger one.

"Have there been more complaints?"

In order not to have to look at him, I studied the files on the shelf next to his desk, each of which had a year written on it and which contained his day-to-day records. It was rumoured that not only was every meeting meticulously recorded there, not just who had said what and then an overall assessment, but banalities too, petty observations about the weather or what he had eaten on this or that day and whether he had been to the toilet or not. At the thought of this I turned away, focusing my gaze on the framed picture he had in front of him, which I could only see from the back but which I knew was of him with his wife and son. Next to it was a small vase of flowers, and I had to look at them twice to dispel my doubts that they weren't plastic flowers.

"Is it the Parents' Association again?"

He shook his head.

"In one of your classes you talked about the bomb threat."

His informers and spies were everywhere, and I was not in the slightest bit surprised that it had already reached his ears.

"I'm not going to tell you what you should and shouldn't do, but I do wonder why you immediately feel a need to show that you understand it. A little restraint wouldn't go amiss. Nor can I ignore the fact that you offered to fourteen-year-old students a theory that it was sometimes a longing for innocence and purity that motivated a person to shoulder the burden of guilt."

It was exactly what I had said, and exactly what I had thought, but of course he was right about school not necessarily being the place for utterances of that kind.

"Apart from the fact that you ought to leave such fantasies of redemption to the Church, you can make any troublemaker a saint that way," he said. "If that was your aim, you seem to have succeeded."

He was silent for a time, then he wanted to know when I had last seen Daniel, so I told him what I had told Agata.

"At Judith's wedding?"

It was obvious that he did not believe me.

"That's a while ago now," he said, looking me straight in the eye for so long that I had no choice but to look away. "Are you sure that was when it was?"

I said yes, and he retorted that he trusted I wasn't hiding anything, and while I thought about who he might have heard about Daniel's later visit to my flat from, it suddenly became clear that our conversation was teetering on the brink of an interrogation. He had started drawing small, invisible boxes on his desk with his index finger, which he then immediately wiped away with his sleeve, as though he could really see them, and I wanted to ask him to stop. At last he turned away, took a black double-flapped folder out of a desk at his side and put it in front of me. While I hesitated, he flipped it open, and I only needed a second to see that it was the first of the three follow-up articles that Daniel had written about his trip to Israel.

"This has only just come into my hands," he said, with a rather too deliberate casualness. "For you it can't be anything new."

It was plain that he had made enquiries, and that my acknowledgement was a matter of form that he needn't linger on, so he could just carry on talking.

"Until a few days ago I didn't even know this existed, and to tell you the truth it didn't really interest me either, once the whole business had blown over."

I had already had Daniel give me the article in his own time, and had been surprised how little it seemed to have to do at first sight with the original report. He had written nothing in it about the Hebron massacre or the two suicide attacks in its wake, and, more surprisingly, it did not focus on the tourist-oriented itinerary of the Stations of the Cross that he had trudged around with the other pilgrims either. Of course they had walked the path of the Cross in Jerusalem, of course they had been in Bethlehem and Nazareth, of course they had been to Tiberias and the biblical sites on the Sea of Galilee, but he skated over all that, dealing with it no more than dutifully, although if you read between the lines you could tell how much it had preoccupied him. But the heart of the piece was an intense celebration of the desert, glowing descriptions in which he wrote, enraptured, about its barrenness and purity, and which immediately recalled for me individual scenes from the Negev that I still remembered after all these years as if they were yesterday.

"It's wonderful how he conjures up the evening light at the edge of Be'er Sheva, or a sunrise on the way to Masada," I said. "You can literally see in every sentence how affected he was."

The head nodded, looking anything but convinced. He propped his elbows on the desk and leant towards me, as if he wanted to examine me more closely, and I saw the wrinkles in the bags under his eyes, which seemed to be constantly in motion, and my nose registered the faint scent of an aftershave, not unpleasant but not pleasant either in the context of this sudden outbreak of intimacy.

"If he would only confine himself to descriptions, I'd agree with you," he said. "What bothers me is the metaphysical slime he has to underlay everything with."

I asked him what he meant.

"All that religious wilderness-worship that's past its sell-by date outside of the walls of psychiatric institutions," he said. "The desert as the most godforsaken place in the world, where a searcher is closest to God, with nothing except himself between heaven and earth."

It was all well and good, he said: he could understand that in the desert Moses had received the Ten Commandments, that Jesus had fought with Satan in the desert and Mohammed too had doubtless had his key experiences there, but as a human being in the twenty-first century his own requirements were either for no more than homeopathic doses of it or, best of all, not even to be bothered with it. Then he added that what was much more interesting was the unsuccessful founders of religion; that if you wanted to get a real picture of the desert, a real idea of what kind of a place of desire and faith, and superstition and delusion it had been for centuries, then you should restrict your attention to the hundreds or possibly thousands of enlightened ones who had given up everything to go into the desert and whose traces were mercifully lost in the sand or the void of history.

I knew I had to let him talk. It was his way of gathering speed, and over the years this need of his, to encompass a subject as widely as possible before getting to the point, seemed only to have increased. I had had conversations with him in which the essence was dealt with in two minutes, but before and afterwards he had used the time to pontificate about nothing less than the situation of the country or the state of the world. He had long resisted the internet, long resisted computers of all kinds, but recently I had gained the impression that he had started to prepare himself obsessively for every appointment by typing out the keywords that applied to it with two fingers on his keyboard and then persistently tossing at his interlocutor whatever barrage of words came up on the screen.

What was more, I felt that he was misjudging Daniel by reducing him to a god-bothering Bible student; in the follow-up article there were plenty of instances where there was no sense of any false dignity developing. For example, he regularly turned his attention back to the tour group with all their earthly quibbles, and on the days that they spent in Galilee the Israeli air force had ensured that his account remained temporal and not spiritual. Practically every hour there were fighter jets patrolling the Golan Heights on the border with Syria, and even the most devout silence could be shattered without warning by their roar, as happened once when Herr Bleichert was reading the Sermon on the Mount in an olive grove above Magdala and above the clouds an invisible pilot, as if in response, decided to break the sound barrier. Someone wholly wrapped up in their experience of the transcendental would not write that way, nor would he write that the smell of kerosene that hung in the air seemed to belong as much to the smell of incense and scent of candles as the roar of engines belonged to the praying and singing – which inspired in him the blasphemous suggestion that the Holy Land offered the widest variety of means to get to heaven.

I can still remember saying that it would be a mistake to underestimate him, and the head pouncing on the word, replying that precisely the opposite was true and the danger lay in overestimating him.

"Whichever way you look at it, I rather doubt whether he wrote it all for himself," he said. "They're not the views of a sixteen-year-old."

That was true, and when I was reading the thought had of course gone through my mind that Herr Bleichert had probably contributed his share. I had just seen him in the staffroom, and the way he had immediately come over to me had already aroused my suspicions, but now I was sure it wasn't a coincidence. He had asked how I was and wished me the best of good luck, without saying what for or what with, and seeing as we more or less avoided each other otherwise, and for months didn't exchange a word, it was unusual to say the least.

"Some of it sounds a lot like Herr Bleichert," I said. "It would be wrong to lay everything at his door, but he's had a great deal of influence on Daniel."

The director looked directly at me, laughing.

"That's exactly what Herr Bleichert says about you."

He leant even further across the desk than he had before already, and I shrank back involuntarily.

"You don't seem to like each other a great deal."

To set the record straight: I would rather not talk about mutual dislike, I prefer to say that he was always suspicious of me, and I of him, and whenever I tried to get to the bottom of it I always came back to the two occasions he had turned up that summer by the river, and how Daniel had told me to say he wasn't there, how he had asked me almost in front of the chaplain to tell him that he was not to speak for him.

"Two years after the Israel trip, Herr Bleichert was still trying to recruit Daniel for the priesthood, although he should have known it had been out of the question for a long time," I said. "He wasn't particularly sensitive about it either. He stalked Daniel like a lover."

The moment I said it, I regretted using the word. I had no grounds to make dubious allusions, certainly not the sort that I had suffered from myself, and I was relieved at the head's circumspect reaction. At first he looked at me as though he might be about to revise his opinion of me, but then said soothingly that it was an occupational disease among priests, though certainly not a crime, that they thought every lad ought to belong to them as soon as his voice broke and he was shy enough and pimply enough and perhaps getting good marks in one or two subjects.

His words reminded me of a photo that Daniel had shown me of Herr Bleichert. Taken by the Sea of Galilee, very near Capernaum, it showed him standing with outstretched arms on the shore. He was wearing a white tunic like a nightshirt with a large crusader cross and the letters "PAX" on the back, which he had just put on in a changing cabin on the beach, and he seemed to be relishing the occasion. A second later and he would be submerged, swimming a few spluttering strokes to cries of "Hallelujah", but for the moment he was still wondering whether the surface of the water might not bear his weight and let him walk on it. The photograph in any case had been composed so that one should think exactly that, and I remember Daniel saying that it was one of the few occasions on the trip in which Herr Bleichert had allowed himself a joke and not behaved like some grim messenger of the eternal truth.

I did not say anything to the head about the picture, though I was sorely tempted to undermine his air of certainty. I suggested that he should not take Daniel's extravagance so seriously, and earned myself a look that suggested that I had insinuated that he too was stuck in the mindset of an altar-boy. I was familiar with this ambivalence among many who had been raised as religious – a need to distance themselves that alternated with a readiness to turn around and defend something that was not easy to pin down, unless it was a sense of right and wrong that had its source in their childhood and therefore somehow explained their indignation. He told me that I could safely let him be the judge of that, and it was only then that it struck me that his drooping cheeks seemed to move with a slight delay when he spoke, as if they had not been properly synchronised.

From the courtyard behind him there was a sudden noise of shouting, but he did not get up as he usually did, knowing it was enough for him to open the window and show himself, but waited till the noise died down on its own. I thought I had missed the bell for the end of break, but then it started ringing and he and I looked at the clock at the same time. He called his secretary and, in the same way that he had ordered coffee for me without asking me, asked her to go to my class and say I would be late. He leant back as he spoke, as though he wanted to make it even clearer that he could command me as he wished, and asked whether I had also noticed the kind of attitudes Daniel had developed after his stay in Israel.

"Attitudes?"

I knew what he was referring to, but had never made up my mind whether Daniel had been merely posturing or whether he had in fact had some kind of awakening – and perhaps ultimately the two things weren't mutually exclusive.

"He was slightly quirky before he went," I said evasively. "The trip just intensified what was already there."

It was true that I had also wondered about his suddenly adopted habit of strict fasting one day a week and his helping out one afternoon at the nursing home and reading novels to one blind person or another, without payment, but I had not given any thought to his motivation and certainly not to whether it was genuine or not. I had heard that the following autumn he had started making regular pilgrimages to a plague chapel in the woods and had taken to going for long twilit walks by the river, plus it had obviously not escaped me that his appearance had changed. He had swapped his thick glasses for contact lenses, started wearing his hair shoulder-length and longer, let a downy growth sprout on his chin and upper lip, and I knew, because stories had already started circulating about him that culminated in this one, that he had appeared at carnival in Bedouin robes like the second coming of Lawrence of Arabia and had been nicknamed Jesus, not just by his classmates but by the teachers in the staffroom too, pronounced American-style obviously.

"What could have surprised me more than that?"

As I was telling the head this, I noticed him becoming increasingly impatient with my loquacious meanderings. He was now actually slouching in his chair, his hands clasped behind his head, and when I stopped talking he said that it had been a ridiculous programme of austerity and self-denial to which Daniel had subjected himself and described his sudden involvement with the poor and weak as "flashy" and "self-indulgent". He boasted that he could quote a whole collection of slogans from Daniel's repertoire of the time, all of them straightforward expressions of his megalomania and proof of what a shameless impostor he had turned himself into; but he would spare me that.

"His trotting out the same nonsense at every available opportunity afterwards, that in the desert he'd had his eyes opened for the first time to everything that had been lost in our world, can hardly be bettered for poverty of thought."

"That comes from his fondness for paradoxes," I said. "He's almost obsessively inclined to equate nothingness with the infinite and the infinite with nothingness."

I said that he had sometimes been so in love with the abstract that he was capable of seeing a simple mathematical as a proof that God exists, but when I was about to give him an example he put his hand up.

"Did he ever read you a passage from the Gospels and then ask you what you most missed from your childhood?"

I said nothing but obviously realised that he had taken a dim view of Daniel sending him a letter asking for a sentence or two in answer to the question; Daniel had told me so. A restless flutter was becoming noticeable in his voice now and I was afraid that he was on the brink of one of those angry outbursts that people talked about, although mysteriously no-one had ever been found who had experienced one. But then he made do with railing against the phoniness of the so-called poetry of disappearance that was so fashionable and goggling at Daniel's chutzpah in having pestered all and sundry with such a pitiful request.

"Apparently when he got home, no-one he knew was spared," he said. "If it's true that he made lists of all the different answers, it must have been a real lexicon of hell."

The pleasure this thought gave him was unmistakable.

"I'm curious to know what you said."

He waited, sure that at last he had me where he wanted me, and when again I didn't say anything, he chose his words as if he wanted to make the room more cramped with every syllable.

"Didn't you recommend Camus to him on one occasion?"

The Outsider was hardly a subversive text, not even in the provinces where we lived, but it was not only the first of Robert's books that I had given Daniel but also the book my brother had named as his favourite at the same age. I had met Daniel at the football ground and invited him back as it started to rain, and we had sat down in my sitting room with him opposite me in an old sweater I had lent him, rubbing his hair dry. I had told him that it was a book about the desert. Whatever you thought of it, it was absurd that I should have to justify lending it to him now.

"Don't tell me we're going to have another row about Camus."

The head taught physics as his main subject and was not an avid reader, but he'd backed me up when the Parents' Association had gone to the barricades against me for rehearsing *The Just* with the theatre group. It had been Daniel's choice, maybe to please me after I had introduced him to Camus, and looking back I think to myself that without that play, without the rehearsals where they saw each other twice a week in completely different circumstances, perhaps the business with Christoph and Judith would have been different too, or there might not have been any business at all, but that was not the point as far as the parents were concerned. The point for them was that a small group of them seriously feared the seditious ideas that I was stuffing their poor children's heads with and tried very hard to halt our work until it became clear that if they carried on there would be no production at all.

"All over the world there are smart-arses who mock Camus for his harmlessness, yet for us he counts as a dangerous writer," I said. "We're going to make fools of ourselves if we say another word about it."

The head apparently disagreed, and asked whether I had ever read "The Renegade". I said no and he said it was just a story in the collection *Exile and the Kingdom*, but I absolutely must get hold of it, and then he added that it was a story about the desert and I wondered whether it was pure coincidence that he had used the same expression I had or whether he knew what I had said and was just reminding me for the nth time that I could not hide anything from him. He had put on that smile that some people called wolfish but that to me just seemed as if he couldn't manage to maintain the expression and kept having to readjust it, which made him make small snapping movements with his mouth.

"There's a character in it who goes into the desert, not to find grace but because he has lost his faith and devoted himself to evil," he said. "He sneers at the God of gentleness, whose very name fills him with horror, mocks him for turning the other cheek to those who strike him, and says he wants to get his own back on love and on all the people who constantly have the Word in their mouth. He wants to triumph over the Word and over love itself."

Perhaps he was right and you could see a prophecy there, if the discussion was about the axis of evil whose agents would cross deserts and oceans and darken the light of Europe with their black veils. He said that the fact that it had been written fifty years ago made it shockingly clear-sighted, when you looked at the current state of things. I was very afraid that he was going to start lecturing again. He had got to his feet, pacing back and forth between the bookshelves and his desk without letting me out of his gaze, and now he stood behind me and I felt him staring at the back of my head. It was one of the last gestures a teacher could resort to, to show a student how powerless they were, and I sat motionless, trying to show no emotion as he said that he did not wish to overstate matters but that if we were talking about Daniel, then we ought to talk about that.

Then he mentioned the bomb threat again, and I remember turning to him sharply and looking at him as if I had had enough of his insinuations once and for all.

"You can hardly make someone a suspect on the grounds that they read or didn't read this or that book ten years ago."

He started by agreeing with me, then contradicted himself.

"Why not, actually?"

"Because then we could all be instantly arrested for what we thought," I said. "What that would mean I would rather not spell out."

I felt that the discussion had become pointless and had finally become annoyed.

"How stupid does a person have to be to choose for such an act the railway station in the same town where he went to school?"

I stood up, and saw how startled he was that I had taken the initiative and had not waited to be dismissed. He seemed to be making every effort to accept my departure as I excused myself, saying that if he had nothing else to discuss I would be on my way and go back to my class, and I was already at the door when he said, "One more word." I let go of the door handle and turned around, and he had that smile on his face again, or a frozen version of it.

"I know about the novel he wrote about your summer out at the river," he said. "If you don't want to, we don't have to talk about it, but it would certainly help if you could say a few words on the subject."

So that was it; and I would have liked to see my face as I stood there and tried to look relaxed. There were three copies of the manuscript: Daniel had kept one himself, one was in my possession, and he had promised me that he would destroy the third after at first saying mockingly that it was "for the world". I tried to think how it could have got into the head's hands. I stared at the floor because I didn't want to see the triumphant look on his face, but his voice was enough for me to be able to imagine the rest.

"Don't worry, I didn't make the mistake of taking everything he wrote literally. Much of it is obviously his imagination embellishing things, and that deserves to be taken into account. However, I also don't believe he simply invented it all."

His words sounded as though they were pre-prepared, and as I waited, undecided about whether to contradict him, he said goodbye.

"Perhaps you'll think again as to whether something occurs to you, and call me if it does," he said. "I wouldn't know what you have to hide."

I left his office then, and it strikes me now as particularly ironic that the first person I bumped into in the corridor was Frau Pfeifer, who asked me how it had gone. I was not surprised that she was apparently in the know, but standing there in her dark blue suit, intended to provide authority in the classroom, blinking excitedly behind her glasses but nevertheless looking at me thoroughly affectionately, she seemed like a creature from another world. She had cooked dinner for me almost as soon as she had arrived at the school, and even though the evening had ended awkwardly we had stayed on good terms. (That evening she had, without any warning, sat her three-year-old son on my lap just before his bedtime, a true bundle of joy, as one always has to say, as innocent and stupid as a lamb, and I could count myself lucky that she forgave me for overreacting the way I did. I had dutifully bounced him backwards and forwards, gently thrown him in the air and caught him again, expertly squeezed him a few times and coaxed a squeak out of him, and had then jumped up and said that I had to go home. It was her blissful smile that had tipped me over the edge, making me feel exactly as if I were the boy's physical father, mature version, or if not him then at least Saint Joseph or God Himself, and I didn't make the slightest effort to hide my dismay. I rushed out, as if otherwise it would be too late to get away and I would smell of milk and urine and ineradicable good fortune that would be indistinguishable from misfortune; but that, evidently, is another story.)

Second Part

THE REVEREND

1

TO RECOGNISE YOURSELF IN A NOVEL IS AN EXPERIENCE THAT probably no-one enjoys, but to talk your way out of something you have been written into seems to me to be a hopeless undertaking and one that I am not even going to attempt. I have followed recent lawsuits brought on those grounds against literary works, if you want to call them that, and in every instance all I can see is a grotesque paradox. A plaintiff must simultaneously assert that it is him and is not him; he has to make known his displeasure at a portrayal that he feels lets him down badly while at the same time, by all appearances, piercing him to the heart. Clearly the range of humanity is less wide than we think, and although everyone is very proud of their individuality, a few strokes are all that is necessary to create a caricature. So our counterparts who exist on paper are really only greater or lesser than us to the extent that we make them greater or lesser, and we can comfort ourselves that in the end we alone decide for ourselves whether we want these Doppelgängers or not.

I am writing this at some distance from events, and don't want to say that I don't believe a word of it, but it's a wretched sort of detachment I've imposed on myself, and one that fails me when I'm faced with reality and failed me entirely when Daniel pressed the manuscript into my hands and warned me that I should decide for myself whether I wanted to read it or not. That was four years ago; he had let me know yet again that he was in town, had been passing through and for the first time in a long while had even stayed the night. He was on his way to Elba, where he was going to meet friends he had got to know during his time in Bosnia. After dropping out of university and the two winter months he spent at the house, which he described both as a form of survival training and an act of asceticism, he had wanted to make a trip to Albania, but on the way there had hooked up with a group of young Italians who worked for an international organisation and were building a settlement near Sarajevo for returning refugees from the war. He had got himself taken on in return for board and lodging, initially as a handyman and jack of all trades and then as a roofer's assistant, and it had turned into his longest stretch of continuous employment, more than eight months, about which he wrote me enthusiastic letters saying that he had finally found an activity whose usefulness he did not question, something that for once you didn't put down as easily as you picked it up.

Why he held forth about the job in such detail, I understood only when he mentioned the reason for the meeting, and I recognised the old pattern in it. It was the wedding of a former colleague to a young Muslim woman whom he, Daniel, had also met during the project, and from the way he talked about her he might have been in love with her himself, mentioning her with an almost holy veneration. Because of his skewed appreciation of women I was also aware, far too well to ignore, what a powerfully erotic charge the meeting contained. Cracking his code was, as usual, a piece of cake: when he said her gaze was "shy" he might just as well have said "seductive", and although the headscarves and long dresses that she wore perhaps weren't the exact equivalent of lingerie, I guessed that they triggered everything but pious thoughts in him.

For the rest, he told me what was going on – as always when it came to what he was doing – impulsively, and as though he wanted to whip up a storm in order to blur the implications of the individual steps he was taking before they could become apparent, by which time he had already moved on and did not need to bother himself with thoughts about the fragility of his enterprise or the homelessness and rootlessness of his life. It reminded me of the way he had once treated paperback books, at some point starting to tear out the pages he had read, crumple them into a ball and throw them in the bin, after having for so long treated books as shrines, even preferring to handle my most tattered novels with gloves, given half a chance. (This even applied to my "blow-dried books", of which I had a whole shelf-full – novels I had dropped in the bath while I was reading and that I had actually dried with the hairdryer until they were on the brink of falling apart.) He had torn out the pages like the leaves of a tear-off calendar, and that was how he talked about himself too, as if the telling was not linked to an affirmation but an extinction and that what was being described was, at the moment of its describing, already gone from the world.

I read the manuscript that night, while he was asleep in the next room, and I will never forget the feeling of betrayal that came over me; more than that, I felt that in a very physical sense I would never be free of it again, that from then on it was a part of me. Lying in bed, I found myself several times on the verge of breaking off my reading and going over to him to shake him and tell him that he had to leave immediately and I never wanted to set eyes on him again. I imagined hurling myself at him and hitting him, and knew at the same time that I would not even be able to remonstrate with him but would, as I always did, play the role of the sympathetic teacher, which I was not and did not want to be and which cost me an increasing effort to play in the classroom, would perhaps say that it saddened me, naturally, but that it was his right to write what he wanted to write and I certainly would not try to hold him back. It was four in the morning when I finished reading, the time of night when I had often started reading in Istanbul when I couldn't sleep, whether I went to bed early or not, and I imagined I could hear him coughing through the wall, followed by other sounds, and suddenly thought that he might have been lying awake all night too and been unable to close his eyes because he was awaiting my verdict and in his youthful conceit expecting, in all seriousness, to be praised the way I had always praised him at school for his essays.

It wasn't the homoerotic passages that struck me, and personally I would never use the word anyway and do so now only to provide clarity. I stress that I point that out only because it worries me that it will be the first thing to occur to some people, before they know any details. There is nothing to deny, we were together almost every day for several weeks that summer, and nor am I denying anything, on the contrary, even if I don't agree with every aspect of his account I have to admit that he captured the atmosphere of those weeks perfectly and I don't hesitate to avail myself of his version when I try to reconstruct the situation.

After the last work on the mill was finished, we slung two hammocks between the house and the trees next to it, and it was mostly Christoph and Daniel who lay in them while I sat on my folding chair outside the door. What that might have signified to the hikers who walked past almost every day I've already indicated, and I could imagine the kind of fantasies that bloomed in their minds when one of the boys walked down to the gravel bar and fished a few bottles of beer out of the current where we had put them to cool, or we passed a cigarette around and their laughter hung in the air. They had carved arrows and strung a branch with string to make a bow, and when they stood and aimed, barefoot and only wearing their trunks, with one arm outstretched and the other angled behind a shoulder, it was like a stage show for all the uninvited spectators and there was no need to have studied art history, been a lover of statues or felt attracted to young boys to recognise the cliché and simultaneously feel a shiver at the frozen moment and a pang at its impermanence. Once I had become accustomed to their presence I used to take them with me to the river in the car some days, on others they came by moped the way they had the first few times, and their coming to the house became such a routine that on the two or three occasions they stayed away without warning I didn't know what to do with myself and spent the day wandering restlessly up and down the river bank. Until then I had not admitted it to myself, but some days I actually only drove out there because of them, just to have those hours with them, and would probably quickly have abandoned my attempt to play the hermit if they had not been there.

Obviously I don't remember every individual scene, and nor can I judge what Daniel thought when I let my gaze linger on him and he suddenly looked up and noticed, but I didn't have the impression that he found it embarrassing in any way. I avoided nearly all physical contact after the one time when I had chased after him in a fit of exuberance and caught him and hugged him. After that I may have once absent-mindedly stroked his hair or touched him on the arm when he fell asleep in the sun and I wanted to draw his attention to something, but then I immediately withdrew my hand again.

The tensions did not come from us, they came from outside. At the weekends a constant stream of hikers walked past the edge of the property, and at times the curious looks were so numerous we began to feel we were in a zoo. Once forestry workers came, and we wondered on whose behalf they were marking the trees around us with white chalk crosses – trees that offered us a last screen from onlookers – and another time children came down from the sports ground and started pointing at us. Afterwards a few days went by when nothing happened, and then one morning we found a word sprayed on the mill door that unmistakably targeted us and it was as if all that was lacking was the right description. We discussed whether to leave it there but in the end painted over it with the leftover paint we had used for the window frames without, obviously, being able to banish it from the world altogether.

Daniel would have had all the elements for a sensational story, and it would probably have been easier to forgive him if he had turned me into a low-life figure, if his story had become an indictment of me, complete with allegations that almost conformed to novelistic conventions, if he had only left my brother out of it. I had only told him about Robert once, and then only the essentials, so he must have asked around or perhaps he hadn't even had to, either because there were rumours going the rounds and I was the only one not hearing them, or because he felt free to fill in the facts with something supposedly approaching them. I found it banal that he should write that I would sometimes stare at him that summer as though I was seeing my brother in him, but for him not only to reconstruct a plausible sequence for his ending but also to posit a conclusive reason for it, I found not just banal but monstrous.

For a long time I had racked my brains about why Robert had not left any farewell note, and ultimately had consoled myself with the thought that an explanation was worse than no explanation, but now, thanks to Daniel, I could read that it had been because of an unhappy love affair; now I could read that when Robert had stayed in the USA he had conceived an undying love for the daughter of his host family; and it wasn't just that word, it was the way that the motive was apparently romantic which I found repugnant. She had the same name in his manuscript as she had had in reality, and I remembered how I had met her. We had postponed the funeral by two days so that she and her father could come, and she had appeared at the graveside dressed completely in black and thrown a white rose and a book into it before trickling a handful of earth over both. I was standing near her and tried hard but in vain to see the book's title, and even though I wouldn't go so far as Daniel, who claimed that I had only read Robert's books during my time in Istanbul because I had not been able to read that book, I would obviously have liked to know what was so important about it that she had had to give it to him in death. I had shaken hands with her and thought about asking her but then hadn't, and at that moment she had said something that I didn't fully understand, either that it had been his choice or that he had had no choice. In Daniel's version she bowed her head as she said it and looked at me from under her eyelashes with the eyes of a woman stricken for all time, but that feels more like him embellishing the scene with cinematic extravagance. His need for completeness also made him go too far in inventing a chronology for Robert's last day and attributing thoughts to him that he was supposed to have had in the minutes and seconds before he put the barrel of the rifle in his mouth and pulled the trigger. So his life had ended with memories of good times on the Mississippi, on a trip from St Louis to Memphis that included a sunset somewhere along the line and, worst of all, with nuggets of wisdom and maxims that I would rather not repeat and the fatuous question of what women really want, whether it was the instant of love, even if it could not be made to last, or the flat happiness of continuity.

I cannot say to what extent Daniel was also talking about his own difficulties with Judith, but when I thought back to her two trips out to us by the river, the parallel was obvious. She came in the late summer, long after she had come back from Italy, and I remember both times clearly. On the first Herr Bleichert had just gone away empty-handed, and the mood he had created still lingered, a mixture of unspoken reproaches and the kind of doomed hope that only a priest can possess. On the second occasion the boys had disappeared into the woods and I had had half an hour alone with her, during which she questioned me ironically about whether the padre had again put out feelers in our direction, and what we were intending to achieve at our hideaway – whether we were constructing a training camp for would-be hermits or just killing time because we didn't want to grow up. It must have been late afternoon or early evening, because she worked during the day, and she looked around as if she was not sure what she had got herself involved in. She had arrived on a bike, and the skin on her upper arms and thighs glistened with perspiration as she stood there, hands pushed into the pockets of her cut-off jeans, her shoulders hunched, shifting from one foot to the other. She was strikingly boyish anyway, but she had had her hair cut short too and when I saw her later, walking along the bank with the boys against the setting sun, their silhouettes were indistinguishable from each other. She must already have known she was pregnant, and maybe that had something to do with the fact that it occurred to me more than once that she had turned up to say goodbye to them both. I watched her messing around with them, and the way she nudged and poked them, ran away from them and urged them not to be so boring had a strained quality, the way adults sometimes are when they join in with children's games. Then it was as if her concentration had gone, and when she looked back at them again a moment later, with visible regret, I felt their responses were as strained as hers. She let them show her the work they had done on the mill, then went out to the gravel bar with them and piled up a cairn at its tip as a signal for the rafters, of whom there seemed to be swarms going downstream that day, and she was the one who suggested spending the night by the river. Nothing was said, but it was clear that this was the last time she would appear in the boys' world, and when she started to collect wood for a fire they refused to help her at first and she had to goad them, saying to them that they weren't going to turn out to be slackers and weaklings, were they, and start flagging just as she was offering them the prospect of an adventure they could hardly have dared dream of till then?

A conversation that I had with Daniel that evening comes closest to conveying the atmosphere. He had come up to the house on his own to get something to drink and paused before going back to the river, where Christoph's and Judith's laughter could be heard as they stood up to their knees in the current, splashing each other. He seemed to enjoy the scene but at the same time be tormented by it; I saw the effect it had on him, and so what he said surprised me.

"I suppose I should be happy."

It was at that moment that Judith called to him. She had come out of the water and was standing on the gravel obviously shivering; she called out the first syllable of his name loudly, filling it with air and letting the rest of it collapse on itself. Having been half-hidden behind the gravel bar, she was now fully visible and seemed herself to become conscious of the fact at that moment. I had the impression that she was displaying herself to him, with one leg in front of the other, arms folded and – which at that distance could only be guessed – an expression of impatience on her face, the suggestion of a pout perhaps and her snub nose tilted mercilessly upwards. She called him again, and again, in that way that had an undertone of command beneath its playful sound, and as I turned to him it did not escape me that he was looking less and less relaxed and deliberately not moving from the spot.

"What does that mean, do you suppose?" he said.

I tried to sound as casual as I could.

"Aren't you? Happy, that is."

I had been struck before by a shyness and anxiety in him, which he seemed to have got over in his relations with Judith, but now they came straight back to the surface.

"I don't know," he said. "If it feels like this."

"You must know."

"If it feels like this," he said. "I know exactly what situations like this are like in books, and I also know what's phoney about them."

"Forget the books."

"You saying that, of all people."

"I should know," I said. "You can read books later."

I looked at him out of the corner of my eye.

"You can read when you're dead."

He gave me a quick but unmistakably dismissive glance, then looked back down towards the river where Judith was waving her arms over her head imploringly one last time before letting them fall resignedly. She turned around and walked step by step towards the water and I saw that Daniel's gaze was glued to her. From the far bank came the sound of an approaching train, and in the same moment I knew that the situation would drag on for him and that there would always be that same image of her in his memory, standing there, turned away from him, a memory accentuated by the rhythmic swelling sound of the train's wheels, because with his gaze unswervingly fixed on her back he could only wait, as carriage after carriage clattered past and for several minutes everything else seemed to stop moving.

"It was one of the moments in books I most wanted to keep going back to afterwards," he said finally. "Do you remember the writer in 'The Snows of Kilimanjaro'?"

"Yes," I said. "A broken figure."

"More like sad," he said. "You remember him?"

"Yes," I said. "I remember."

"Do you remember him lying there dying and thinking about everything he would have liked to write and now wouldn't?"

"Yes," I said again. "Always the same subjects."

"That's what it feels like."

I could have shrugged it off as youthful angst, but what he said made me think of Robert. Robert had been dead set on this idea of literary longing and literary happiness. To picture yourself in a situation, thinking about the way you would remember it later, only to realise at that later moment that you could no longer have the thing that you remembered, was a two-fold extinction. You pushed the moment into the future in order to possess, from that vantage point, everything in the past, in which it was then, naturally, lost, and what was left to you rose into a leaden limbo of melancholy. I had never explained this properly to myself up till then, and of course had never spoken to Robert about it, and the realisation hit me like a blow.

I didn't stay out by the river with them that night, and when I drove out again the next morning with fresh rolls, the first thing I saw was that they had had visitors. They were still asleep, their three sleeping bags spread out on the veranda, although the ground had to be damp, and the sun was already up and it would not be long before it reached their faces. What immediately struck me was that Judith's sleeping bag wasn't between theirs, but I didn't bother to speculate why. I started collecting up the beer bottles I found scattered around the ashes of their fire, which had a few hardly burnt logs on it but the embers were cold. I came across a jacket that I didn't recognise as belonging to any of them and hung it on one of the nails that we used as a wardrobe on the mill's back wall, after having searched through the pockets without success. Then

I sat with my back against a tree stump so that I could see their faces, and waited for them to wake up.

It was Daniel who told me what had happened, almost the minute he opened his eyes, and I'll try to reproduce the conversation exactly as I remember it. What he said was so completely unexpected that I listened to it as if it were the most normal thing in the world; any commentary would take away its authenticity. For me it was one more proof that apparently entirely rational circumstances could lead you into an irrational world, and that that was just what Daniel seemed to be savouring too.

"You won't believe who was here," he said. "Can you guess?"

I assumed it was the police, because they had been too loud or someone had reported them for making a fire, but he shook his head.

"It was the cult people."

I knew straight away who he was talking about.

"The Americans who've rented the farm in the village?"

He nodded and seemed simultaneously to lose himself in his memory as he talked about them.

"We'd heard their voices getting closer through the trees for a long time in the dark, then we finally saw them," he said. "It was a proper procession, with them moving downriver in a line and praying."

"What did they want out here?"

"I ask myself the same question. Supposedly a girl from their group disappeared, so they rushed out with torches to look for her. I have my doubts as to whether they were telling the truth."

He glanced at Christoph and Judith, as if to check whether they were really still asleep. They lay turned towards each other in their sleeping bags, and he tilted his head and contemplated them with feigned benevolence. Then he placed a finger on his lips, and as he went on talking in a whisper I wasn't sure whether they weren't supposed to hear something or whether he was just being careful not to wake them.

"They combed the undergrowth along the river bank first, then came to join us around the fire, but right from the start I thought there was something fishy about it," he said. "I'm sure all the searching was just a pretext and that from the start they came for another reason, or they wouldn't have sat down so calmly."

He glanced at me suddenly with a sharp look.

"You've heard the stories."

I wondered whether to pretend that I hadn't, but it was too late.

"They wanted to save you?"

He didn't answer, and I asked him again. He stood up, walked over to the fire and poked the ashes as if he could rekindle it. Then he came back and I sensed his embarrassment as he sat down again, further away from me than before.

"It's always the same with them in the end, isn't it?" he said, uncertain how much he should confide in me. "Didn't they try it with you too?"

2

"THE CULT PEOPLE" HAD BEEN KNOWN THAT WAY SINCE THEY FIRST turned up in the village two years before, and the description alone showed what an arm's length relationship people maintained with them. Hardly anyone bothered to find out exactly who they were, and when they came up in conversation they were most likely to be described as the crazies who had rented the farm on the outskirts of the village, who had actually been prepared to pay good money for the building with its leaking shingle roof that let in the rain in several places, and its half-derelict stables. The old owners had died, their children moved away long ago, and for years the farm had failed to find a buyer, although until recently a "For Sale" sign had hung at the gate; this alone had ensured that the new occupants were a subject of curiosity.

They had appeared out of the blue one summer's day, in a big estate car with tinted windows, which rolled almost noiselessly up to the gate and stopped, its hazard lights flashing. For a while nothing happened, as though the car's passengers wanted to think about their decision one last time, but then they got out one after another: the Reverend, as everyone later called him, in his black suit that no-one ever saw him without, the wife, reportedly in a headscarf and sunglasses, and the three girls, outwardly unremarkable so far as their appearance went, the two older ones perhaps sixteen and seventeen, the other one a bit younger and – which of course was striking – with darker-coloured skin. They paused, looked across at the house and up and down the valley and back to the house, and here accounts diverge. Some say that the man stretched up his arms and with his head raised, staring into the cloudless sky, turned a full circle, others that they started unpacking their luggage from the boot straight away and that it was absurd to attach any more importance to the scene than that. There cannot have been as many observers as there were alleged witnesses who claimed to have seen their arrival, because the idea that there were more passers-by than usual at the time is unlikely, and the nearest houses were some distance away, all of them properties that had been abandoned and were now occupied by Turkish families and, with their few dozen inhabitants, collectively referred to in pub conversations as Little Istanbul.

The day they arrived, they walked around the village, and accounts of that differed too. They walked abreast down the little used roads, people said, the girls with their arms linked, the woman on the Reverend's arm, and quite clearly they had dressed up for the occasion. That remained the first picture I always had when I thought about them, although I wasn't there either: the daughters in their white blouses and long skirts, their hair combed flat, while their mother, now in black like her husband, still wearing her sunglasses but without her headscarf and half a head taller than him, a self-assured presence and in no way the diffident being whose oppressed condition could be read in her expression that many later made her out to be. Some say the Reverend began there and then to initiate conversations, calling to people over their garden fences, wishing them a good day and displaying a cheerfulness that awakened feelings of mistrust everywhere. Others say that that can't have happened because no-one was outside, or the few who were sitting on their benches or fussing in their gardens had, on seeing the mysterious contingent marching through their village, retreated into their houses.

Rumours multiplied rapidly about them, of course, and eased only because they were from America and nobody could work out what might make a family from America want to spend a summer here of all places, where once in a while an elderly couple might take lodgings, or some overtired tourists break their journey overnight on their way to the coast, or parents take their children into the surviving farm buildings to show them first-hand what a horse looked like, or a cow or a pig. The Reverend went to the pub that evening, but no-one found out more than his name; the next morning he asked at the service station where the best place to go shopping was, and at first gave far too big a tip but then came back and demanded his change but for the last ridiculous Groschen, and a few hours later was observed parking his big estate at the supermarket and loading it full to the roof. The girls meanwhile had started to do what they would do in the weeks that followed, or at least what people said they did. They played badminton and set out the hoops of a croquet game all over the orchard that belonged to the house, so you could see them now here, now there in the landscape, holding their mallets, as though they had a tricky challenge to overcome. When they were not doing that, they found themselves a place to read, in a hollow, on the step in front of the sunny wooden wall where the firewood had once been stacked, on the bench seat of a car that they found in the barn and put under a parasol in the middle of the meadow. It had not been twenty-four hours since they arrived and they had already settled in, even if no-one was asked inside and so no-one could imagine what the house looked like, after standing empty for so many years.

It was a swift takeover, by which they marked out a territory that they then rarely left, the great exception being when, after their first walk to greet their neighbours, they occasionally ventured into the village again, always the three of them together, the two bigger girls flanking the smaller, darker one in the middle. So it wasn't long before the first mopeds turned up at the half-rundown property, their distant clatter announcing their arrival, and at any time of day you could see boys staring over the hedge at the girls playing unhurriedly, moving away whenever the Reverend or his wife came outside. Some of the boldest stood their ground and chatted with them, and a few even accepted an invitation to go in and subsequently reported that they had sat down with the whole family at their big wooden table outside and been served lemon cakes and tea, though they had hardly dared to address a word to any of the three girls directly within the family circle.

The rest came later, the stories of the Reverend accosting people in the pub and the street and starting conversations by asking his startled interlocutor whether they believed in the Bible or Jesus Christ. To a worker on his way home from his shift at the cement works, of all people, he would make a couple of innocuous remarks about the weather and then ask if the man had any idea where he would go if he were to die at that moment. Someone else, strolling down the road without a care in the world, would suddenly be asked if he knew that he was a sinner; another whether he would like to pray with him, and if that person refused he would offer to pray for him, and if that offer also met with a refusal, he would assure him that God would still love him in spite of everything and one day hopefully he would open his heart. His German was astonishingly good but nevertheless sounded as if he had learnt his few opening gambits by heart, which gave his approaches an additionally grotesque quality, and it was not long before people started running away whenever they caught sight of him. He succeeded best at buttonholing the women, either outside the one remaining village shop or by actually ringing their doorbells in the morning when he thought he might find them alone, and they then reported that he would offer them the choice of whether they wanted to be saved or not and would swear to them that he had a totally foolproof method and would only take up ten minutes of their time to save them from the fires of hell.

On one occasion they were all seen together at the cemetery putting flowers on a grave, which naturally triggered speculation but only made the riddle that surrounded them all the greater. The grave on which they laid flowers was that of a forester who had died three years before leaving no family to take care of it, and no-one could imagine what connection he of all people could have had to the Reverend and his family – a loner who had never in his life stepped far outside his forest, so it was said, and probably could not have found America on a map. They were seen barbecuing in their garden, and on these occasions the Reverend would invite passers-by to come in for a lemonade and a chop, and people would report that he made a great song and dance about breaking the bread as soon as anyone showed an interest, but then held back from asking his questions or – if he tried to ask them – would be ticked off by his wife. They were seen getting into their estate car early in the morning and driving away, only coming back late in the evening, and it was also observed that every two or three days they went for a walk along the route of the autobahn that was then under construction, although others did that too, as if the land needed to be reclaimed one last time before it was handed over to cars. The family walked abreast, the way they had walked around the village the first day, the Reverend in his black suit, even if reports that his wife was also always in black on these occasions and that the girls wore their long skirts and white blouses were probably an embellishment after it became clear what they went there for. Mostly they strolled the short distance to the service area, which was still a shell too, spread out a blanket and picnicked or just rested there for a while. The weather was good as a rule, but they did not give up the ritual when it rained; instead they took umbrellas with them and stood with bowed heads in a circle. The Reverend supposedly lifted his arms to the heavens on these occasions too, and there were passers-by who swore they had seen him reading aloud from the Bible to the others and heard them praying: the dark, loud male voice and the chorus of much brighter and quieter voices of his wife and the girls, who always started off hesitantly and a little behind their mother.

Despite these stories, there were ultimately so few facts to go on that gossip about them quickly became rife, conjecture that they definitely had not left America of their own accord and about what they therefore had to hide, until in the third week of their stay a long article about them appeared in the newspaper, which added genuinely novelistic elements to their story. As the piece related, they had not stumbled on the area by chance but had come because of the bomber that had crash-landed in the Au countryside in the year before the end of the war. That summer was the fiftieth anniversary of the crash, and the Reverend not only turned out to be the son of one of the bomber's crew, he had also been born only a few days after the landing and so for him it was a double anniversary. He had always wanted to see the place where his father had cheated death by a whisker, and apart from reporting that he had made a vow to do so, the article remained free of all other mystical overtones.

It was illustrated with three photos, which did not substantiate any of the story but still fitted the facts. One was a photographic portrait of the Reverend in his twenties; it would not have been surprising if he had had a military background, given the uniform-like shirt he wore, his brush-cut hair and too-direct look, yet it was there in black and white: at the time of Vietnam he had been an outspoken critic of the war. The second picture showed the bomber crew, supposedly taken shortly before their last mission, nine men who had only just reached adulthood, it seemed, posing like a slightly reduced football team, four in front, five behind, his father highlighted with an arrow and all of them looking with assurance at the camera, as if it really was just a sporting encounter that they faced, in which the winner had already been decided. In the third picture a young woman posed with a hand on her hip and her head thrown back – the way she had seen actresses pose on film posters? – in front of the stranded aircraft, which lay like a felled monster in the meadow, with two twisted propeller blades pointing up into the sky behind her and the empty skeleton of the cockpit.

It all felt more like a curiosity than anything else. The end of the war, nearly half a century before, would no doubt be marked by more important memories than this personal mythology of an American God-botherer. I read the story, half amused and half shaking my head at the Reverend's obsessiveness in assembling his own private world (and the more I discovered about that, the less I felt it said anything to me: that applied above all to the religious background). There were apocalyptic visions of the Second Coming, which was to be expected at any time, and I could not make any sense out of the piecing together of rational elements with irrational ones, in which the bomber's crash-landing was hailed as a miracle and its survivors born-again beings. What interested me more was why the Reverend had kept the reason for his being here secret, why he had not told anyone in the pub or on the street anything about his father's story and it had all had to be learnt from the newspaper, but the only answer I could get was that he had set himself the task of saving at least ten souls before he did, and then he just didn't want to talk about it anymore. At least the riddle about the forester's grave was cleared up: as a boy, the forester had arrived at the wreck before the first soldiers and the ambulance reached it and had told the crew their exact location, how far it was to the Swiss border, and whether there was anyone who could lead them there.

It was probably because of the article that there was a small celebration on the day of the anniversary. The band marched out, as it always did, in broad formation across the path of the autobahn as far as the landing site. There a small crowd of curious spectators had gathered around a lectern, no more than eighteen or twenty, and a number of them probably because they had been ordered to go so that the ceremony (which took place against the noise of construction machinery that had been coming ever nearer in recent weeks) would not be entirely unattended. A representative from the town council gave a bold speech in which he talked about terror-bringers and liberators, as though the words were interchangeable, but everyone applauded, and then the Reverend read something from a piece of paper before burying, then and there, a metal plaque bearing the names of the crew members. Following this, the band played again and after those who had been summoned had withdrawn once more, he stood alone with his wife and the three girls in the field. It was half past three in the afternoon, and everyone who saw them said it was a poignant sight as they held hands, raised their heads and looked up at the sky.

The following summer they came back, but the new section of the autobahn had been completed by then and they could not get over to the other side. There had also been a multiple pile-up in the fog very close to the bomber's landing site, with almost three dozen cars involved and four dead; withered flowers were still strewn across the embankment and pieces of wrecked cars could still be found in the fields not far from where the bomber had lain. They often went to the service area to eat, and to do so they had to use a gravel path that ran parallel to the carriageway. There were no more attempts at conversion now, no promises of salvation, and if they ever came up in conversation it was mostly to the effect that their disputes with their Turkish neighbours had increased – complaints that animals were being slaughtered in their backyards, reciprocal allegations – of which the highlight was that the big estate car was found one morning with its tyres slashed and windscreen wipers ripped off. After that, the Reverend took the girls into the house whenever the boys turned up on their mopeds and they were rarely seen in the garden, with the lads listening vainly for the soothing plop-plop of shuttlecocks that for a few weeks had started up at all sorts of different times of day. The girls had obviously been told to be careful of the effect they were having, and instead of playing or lying reading in the grass they sometimes sat on the bench next to the farm's entrance, the way older women do, although when they came to the village nothing seemed to have changed. They still at least walked together with linked arms, the two bigger girls flank-ing the smaller, darker one, and looked just as serious as they had the previous summer, just as strict with their narrow faces which despite the warmth of the first sunny days looked irritatingly pale.

That was also the year that I saw them for the first time. The previous summer there had not been anyone home when I went past their house, but now it was almost inevitable that I should see them at the service area. I kept driving out to the mill just once more, each time unable to make up my mind what I ought to do with it, and when I made my habitual stop at the services on the way back I sometimes bumped into them. From everything I had heard about them I had imagined them quite differently, and I was amazed at the picture they presented. All right, it was absurd, but I really had had a Quaker or Amish family in mind, with all the rigour and narrowness I had seen in photographs, and I had to admit that reality taught me a lesson. The Reverend was a bulky man, easily more than 120 kilos, a good eater, with big hands – he was always looking for somewhere to put them down and only in the absence of another resting-place did he fold them in his lap; his wife was not brittle at all, having a soft face and soft brown eyes; and the girls were the way girls of that age tend to be, and no more talk of their being especially withdrawn or still having an unhealthy pallor after several weeks' holiday. The thing that most struck you about them was that they always sat at the same table and were not in a hurry like everyone else who only stopped to refuel and swallow a snack and then vanished again.

I rapidly gained the impression that the Reverend had noticed me, that he made a point of nodding to me when I came and went, and that it would not be long before he started a conversation with me, which he did but only the following year when they spent the summer in the village for the last time and I was driving out to the river every day and dropping in at the services almost as frequently. I was sitting at the bar, not having seen him come over, when he was suddenly standing behind me and asking if he could offer me a coffee. His voice was deep and, even when he lowered it, still sounded as if it was audible throughout the dining room. He didn't wait for me to answer and ordered as he pulled up a stool next to me and laboriously settled himself on it. I had not fully turned towards him and remained with stiff shoulders in my half-twisted position that he could only interpret as an affront, but he pretended not to notice, lit a cigarette and pushed the packet towards me with a barely perceptible nod.

"You got a house down by the river."

I saw that his wife and the girls had stayed sitting at their table and were observing us, but their faces gave nothing away.

"I can't say that," I said. "It's only an old mill, and the state it's in, it's going to fall down soon if I don't do something."

I don't know if he was angling for an invitation when he said that they were sometimes in the area, but I did not react. The coffee came and I nodded to him, although I still had my back half-turned to him. He smoked for a while and then told me that his grandfather had owned a house by a lake where he had spent all his summers as a child, and I had even less idea what he wanted from me.

"There must be wonderful places for fishing there," he said, just as I thought he was going to dissolve into outright sentimentality. "Do you fish?"

"No. But why are you asking me?"

"You don't fish?"

"No," I said, getting more irritated. "I don't fish."

"So you got no idea what it's like when you got a really big one on your line?" he said, and I could not think of anything else but his grotesque attempts at being a missionary and that in his own understanding of himself he was probably a fisher of men. "It's life itself you can feel in your hands. You feel it wriggling. You see what you're missing?"

His persistence made me obstinate, but when I said I did not even know if there were fish in the river, he just laughed.

"Sure there are fish."

He looked at me pityingly.

"So you don't hunt either?"

That was an excuse for the story of his first rifle, which he had been given as a present for his tenth birthday. I could not shut him up, and he described blissfully to me how he and his grandfather had gone hunting on clear starry nights together somewhere in the American south. He declared that he had never been happier than he was there, or more filled with the certainty of being made in God's image, and then he talked about the innocence of the land that only a few generations before had still belonged to the Indians.

"You don't fish and you don't hunt," he said finally, and he made it sound as if he'd said I didn't drink and didn't eat. "So what do you do down there?"

Apart from the father and daughter at Robert's funeral, to whom I had hardly spoken, he was my first American. I had known him for barely a quarter of an hour, but he had already shown himself to be an unusual kind of man, with his rather square face and the doggedness with which he kept on talking to me. I waited for him to pause before I completely turned my back on him. I did not think it would be sufficient to cow him into silence, but something in my gaze must have communicated to him that he had said enough, so hurriedly did he then swallow his untouched coffee, pausing after each gulp and keeping alarmed eye contact with me.

"If that's to be your new strategy for putting the moves on someone, then maybe the full frontal version's better," I said. "Why don't you just ask me whether I believe in Jesus Christ and the Bible and spare yourself all this talk?"

"Look, no offence."

"Why don't you ask me whether I want to be saved?"

"I get it," he said. "I'm not asking you."

"But I want to be saved."

"I get it."

"Ask me if I want to pray with you."

He looked at me open-mouthed and I had to stop myself from laughing in his face, the situation seemed so absurd.

"I want to pray with you," I said when he failed to answer, and I could not tell whether I was talking loudly or quietly. "You start and I'll follow you, word for word."

How angry I was I could only tell from his reaction. With an agility I would not have expected from a man of his build, he slipped down from his stool and went back to sit with his family at their table as I stood up and walked out. I thought about going over to them and saying something conciliatory, but then instead I waved to him and he waved back, while the three girls gave me hostile looks and his wife rummaged in her handbag. They could not have heard our conversation, but they had obviously seen him defeated and rebuffed somewhere along the line and had developed a reflexive habit of showing solidarity with him. I saw that his brow was beaded with sweat and that he had damp patches under his armpits, and I was glad to get outside. I stood next to my car for a while, taking deep breaths before I got in, and then as I drove onto the autobahn and changed up from one gear to the next I could not work out why I was suddenly gripped by a feeling of freedom, by an overwhelming feeling of escape, just at having got away from him.

3

I NEVER THOUGHT I WOULD SEE THE REVEREND AGAIN AFTER THAT
conversation at the services, and definitely not that after his nocturnal visit to the river he would turn up again the very next day
with his wife and the two older girls, supposedly to retrieve the
jacket he had left behind. It was a strange day anyway, and probably
no coincidence that I associate it in retrospect with the first hint
of autumn, though this is probably more as a result of my mood
than the fact that it was appreciably cooler before the sun was up,
because when I drove out to the house that morning I was wavering
between anticipating another fine summer's day like all the rest we
had had and a sense that something could have changed for ever. I
had left the two boys alone with Judith the night before without a
second thought, and had gone away with a light heart, as the saying
goes, but now I felt like an intruder. Up till then it had not been
the years that separated us, but now the few hours of my absence
were enough for me to approach the house hesitantly, as if I was
afraid of finding that there was no time or place there for me anymore. I had not expected that they would still be asleep, and they
presented a peaceful picture despite the empty beer bottles and
cigarette butts, despite the carelessly scattered clothes, even though
the idea simultaneously forced itself on me that this was just how
they would lie after a catastrophe and that a murderer had possibly
arranged their bodies like that.

I had wanted to return to my conversation of the previous after-noon with Daniel, in which he had sounded so disillusioned, but the Reverend's visit put everything else out of my mind. While I was talking to Daniel I felt that he could not wait for Judith to be awake, and later it struck me that he seemed to be both trying to stay away from her and get closer to her. He had never seemed so fragile to me before, barefoot, wearing rolled-up trousers and a T-shirt that was much too baggy, practically unchanged from our first encounter four years before, and the way he fussed around Judith and then, when he sat quietly, seemed to be sitting only for her, had something helplessly childlike about it. He obviously did not know how to approach her, and she did not make it easier for him by greeting each of his attempts with an ironic smile. It was only with great difficulty that we persuaded her to stay for coffee and then she jumped up to go straight away, and I remember how she said goodbye to him. It was an extraordinarily tense moment, as she went to sit on her bike but then stopped halfway and came up to him and I abruptly realised what must have happened in the night.

"Good luck in the rest of your life," she said, and it couldn't have sounded more scornful. "Now that you've been saved, nothing else can happen to you."

I heard her call him Jesus very clearly, and it rang as false as the hug she had just given Christoph, throwing her arms around his neck. The scene reminded me of the rehearsals they had had in the theatre group and her playfulness when she sometimes went off-script and started saying, in a trance that was more concocted than real, the first things that came into her head but which were nowhere in the text they were rehearsing. She had placed her bike as a barrier between her and Daniel and for a moment I felt any-thing could happen, that she was about to slap him on a sudden impulse or that she would burst into tears.

He did not say anything and watched her as she picked up a book that was lying on the ground. It was *Repetition* by Peter Handke, whoever had brought it with them, and the way she started to leaf through it came across as sheer provocation. She even looked as if she was about to start reading at one point, then she clapped the pages shut and held it up in the air.

"Does somebody want this?"

When she got no answer, she tucked it under her arm, changed her mind and fastened it onto her luggage rack. She got on her bike and looked around again. She had already ridden a short distance when she turned around, took a hand off her handlebars and waved. She rode in a circle to do it, and for a moment her hair blazed in the sunlight, with the forest deeply in shadow behind her.

"Enjoy the rest of the summer," she called, momentarily indecisive as to whether she should make an especially light or especially dramatic departure. "If you get bored, you know where to find me."

I saw that Christoph was waving back. I did not dare look at Daniel, who was standing next to me with his head lowered, but instead called out to her for him, as if she was about to vanish from the earth at any moment.

"Come and see us again." I heard my voice die away unfamiliarly in the morning air, but instead of defusing the situation it sounded a jarring note. "You're always welcome."

We watched her go until she was out of sight. For a while her white blouse continued to shimmer between the trees, and then we stayed standing there, motionless, as if we were waiting for her to reappear further on, where the meadows began, although the track did not go that way. Maybe I was imagining things, but I had the impression that the boys were avoiding each other's gaze, and I did not look at them either. We walked back to the house, and I remember that for the first time since we had been together by the river I did not know what we should do, and they too both seemed robbed of their spontaneity, not going to lie in their hammocks as they usually did, or read or stroll down to the water deep in conversation, but standing there stiffly, saying nothing, as if any word would be an offence.

I did not try to talk to Daniel about his having allowed himself to be saved, and perhaps that was a mistake. I cannot explain it any other way than by saying that I silently went along with the shamefaced way the two of them behaved towards each other that day, respecting their apparent taboo, although it's possible that there wasn't one at all. It was the first time I had seen Daniel so closed towards me, and because I did not challenge him perhaps I missed the one opportunity to ask him in a completely natural way the questions that were weighing on me. Because whenever we touched on the topic afterwards, he withdrew again into the embarrassed mood of that morning and a silence spread between us exactly the way it had back then. Mostly he treated it as if it had all been nothing but a joke, and for that reason alone it seemed to become increasingly unreal with every – albeit hesitant – attempt to discuss it on my part.

To be honest, I don't know how we spent the two or two and a half hours till the Reverend and his wife and the two older girls appeared at the house, but it seemed like a long time to me and the fact that I was willing to spend time with the Reverend was almost certainly because of my relief at the way his arrival broke the oppressive atmosphere. He called out to us when he was still a long way off, as if he found himself in enemy territory and wanted to advertise his friendly intentions before getting too close. When he was finally standing there by the ashes of the fire, he was breathing heavily. His wife handed him a handkerchief which he used to mop the sweat from his forehead, and the two girls stood close by, partly as though they expected a scene but also partly as though there could not be anything about this father that was alien to them.

It was striking that from the outset he treated the two boys as if they were not there. A couple of times I let my gaze switch between Daniel and him, but there was no sign of recognition between them and the Reverend directed himself towards me with a conspicuous exclusivity. He apologised profusely as he tried to get his breath back, then stared around unashamedly.

"Could I have left my jacket here?"

I did not respond and instead asked smoothly after the other daughter. The question seemed to surprise him. He blinked nervously and for a moment I even had the impression that he was trying to work out who I was talking about.

"You must be thinking she's adopted," he said, as if it was part of my question. "She's always running away and turning up again a few days later."

Obviously I could put two and two together, but it still sounded very weird to me that a night-time search along the river bank should so quickly turn into pleasure. He must have known how far he wanted to take the game he was playing, but for my own peace of mind I nevertheless asked him whether he had at least informed the police. He shook his head and put his hands together and raised them in an imploring gesture to his chest while he went on speaking.

"There's no need to worry about her at all. She'll be sitting in the woods somewhere watching us, no doubt about it. It's her way of attracting attention to herself."

I only learnt the following day that she had been at home all the time, which explained his composure, although not why he was going to all this effort. If he had actually invented the story of her disappearance in order to have a pretext to come out to the river, he could have made it a lot easier for himself, but in any case his relentless talking made me drop the subject. Indeed, it was more as a gesture of embarrassment than because I wanted to, but I invited him to sit down for a minute, and he apologised again, but then sat and introduced his wife as his wife and the two girls by their names. A glance was enough for the elder one to communicate with the younger, and both gave the hint of a nod before they sat down, by all appearances happy to be able to fade into the background while he got properly stuck into me.

"I know you don't want to be saved," he said. "So I find it all the more pleasant to meet you again in these earthly realms."

It was an unctuous opening, and I was relieved that he followed it immediately with the topic of the bomber's crash-landing, starting with the irritating remark that, once he was safely on the ground, his father had felt that he was in paradise despite being in the middle of enemy territory. I complimented him on how well he spoke German, then let myself get a bit carried away, telling him about my mother and how she, with some other schoolchildren, had been one of the first to reach the crash scene. I spoke without thinking, but I sensed that it was a mistake when he replied that he was not in the least surprised to hear it because he had already had the feeling at our first meeting that there was a special bond between us.

"My father told me about the children," he said. "They stopped and stood a way off, then started yelling as if they'd been told to."

I had never thought about it, but for some reason I had imagined a scene with no sound, and so I was surprised by his description.

"They were yelling?"

"There was a guy who got to the crash site before them and was yelling 'Schweinehunde' over and over again, and they just copied him."

"They were yelling '*Schweinehunde*'?"

"The boldest ones dashed forward a few steps, then retreated quick," he said. "They were all trying to outdo each other, and kept getting closer and yelling louder."

I wanted to ask him if the girls had done the same as the boys, but didn't. If he had said yes, the pathetic hope I nursed would have been too transparent and my sentimental memories of what my mother had told me would have been lost for ever. It felt like a rewriting of history to me, but for him it seemed to be just a funny anecdote, whose punchline was that this was how he had learnt his first word in the German language, albeit in its wrong meaning.

"The truth is that it took me a long time to grasp that it was an insult, because my father said it with such gentleness," he said. "When I was a kid he used to sit me on his lap and call me 'little *Schweinehund*' in his softest voice."

I was silent, and in the silence I looked at the two girls who listened with blank faces as he spoke. The glances of his wife gave nothing away either. There was a moment when I had the impression that they flinched, but if so they immediately got a grip on themselves and resumed their pose of indifference; it came when I offered him a beer and he hesitated for a second before saying that the Lord had freed him of this vice and added that it had been the moment of his own salvation and rebirth when he had given up alcohol for good. It was not the first time he had deployed the jargon, but it was the first time I thought I detected a reaction. Otherwise these interjections were striking for the fact that, at the same time, there was evidently not one technical detail of the bomber that wasn't familiar to him – and for how he kept switching from one subject to the other seamlessly. So one moment he might be waxing lyrical about the plane's range and payload, with precise figures for distance and weight, or recalling the type and number of missions flown and, litany-like, underlining its key capability for being literally shot full of holes and still able to stay in the air, and then the next he would suddenly start quoting a psalm or, without drawing breath, move from the Garden of Eden to Sodom and Gomorrah or from Sodom and Gomorrah to the Garden of Eden.

Even so, all of this would have remained no more than a bizarre episode if he had not raised the question again of what had brought me out to the river. It was barely two weeks since our conversation at the service area, but he put it differently this time, and I thought to myself that he had been doing some research. I realised straight away that he wanted something from me that I could not give him, an ideological justification of some kind. Perhaps it was because he was American, or perhaps it was just because of his excessive religiosity, but he seemed unable to comprehend that I was following no deeper impulse than that of creating a place where I could be myself for a few weeks, and when he started to dish out his apocalyptic visions – declaring that there were more and more people going back to the woods, as he put it, more and more withdrawing from the world because it was no longer their world, leaving it to its fate and hoping for its speedy end so that something new could rise out of the ruins, or the old ways all over again, from way, way back and in virgin condition – I immediately tried to cut the conversation short. His voice had taken on a soothing tone and it was clear that this was his pet subject, a set piece that he might have delivered a hundred times, perhaps not even conceived by him but by a centre somewhere out in the Midwest or God knows where, that had sent him out to save a few last souls from the coming inferno. I could have given him plenty of prompts if it had just been the usual lament about disintegrating morals and the decline of the West, but there were two or three sentences that made me sit up. It started when he said that we were overdue for a new world war, and that the tragedy was that so few had noticed and most were carrying on with their lives as if they could not see the abyss on whose brink they stood and would carry on dreaming that they were flying when they fell into it.

At first I thought he only intended this figuratively, but when he went on to say that the new world war would be a war for Jerusalem I realised that he was picturing a concrete scenario.

"It's a war that'll be waged at every second and in every corner of the world," he said. "Every person will have to decide, sooner or later, which side they're on."

He looked at me as if he was unsure which side I was on and wanted to assess what sort of contribution he could expect from me.

"Have you been to Jerusalem?"

"No," I said. "What would I do there?"

"It's one of the holiest places in the world."

Still short of breath from excitement, he seemed to be under-lining not just every syllable but every letter, and his eyes radiated aggressiveness. Sweat was starting on his forehead again, and when he raised his arms as he spoke you saw the dark circles around his armpits. He was gesticulating with short, sharp movements, throw-ing out his hands, making arbitrary snipping cuts in the air with his index and middle fingers.

"Of course that means that it's also one of the most terrible places in the world," he said. "That's why the struggle for Jerusalem won't take place on the Temple Mount, the way everyone thinks."

Until that moment his gaze had not left my face but now he assured himself, with a sweeping look, that everyone was listening and raised his voice.

"This isn't about the Jews' earthly Jerusalem. It's a struggle for each and every one of us and will be waged, at every hour of every day, nowhere other than inside ourselves because it's about the heavenly Jerusalem that is the Jerusalem of angels and saints."

I knew that such conversations rarely ended well and was relieved that his wife joined in at that moment, softly, almost inaudibly, yet with an unmistakable firmness and, paradoxically, as if her voice were emerging from the darkness. She said that he should let it go now, that everything had been said, and when she spoke his name it was enough to calm him. If I understood her correctly, he was called Abner, and although nothing could have been less relevant I suddenly had the absurd idea that the Lord must have revealed Himself to His prophets outdoors in the same way. I had never heard the name before, but it sounded as if it came from far away and there was no mistaking the effect on him. In fact he started up again, saying that the struggle for Jerusalem was a struggle between the forces of light and the forces of darkness, but then admitted that he was beaten and let her speak.

"There's a time for everything," she said. "Just calm yourself."

I can still hear how her voice wrapped him up in its softness, and I couldn't help noticing how naked he seemed to be in front of her and what power she had over him because of it.

"You've got nothing to prove to anyone. There's a time to fight, and a time to stand back from fighting. How you work that out, only you can decide."

It was as if she had given a sign, but even today the haste with which she stood up and walked away still puzzles me. The Reverend was already on his feet when she said that it was high time they went. He had jumped up again with that same nimbleness that looked so incongruous in a person of his bulk, and urged the two girls to do the same; they came to life with languorous movements, reminding me of aquatic plants wafting back and forth in a sluggish current. I thought at first that they were not going to react to his urging, and watched them with fascination. While they had been sitting, motionless, with their backs straight as candles, I had asked myself how they kept it up, and as they stood their upper bodies were just perceptibly out of true, now slightly bent to one side, now to the other. When they came closer to me I was struck by their dark, nearly black eyes; I tried to imagine what they had looked like the night before by the fire. Their graceful stiffness gave them a spaced-out quality and with the forest and river in the background, and the almost cosmic stillness that can make itself felt out here from one second to the next, they made me shiver.

I would have liked to say something, but stood there mutely. They silently gave me their hand before going over to the two boys, to whom they also said nothing, and only the Reverend spoke, again urging them to hurry up, until his wife interrupted him. He murmured an apology, took a few steps, then came back and stood in front of me.

"One last question."

I nodded.

"Is your mother still alive?"

I don't know why I hesitated. I am not superstitious but I felt that everything hung on the right answer, except that I didn't know what it was. For a moment I even considered asking him to list the possibilities, as if there were plenty to choose from.

"She's still alive," I said. "What about your father?"

"What about him?"

"Is he dead?"

"He died last year," he said. "He wasn't that interested, but anyhow he knew we were here."

They finally went away, without further ado, but no proper explanation was forthcoming then, or that evening, when Daniel came over to the flat and we talked about it. I went after the Reverend to give him his jacket, and directly after he and his wife and the girls had gone the two boys also made moves to go, as if they wanted to stop me putting them on the spot. I stayed on my own for a while at the house, going over everything again step by step, every question and answer, but only ended up understanding their behaviour even less. Of course I hadn't been able to help noticing the unease that they had shown during the conversation. Christoph had been sitting diagonally behind me, so I had not seen him, but I had been aware that he was close by; Daniel had been poking the earth with a branch and staring at the ground like a truculent child. Throughout the conversation I had been waiting for the Reverend to address him directly, but I suddenly understood why he did not. So long as Daniel did not spontaneously declare his own faith, what had happened between them remained embarrassing, and when they bumped into each other again they were like two men who, having met under dubious circumstances, pretended not to know each other.

When he rang the bell that evening it was after eight. First off we chatted about the book I had spent a long time searching for among Robert's books late that afternoon when I had come back and that was still lying on the kitchen table and immediately caught his eye. I still had the Reverend's phrase in my head about how there were more and more people going back to the woods, and if the obvious connection had not dawned on me out by the river, as soon as I was driving home I had thought of Thoreau's *Walden*, his book about his life in the woods, and then, having located it, dipped into it, although without being as carried away as I had been the first time. I had not found it immediately because it was not with Robert's books where I had thought it was, but when I did, I discovered that he had even written his name in it, which was a rarity, and that there were underlinings on several pages which were probably his, and this then formed the basis for a game in which I became more and more engrossed.

It started when Daniel picked up the book and began to read the underlined passages aloud and then, when he had had enough of making his own comments on them, demanded a verdict from me. He would read a sentence or two and I was supposed to say true or false, he would declaim in a formal voice and I had to give him a thumbs-up or thumbs-down, or he would quote a few words that were clearly absurd from a contemporary standpoint and all I had to do was laugh, but then as we went on my laughter died in my throat more and more often. I remember that I fell silent at the point where Thoreau says that living is so dear, and I know I just nodded when Daniel read out his reasons for going to the woods, because he wished to live deliberately, to front only the essential facts of life, so as not, when he came to die, to discover that he had not lived. There was the exhortation not to come to grief by a false position, about which Daniel himself was silent, and what I particularly liked was the idea that if you built castles in the air, your work could not be in vain, because that was where they should be and you only had to put the foundations under them.

I know, I know, it's the easiest thing in the world to defuse with irony a book that poses the question of the right way to live more directly than almost any other, but that was how the evening started, even if it turned out completely differently. It was a conscious sacrilege, committed in the hope that one would thereby rob it of its seriousness, yet at the end the plainest sentences struck me again with all their force. Our attitude had already swung around and we had stopped joking when Daniel found the passage where Thoreau talks about the Atlantic and Pacific of one's solitude and showed me Robert's long exclamation mark in the margin – at least four or five centimetres long. Daniel had walked around the table, because I told him I did not believe him, and he held out the open page to me. I stared at it for a while without saying anything and held my breath, I remember that. Then I got up, opened a bottle of wine and raised a glass to Daniel, but I don't remember stroking his hair and calling him "my boy", as I read later in his manuscript in which the scene is described in detail, including what I am supposed to have said.

"Daniel, Daniel, my boy, my dear boy."

Anyhow, straight afterwards he quoted the passage where it says that only from the summit of a pile of books can we scale heaven at last.

"True or false," he said. "What do you think?"

This was also a reference to our conversation of the day before in which I had recommended that he forget books, that he could read them later, read them when he was dead, and I shrugged. I had the impression that he would not forgive me for that, and when I subsequently told him that he should try, just once, piling on top of one another all the volumes that might conceivably supply him with meaning in the course of his life and that in the best-case scenario he would get no higher than an average tower block, never mind a skyscraper, he looked at me aghast. The mood had become much less relaxed than when he arrived. Then he had seemed no different from the many times he had come over to see me before, but now something seemed to have clenched up in him. He did not feel he was being taken seriously, and that probably had something to do with why he initially ducked my questions when we started talking about the Reverend again, until he suddenly revealed why his wife had shut him up so hurriedly at lunchtime. He said she had wanted to stop him delivering yet another inflammatory speech of the sort he had made the night before, and when I put it to him that that was exactly what it had been, he shook his head.

"That was only the start of it, you've got no idea what tirades came after," he said. "He said that for every person there are only two possibilities, and they don't choose the better one."

It was exactly as I had anticipated, and I really could not see what he was worrying about when he spelled out the Reverend's possibilities: that you could be close to the Lord or not, and if you weren't then you were doomed to damnation.

"What's so special about that?"

"You don't know what he meant by damnation."

"What did he mean, if he didn't mean hell?"

"Of course he meant hell, but he got a lot more detailed about how you end up there," he said. "He talked about the worship of Mammon, and about homosexuality and harlotry."

4

IT IS ONLY IN RETROSPECT THAT I HAVE REALLY UNDERSTOOD how, from the outset, this conversation with Daniel was also about Robert – not just on account of Thoreau's *Walden* and the passages he had underlined in his copy, but because all the time I had a question that I only managed to ask just as Daniel was about to leave. He was at the door when I asked him whether the Reverend knew the story about my brother. It was not premeditated, the words just came to me, but precisely because of that, and because Daniel looked startled, we realised simultaneously that the answer could harm me. I couldn't say exactly why, but I knew I had to keep Robert out of this madman's grasp. I had to protect him from the Reverend including him in his prayers, as was his wont. But Daniel did everything but calm me down.

"Afterwards the Reverend walked on down the river with his wife and the girls," he said. "We tried to put him off, but we couldn't."

At first I could not understand what he was trying to say.

"He walked on down the river?"

Daniel nodded.

"But not to look for his daughter?"

"To be honest, I don't think so."

For some reason he nodded again, and I wanted him to stop nodding, but I saw his agonised look and it struck me that it was not his fault.

"He walked on down the river, but not to look for his daughter,"

I said, as if I still found it impossible to grasp the most elementary facts. "What on earth was he looking for down there then?"

The sudden awkwardness in Daniel's expression was answer enough for me. There was no going back, and I had hardly said goodbye to him before I was in my car. From my flat in the town to the house in the village that the Reverend had rented with his family was perhaps twelve or fourteen kilometres, and only a few minutes later I was sitting outside it. I parked behind the big estate car, left my headlights on and the engine running and sat with both hands on the steering wheel, motionless for a time. It was before midnight, but there were no lights on in any of the windows and as I wound down my side window I felt I could hear, over the diesel's continuous rumble, the noises of the night, the sounds that as a child I had thought came from extraterrestrial beings. I got out, leant against the car's wing and quietly smoked a cigarette, and if anyone had peered out of a window they would have seen me staring across at the house. Then I walked the few steps to the garden fence and swung myself over it. I landed on a plastic bucket, which cracked under my feet against the stone paving, and when still nothing moved in the house I was sure I was being watched. I stood upright and stayed pointedly standing there, less than ten metres from the front door. It was completely silent, and as I started to move towards the door I hardly noticed the gravel crunching under my feet. A shadow darted past ahead of me, a cat probably, and disappeared into the bushes. I stood at the door, hesitating to take hold of the handle, and then left it. I walked around the whole building, letting my fingers run along the stone walls as if I wanted to take possession of it, and crept past the lower windows until I was back at my exit point and stood with a beating heart under the starry sky, which seemed to be retreating from the earth at an immense speed, every time I looked up.

I cannot describe the state I was in, a sort of trance, as if I were outside the human race with only a night-life that by day would vanish into nothing and a dark foreboding, a bright terror, that I was perfectly capable of feeling, and yet this nocturnal occupation, or conquest or whatever you want to call it, was responsible for the fact that the next morning, standing in front of the house again, I no longer hesitated. I only had a vague memory of how I had got home the night before, and I could easily have imagined the whole thing, if my forehead had not been scratched by an overhanging branch and I had not picked up a book lying by the doorstep and taken it with me, but now I was bathed in bright daylight and it could not have been more real. The two older girls were already out playing badminton in the garden, as if they had been put there to suggest normality, and they stopped their game to watch me as I got out of the car. They stared as if they were expecting me, and so I took my time, waiting until they resumed their game before walking up to the entrance, hearing sharp pocks behind me that reminded me of the hiss and crack of whips. Inside, in the hall, I was met by moist, cold air like in an underground vault and it took a moment to get used to the bottle-green light that filtered through two stained-glass windows. Against one wall there was a wooden chest with iron fastenings behind which the stairs, carpeted with a once probably red but now yellowish-grey runner, seemed to rise into a void, while along the other wall there ran a low shelf made of planks and bricks on which empty bottles had been lined up. Of the four doors, two were wide open and one was ajar, hanging crookedly on its hinges. I glanced quickly into each of the rooms, which were evidently unused, two of them without a single object in them, the third crammed with junk, and then I opened without knocking the closed door that led into the kitchen.

The need to confront the Reverend evaporated as soon as I saw him. He lay on a couch that was pulled up very close to the stove (and easily movable, as I found out, because it was made of inflatable cushions). He didn't get up, just folded the newspaper he was holding, put it on the pile of other papers next to him and watched me with a put-on air of unconcern that was not even provocative. The girl who was sitting writing in an exercise book at the table when I entered was of course the missing daughter. She cleared away her things and walked out without being asked, and the woman, who was leaning against the sink, washed out a cup, rinsed it at length and then dried her hands thoroughly while I looked around and finally said the first thing that came into my mind.

"So your daughter's back."

I had turned to the Reverend, but he made no move to reply, and the woman also only answered after a pause, as if she were still undecided as to how she should deal with the unwelcome guest. But the next moment she offered me a coffee, and faced with her friendliness everything I had prepared on the way there fizzled out. She was apparently perfectly clear about her mission, and from one second to the next swept me up in her look – literally as if at the flick of a switch – with a solicitude that frightened me.

"She was hiding in the barn," she said. "When we got back to the house she was lying reading in the meadow."

What had happened to the girl seemed to interest her as little as it had interested the Reverend the day before, and she seemed to shoo her words away with a brisk but light and barely explicit hand movement.

"But that's not why you're here, is it?" she said. "You're here to find out what we were so keen to look for down there by the river."

She laughed and immediately stopped, as if realising how false she sounded. She seemed to be listening intently for something, although there was nothing to hear. She turned her head round to the window behind her, and as she turned back to me again I could still see in her eyes the brightening of the light that had only fallen on her face for a very short time.

"Why do you fret so?"

I said nothing but held her gaze. She was speaking English, but it felt more as though she was speaking a language from another time. It could have come from a medieval epic poem and I might have been a knight returning home after a long odyssey, standing before the answer to the riddle that had driven him all around the world.

"You mustn't fret, everything's all right," she said, "We went down there to the river to pray."

She hesitated and her voice became very soft.

"There's nothing for you to be frightened of."

I cannot say why I simply accepted from her lips precisely the story I had wanted to confront the Reverend with. She told me that the flood had washed several logs ashore and someone had put up a cross there. I just nodded. I nodded again when she said that it was a beautiful, peaceful place, a description that, coming from anyone else, I would have rejected but that from her, despite its transparency, only further reassured me. As she spoke she left her place at the sink and came nearer to me, standing so close that she only had to reach out her hand to touch me. She asked me to sit down, and after she had poured coffee for me from a Thermos and made small talk for a while, she returned again to the visit to the river.

"They're fantastic boys you have there," she said neutrally, as if otherwise she risked sounding as if she did not mean it. "They're so full of admiration when they talk about you."

I looked into her eyes, but there was nothing, not a trace of mockery, no ironic smile, definitely no contempt. She was wearing sweatpants and a faded blouse, and at its neck I could see her clearly defined collarbones and the skin stretched over them. She was not more than forty but looked younger, and it seemed hardly imaginable that she was wearing a headscarf for anything other than practical or possibly fashionable reasons. She had clasped her hands together, slender fingers with strikingly broad joints, slender wrists and strikingly strong elbows, and judging by the way she reacted as my gaze moved over her I was obviously not the first one to have appreciated them. She stroked the backs of her hands, as if she wanted to reshape them, and looked away with feigned embarrassment.

"The boys say that you're different from the other teachers."

"Different," I said. "What does that mean?"

"They say you don't lie to them."

I laughed, and she laughed back as I said that perhaps I was not quite that pure – a deep, full laugh in her narrow, powerfully boned face.

"In any case, what have I got to lie to them about?"

She did not need to reflect for long.

"There is one thing," she said. "You could pretend you knew how to live, and build yourself up as too important."

It could have been a criticism, but there was no indication that she intended one, it seemed more as if she had made the remark for its own sake and there was nothing else to it, apart from the paradoxically calming effect her way of speaking had on me, which in turn reminded me of the conversation I had had years before with the head during his visit to Istanbul. The others had stayed at the hotel, keen to manage things so that we could be alone, and we had caught a ferry as far as the First Bosphorus Bridge and there looked for somewhere to sit in the autumn sun with a view out to the broad arch that spanned the strait and drew the traffic apparently almost noiselessly across it, high over our heads. I had told him that I was reading Robert's books when I couldn't sleep at night, and he took me to task, as though it was just the opportunity he had been waiting for.

"Of course you must decide for yourself what to do, but it can't help if you keep agonising over it," he said. "Why do you want to keep the wound open?"

What came next has stuck in my memory like a language exercise, and I explain it to myself today by thinking that he instinctively chose this form because I was not open to any other approach. Diagnosis would be followed by absolution, his finding that I felt Robert's death was my fault would be followed by his not-guilty verdict all of it delivered in half a dozen variations, as if he wanted to demonstrate how easily each phrase could be formed in the negative. Finally, he asked which books they were. When I started to list them, he interrupted me, perhaps because my scrupulousness made him nervous but possibly also because he wanted to express his dislike of such obsessiveness.

"You don't really think they were the reason."

Perhaps I was imagining it, but I thought I heard something almost like jealousy in his voice, as if we were talking about long departed lovers that he had never had.

"Sometimes I think they were, sometimes not."

I knew how much my answers must infuriate him.

"Believe me, they weren't the reason," he said, as I had expected, without letting any of his feelings show. "It's only you who ascribes that significance to them."

Then he was silent and I looked out across the water to the Asian shore, where I had never been, although all I would have had to do was take the ferry, which ran all day, from Karaköy to Kadıköy. I didn't manage it until months later, and when I think about the hours I spent with the head, it feels like a terrific over-reaction that afterwards I immediately took the Baghdad Railway to what was the end of the line in those days, as far as the Syrian border. On that particular day, however, I could never have imagined doing such a thing, on account of the way he treated me like an invalid. On the ferry he had bought me one glass of tea after another, whenever the waiter came past us with his tray, and now, with the same attentiveness, he wrapped his scarf around my shoulders and contemplated his work with satisfaction.

"I'm sure it'll all get straight in your mind," he said. "Once you decide to give up your all-night reading sessions, you'll be your old self after a couple of months."

The two years in Istanbul had always been a gloomy time in my memory – what I want to say is that I would have preferred to avoid remembering them at all because I never expected anything uplifting from them, but the thought suddenly occurred to me that perhaps that was wrong. I only had to think of the hours I spent reading there, and it all looked different. As long as it was still warm enough in the autumn, and then again in spring, I made sure I found a place in the open air whenever I could, and in winter I went for walks until I crept in out of the cold somewhere, and of course I had favourite places. Either I went straight down to the water from my apartment in Cihangir behind the Galatasaray High School, or I left the Austrian School after lessons and walked out from there. I only had to turn left at the end of the block and walk a few steps up the street to what had once been the English hospital, where there was still a small garden, or go in the opposite direction down the Strudlhof Steps, as my colleagues called the *Jugendstil* staircase at the corner, and in a few minutes I was at the Galata

Bridge, which is certainly no great find but on which I sat, shielded against sun and rain, at all times of day and in any weather, either on the western side with a view over the Golden Horn, or the east, overlooking the Bosphorus. I particularly remember the days at the tail end of the year when it got dark early and a yellowish haze hung in the air as I watched the lights going on along the banks and on the boats everywhere across the water, and after I had been reading for hours I had the feeling that reality was about to dissolve under my gaze and that I would be in limbo, neither here nor there, neither in the story I was reading nor in the world of the people who were commuting between Beyoğlu and Sultanahmet and could not see what I saw.

It was in this mood that I found myself listening to the Reverend's wife, just as I had also listened to the head back then, as though it was not so much what she said that was important but a formula, a ritual. She then also moved straight on to other subjects, starting to talk about her Turkish neighbours, and how the first thing she would do when she got back home was go to their local diner and order a hamburger with fried eggs and potatoes, and about how the two older girls, who all year had held out against spending another summer in the village, now suddenly wanted to stay here, and she went on chatting until she made a remark that led straight back to the starting point, when she invited me to come back soon. I stood for a few moments at the threshold as I realised that the Reverend, who had been gradually retreating and had finally completely disappeared from my field of view, had been keeping watch on us from the furthermost corner of the kitchen where, along with the inflatable couch, he had been moving away inch by inch, and that the oddest thing about the situation was that his wife was basically talking to me as if he were not there and I was not really registering his presence either.

That was the last time I saw him, and however much this encounter brought me face to face with Robert again and started me thinking about things I had avoided thinking about as far as possible, I became even more involved when I read Daniel's manuscript. For in it Daniel had described precisely how the Reverend came up with the idea for his nocturnal visit to the river and what had led him to walk down the bank to where my brother had ended his life, in order to pray for him. He had allegedly felt responsible for him because he had heard in the village that Robert had built an altar before he put the barrel of the rifle in his mouth and pulled the trigger. Of course I knew all the crazy details, starting with the sheet spread on the bare ground and the cross and the two candles on it, but I had forgotten them, or perhaps not forgotten them but just avoided thinking about them, and so they were only revived when I read about them. It was an utterly bizarre scene, the unspoilt riverside with the fast-flowing current at the narrows there and, in the middle of it, the ancient-looking arrangement of objects, that people had made vague references to but which I now had set out on the page in front of me in unbearable detail, because it was Daniel's style to describe everything as if he had been there, and to prefer to write two sentences too many rather than one too few.

I have always held back from attributing any specific significance to the business with the altar, but when I read about it I could not help remembering all over again how Robert used to ask me, when he was five or six, about the story of Abraham and Isaac. It was one of those summers that he spent with his grandmother in the village, and I came down for a weekend visit and shared the bedroom with the mirrored chest of drawers that overawed us both. On it there were not only confusingly similar wedding photos of our parents and our aunts and uncles, but, among some other pictures which included portraits of two relatives who had been killed in

Russia, there was also a wooden crucifix with a tiny olive branch, which I told him had come from one of the trees in the Garden of Gethsemane that were supposed to be more than 2,000 years old. He had been saying his prayers without being told to, as usual, kneeling next to the bed with his head bowed and hands clasped, unconcerned at me standing behind him looking at the top of his head, saying out loud what was on his mind. He was asking why Abraham had been commanded by God to sacrifice his son, and I remember the urgency in his voice when he wanted to know if he would really have done it, if he would really have slaughtered Isaac and burnt him on an altar like a lamb if he had not been prevented from doing it at the last minute by the angel of the Lord.

I was amazed at how helpless, and then how precise, his choice of words was for his age, as he switched without pausing from very tentative expressions to phrasing that could have come straight out of the Bible, and I knew that my answer could only be unsatisfactory, an anodyne sop. Afterwards we lay silently next to each other in the dark for a long time, and I got the impression that he was holding his breath for as long as he could, and then straining to breathe in and out so that I didn't notice. The bedroom was small, almost square, more like a cell, and we had opened the window that looked out onto the orchard and could see the lights of passing cars sliding along the wall. We watched as they moved over the cupboard that contained the practically never-used suitcases of tortoiseshell and cardboard, and plucked out of the darkness the image of the Sacred Heart that hung next to it, whose rays seemed to go on glowing for a while afterwards. We could hear the trains a long way away too, night trains as long as the freight trains in books, which rolled across America from coast to coast and that you could jump aboard as they started up if you were young and agile and didn't care where you were headed. His grandmother slept on the couch in the kitchen and left us the bed, and even though I was too old for it I knew exactly what sort of mysterious world it was for a child – outside the wide-open space with its noises and then sudden silence, inside the play of light and shadow on the walls. It was one of the nights when Robert begged and then literally implored me not to make him go to sleep, and I remember his terror that could not be soothed, his incessantly asking the same question – how could God demand something like that from somebody? – and finally his gentle breathing against my chest and his small body, twitching as it pressed itself against me in sleep and wrapped its arms around me.

The only time I saw him similarly distressed was when his grandmother told him that in the early 1930s she had almost emigrated with her husband to Brazil. He asked if that meant that he would be living in the jungle now, and she answered that no, he just would not exist, and I had to explain it to him. He was a few years older then, maybe nine, but otherwise the situation felt very similar, lying in her bed again, night again and summer, and the longer we talked about it, the more the idea aroused in him a sort of spooky pleasure, which much later I thought I also detected in one of the few letters he wrote home from his year at school in America. It was about the euphoria that sometimes got hold of him when the thought suddenly sprang into his head that he was on another continent, surrounded by complete strangers, and he imagined that no-one knew where he lived and that he could drop dead and everybody at home would go on thinking for some time that he was still alive and carry on as if nothing had happened, maybe only for a few hours but maybe for days, and only then find out. I did not think much of it, I certainly did not think it was an alarm bell, more one of his literary fantasies, a flight of fancy to make himself interesting, and it's only lately that I have caught myself having similar thoughts, similar impulses devoid of logic, when I go to the churchyard to visit my grandparents' graves and close by those of my uncles and aunts, all of them within a few square metres and all so beautifully laid out, I want to scream. Then I think that perhaps they should have emigrated, it would have been a second chance for them, and whatever might have awaited them, whatever life of hardship, whatever else might have faced them in Brazil beyond the false promises of an earthly paradise, it could not have been very much worse, all things considered, and if nothing else at least these gravestones and these crosses would not have existed in this place.

I remember that there were bells to be heard from the church as I walked out of the Reverend's house, and that the two girls, racquets in hand, were standing and waiting till they had finished. Even when I was a child I disliked the pealing of bells, the bustle it provoked and then the motionlessness that followed, the immo-bility of village Sundays as the last note sounded, which gave me an inkling of the ghastliness of eternity, especially in summer when everything came to a standstill as though there was no life left in the world and an oppressive heat announced itself over the fields from the early morning onwards and I instantly felt squashed by it. No, it was not Brazil, not a tract of land wrested from the jungle by years of hard work, with poisonous snakes and fever-ridden swamps and possibly even hostile Indians, but I only needed to hear bells being rung and I was back in the world of the grand-mother, with her barley coffee in the morning and her luncheon meat that she bought in seriously excessive quantities at the shop whenever we went to visit her at weekends, and the locked room next to the stairs in which not just Robert but I and all our cousins were born and where our aunt and uncle later slept beneath a huge painting of the Last Supper with its gently slumbering John against the shoulder of the doomed Jesus, whom I envied for sleeping and for being so close. There were always six or seven cows, a few pigs and hens, and whenever I succeeded in avoiding going to church and mass, or otherwise afterwards, I went to find them, still full of grandmother's stories, stories of bereavement and fatal accidents on the road mixed up with the lives of the saints and neighbourhood gossip, and it had always been their placidity, their animal placidity, that chased away the fear of death that the ringing of bells evoked in me. I could still have recited the names of the cows by heart, and thinking about them I recalled how Robert once said that for fun he sometimes used to name them after the attributes of the Virgin, calling them "most lovely", "the comforter" and "our lady of sorrows", "full of grace", "mother of heaven" or "blessed among women", when he stood by them in their stalls and imagined that the adults were not coming back and he would be alone in the world with them. A dog yelped and immediately stopped, and with relief I made out the sound of traffic that came from the autobahn as if it had only started a moment before and taken me out of my thoughts. The two girls watched me go up to the garden gate and then, before I had got back into my car, the pock-pocking of their game resumed, which then I registered with a sense of release but now feels like the sound of mockery.

I didn't know then that that was the end of summer. The two boys didn't come out to the river the next day, I waited for them in vain, and only found out later that the Reverend had invited them on an expedition and that the same afternoon they had driven away in the big estate, wedged in the back seat between the girls like two clueless children who were no danger to anyone at all. It's pointless to air my disappointment, pointless to lament that they stayed away the following day too, and that afterwards only Daniel came, once or twice, while Christoph was nowhere to be seen – so absent that even in the years afterwards, except for two or three permanently awkward chance encounters and at Judith's wedding, I actually heard and saw nothing of him. The boys now sought out the Reverend and his daughters the way they had previously sought me out, and if I think about it, I can hardly complain. They were the last days before the family's return to America, the boys were using the time they had, and when Daniel took himself off for half an hour or so and turned up to see me, I couldn't help thinking that it felt like a duty call and I had to be careful not to say so because that would probably have driven him away completely. I put off driving out to the house a bit more each day too, although by midday at the latest I was always in my car and hurrying to get out there just so that I didn't miss anything, and then I would sit out in my folding chair until the late afternoon.

The idea that the Reverend would go as far as using his own daughters as bait to seduce the two boys away from me sounds nonsensical, even if Daniel's manuscript more or less said so outright. If I felt like it, I could easily conjecture a stealthy kiss planted under the strict father's nose, a hand stealing into a pair of knickers, and plenty of other clichés besides, but it's unimportant whether such things happened or not, there's no point bothering about them, it's just soap opera stuff. That the Reverend did not like me was not exactly news to me, the feeling was mutual as they say, but I was still surprised that his speech about damnation had been so explicitly directed at me. Of course I remembered his claim that the struggle for Jerusalem was a struggle for every single person, but that he could have meant it as being a struggle for the two boys, and viewed it as his duty to lead them away from me and my influence to a place of safety because I was their perdition and would lure them into unspeakable sins and lives of disgrace, felt to me a very poor scenario, and not just because of how I've phrased it.

Perhaps I ought to have made slightly more effort to tear Daniel away or at least demand an explanation from him, but I don't know whether it would have helped very much. It is easy to say in retrospect, but the truth is that they were wonderful days, the mornings sharp and by midday the beginnings of that late summer warmth that reconciled me to the whole world, and I was perfectly good at keeping myself occupied once I had worked out that Daniel would only be coming to visit me sporadically from now on. I started to look for jobs around the house: I marked out a kitchen garden and dug it over, whether it was the season for it or not; I built a nesting box and nailed it to a tree; I cut firewood and was always busy somehow when he stopped by – sat down with him for half an hour and made a point of never asking him where he had been hanging out the rest of the day, made sure that I let him feel that I didn't have too much time for him, and by the time he disappeared again was none the wiser about what he was doing. Seen from the outside, perhaps it resembled a lover's fussing, but there was no outside, at least none that could have played a part for me, and from the inside I didn't consider it. I don't believe in symbols, and also don't think it was anything other than a coincidence, but it must be said that two days in a row I found dead animals very close to the property, once the remains of a slaughtered and half-eaten, half-decayed hare, once a pigeon that looked as if it had fallen out of the sky and might take off again any minute if it felt like it. Then I was busy because someone forced the door one night and I had to replace the lock and the hinges. I thought I would find a shambles inside, everything upside down or excrement smeared all over the walls, but I could hardly see a single object out of place. The bed had been used, the woollen blanket turned back and the sheet and duvet underneath it tangled as though whoever had used it had not slept in it but been involved in a life or death struggle with it, and on the table I found an empty wine bottle with a piece of cardboard propped against it with a spikily scribbled "Thanks". It was one of the last days before the weather turned, and soon afterwards there was the first fall of snow, so I spent another afternoon doing the essential things to make the mill ready for winter. I inspected the roof for leaks, nailed the shutters closed, secured the door with an extra padlock, and then only drove out to the river two or three times more, not staying longer than a few minutes each time.

5

TO REMIND ME THAT FROM THE BEGINNING I CONSIDERED THE business with the Reverend as more or less a grotesque joke, I only have to call to mind the sum of his beliefs. They started with his literal interpretations of the Bible, from the Creation to the Book of Revelation and the Virgin Birth to the Resurrection, the most important of them being that he lived in an end time and would be able to gaze upon the return of Christ with his own eyes. Before that happened, the last remaining prophecies would be fulfilled, particularly concerning – apart from all sorts of general heavenly events – the restoration of the nation of Israel in Palestine, as it was slightly awkwardly called, and the rebuilding of the Temple in Jerusalem.

I had asked Daniel about these prophecies the morning after I read his manuscript, and what he told me gave me an insight into a world that on the one hand could sound utterly fantastical, but on the other hand was more real than I liked to imagine.

"For sure, the Reverend never had any doubts about where the last end-time events would happen," he said. "He may have always emphasised that the struggle for Jerusalem wouldn't happen in Jerusalem, but it didn't stop him going there the summer after the three summers he spent in the village, to be closer to the salvation event."

The striking thing about his perspective was how confused religious myths were with contemporary politics, and how as a result of this thinking everything that had happened in Israel since the state had been founded could be seen as a part of the fulfilment.

"If you accept that", I said, "then it instantly becomes difficult to say what's wrong there and what's right, because at any moment the wrong thing can turn out to be right, so long as it prepares the way for the Lord and hastens His coming."

"Does that apply to wars too?"

"Especially to them. Because it's said that great tribulation will reign before God's thousand-year kingdom dawns. So wars are practically a precondition for it."

I felt that Daniel was speaking with a different voice from his usual one. On the one hand he was quieter and it sounded higher, but I don't just mean that, it was a continual wavering, a trembling as if there were gaps between the individual syllables, and it wouldn't have surprised me if he had fallen silent from one word to the next. He seemed to be listening to himself, and I wondered whether it had something to do with the fact that he himself found what he was saying so outrageous.

"Wars are a sign of impending peace?"

"If you like."

"Crimes are a sign of mercy?"

"You could say so."

"Bad times are really good times?"

I had let myself in for this game, and he treated me like an all too eager student who was going to burn his fingers the minute he discovered fire. He had not showered, he was unkempt and unshaven and had come to the kitchen in his shirt and underpants, which was both not particularly important and a decisive part of the situation, for it seems to me that we could only have had that conversation like that, with him still half asleep and nowhere near presentable and me caught off guard by him and at first less curious than polite, then just curious, and whether polite or not no longer the question. For a long time I did not notice that he was letting me talk on, as though watching to see how far I would go, until I became aware of his smile. It was benevolent and patronising at the same time, and as he looked at me, sitting back to front on his chair with both hands on its back and his chin resting on it, it felt as if he was demonstrating his superiority.

"The only problem is the last step in the whole construct," he said finally. "It foresees the conversion of the Jews to the one true faith, or, if they remain stubborn, their destruction."

He himself had been back to Israel to spend more time there, not that autumn straight after our weeks by the river, but the following winter and spring. I had thought he would start at university at the beginning of that semester, but the more the summer went on, the more uncertain he had become. Instead he kept having ideas by the dozen of all the places he could travel to, and though his longing only went as far as getting hold of a globe and marking it indiscriminately, he did make his mind up to give himself a year, as he said, to have a look around before he committed himself. In the end he decided it was to be Morocco, a trek from one royal city to the other that was planned down to the last detail, with a side trip into the desert, but at the last moment it all fell apart, either because Christoph could not be persuaded to go with him or perhaps it had never been more than a flight of fancy anyway. Then he remembered that the head of the Austrian Hospice in Jerusalem had invited him to get in touch if he ever wanted to come back to the city for a few weeks, and he would see what he could do, perhaps offer him an internship or a temporary job. He had stayed there for two or three days during his Easter journey through the Holy Land with the other pilgrims, and he remembered the castle-like building right on the Via Dolorosa fondly. It had seemed like a haven to him, behind whose walls he could retreat whenever the hustle of relic- and junk-sellers outside on the Way of the Cross became too much and an apple strudel at the Vienna Café inside the building felt like salvation.

He had never told me very much about this second time in Jerusalem, and because he tended to be laconic I tried hard not to seem too interested. I had heard about an incident that had meant he had to leave the Austrian Hospice prematurely, but no-one knew anything for certain, not even what kind of incident it was, and because in the past he had flatly refused any enquiries about his activities, I refrained from asking him. So secretively did he behave generally that I was surprised he answered me when I wanted to know if it had been the Reverend who had given him the impetus to set off on this new adventure.

"You don't really think I needed his babbling to make my mind up, do you?" he said. "It's all just pretentious waffle he uses to big himself up."

This distancing seemed all the more surprising when he happened to add that he had actually met the Reverend in Jerusalem. They had arranged to meet several times, he said, but after the first time he had avoided seeing him in the old town because there was no talking to him there. Afterwards he had always suggested meeting somewhere where there were people who had nothing to do with the whole carnival of faith, a place where the city was no different from any other city in the world, a café on Jaffa Road or Ben Yehuda Street, near modern shops if possible, where you could buy everything, just not devotional goods.

"At least there he'd stop his preaching and missionising for a couple of minutes, whereas as soon as he was inside the old city walls he always got over-excited and no other subjects got a look in because he was always surrounded by loads of other people who swore by the imminent coming of the Lord," he said. "He's been there since Easter, without his wife or the girls, and that's probably had a lot to do with the fact that he's let himself go. After a few weeks he was hardly recognisable."

I tried to picture the Reverend as he described him, and when I asked whether he had really changed that much, Daniel just laughed.

"He's lost a lot of weight. I can still see him, he's a bag of bones. He's stopped wearing his black suit and started wearing a sort of tunic he must have bought at some souvenir stall."

"Not some kind of cassock, then?"

"On him that's exactly what it looked like," he said. "On top of that, he stopped shaving and made himself look like the poorest person you can think of, from every angle."

He himself seemed hardly able to believe it, shaking his head as he spoke and looking at me as he went on without a pause.

"Then the nutter moved out of his hotel in the city centre to some cheap place in the Armenian quarter, and every morning when he didn't have Hebrew lessons he cheerfully strolled very early up to the square in front of the Church of the Resurrection to set himself up for his day's work."

I had a stronger and stronger impression that I had heard the story he was telling me before. I knew that it even had a name and almost every guidebook had its own entry about Jerusalem Syndrome, as it was known, and if Daniel was to be believed the Reverend was suffering from a textbook case of it. It sounded too good to be true, which I pointed out to Daniel, but he waved my scepticism away.

"Just because it's a cliché doesn't mean it couldn't happen to him," he said. "When you hear what else he got up to, your eyes will be popping out of your head."

Unpredictable as I had personally found the Reverend to be,

I could imagine him being capable of a good deal, but to have selected for his attempts at salvation and conversion the Wailing Wall of all places, and even apparently as far as Mea Shearim in the Orthodox quarter, was definitely pushing it.

"Not even a nutter would think that was a good idea," I said. "With all due respect to his penchant for folklore, surely he understood that particular limit."

Daniel agreed, as if he'd expected me to say exactly that.

"Very true," he said. "You'd think so, wouldn't you."

He seemed to find my surprise amusing.

"People in Jerusalem are accustomed to all kinds of things."

"But he can't go evangelising at the Wailing Wall."

"His dire state somewhat gave the game away, and luckily no-one took him at all seriously," he said. "Anyhow he was picked up at his first try and admitted to a clinic."

I knew less and less what to make of it, but if I still had any doubts about the whole situation I was now convinced it was true, even if it had perhaps been rounded out and polished to make a good story. I could easily imagine the Reverend getting himself into the predicament Daniel described, and bearing in mind the untenability of his chosen way of life, it was not even as far-fetched as it appeared at first glance. To be honest, the incident amused me and when I asked Daniel what else had happened to him and he told me, I couldn't help laughing.

"The embassy got in touch with his wife and she came to collect him," he said. "She set the wheels in motion to bring him back into the real world."

Daniel had gone with the two of them to Tel Aviv airport, and in the departure hall the Reverend had thrown his arms around his neck and begged him to stay there and take his place until he returned with his strength restored.

"But he probably knew he had a problem," he said. "He looked a lot more cheerful as he disappeared through security, anyhow."

It was a ludicrous story, but it helped us break the ice, and even though it had occurred to me that he was going on talking so that he could dodge talking about other things, I had also noticed how it had gradually cheered me up, so that when he finished the silence felt strange and awkward. I had wanted to challenge him about his manuscript from the moment I got up, in particular because of the passages that dealt with Robert, but I neither managed to spring it on him when he came into the kitchen nor did I find an opportunity after that or perhaps even want to find an opportunity to bring the subject up. It was nine o'clock by now, and I had originally planned not to cancel any more than the first hour's teaching, but then I decided not to go to school that morning and to devote some time to him. So I was not in a hurry, and when he offered to go and fetch some rolls from the bakery at the end of the street, I said yes. While he was away I took the opportunity to glance around his room. Not much luggage, obviously, as usual, a lightweight holdall that contained some underwear and a couple of shirts, although he was on his way to Italy and intended to stay for several days, and on his bedside table I discovered a book of John Donne's poems and T.E. Lawrence's famous *The Seven Pillars of Wisdom*, which had been one of the books he had been reading back then, that summer out by the river. I picked it up and remembered the stories of how he had allegedly appeared at the next carnival parade dressed in a white robe, white head-cloth and dummy gold dagger tucked in his belt, leaving everyone present with an abiding sense of just how far he could remove himself from reality.

I expect he guessed I would rummage in his things, and what I found was no accident, he had arranged things so that I got a specific picture of him, but when he came back I said nothing and just marvelled at his cheerfulness and obvious good humour that, in retrospect, made the conversation about the Reverend feel incongruous. He had, I thought, been too quick to put the knife in, and had made far more of a caricature of him than he perhaps really was. I wondered what he was trying to hide. Even if he would not allow himself the sort of inconsistencies that the Reverend allowed himself, I doubted whether the piety he had sometimes flaunted as a student had turned into its complete opposite and made him a cynic in such matters. Had he instead put the episode in Jerusalem at arm's length because it affected him more than he cared to admit?

He had seen the Reverend again only six months before, and he talked about that meeting quite differently. He had been in America — a trip I paid for, incidentally — and wanted to visit the family. His descriptions were full of affection and relegated the image of a fanatic and his escapades in Jerusalem into the background. For one thing, he had not expected to meet a pensioner who was living on his own in a small town because his wife had walked out on him and the girls had long ago left home.

"He's still active in the Baptist community where he lives, but he's given up his evangelising. There's a yellowing banner with the inscription 'A THOUSAND SAVED' hung across one of his living-room walls to remind you of his glorious period of activity," he said. "Polaroids everywhere too, showing him with the fortunate ones he has saved from hell."

This was more than I wanted to know, and when Daniel told me there was also a picture on the mantelpiece of the bomber that had crash-landed in the Au, I told him he could save his breath. For me it was sheer sentiment, and while I might have enjoyed him waxing lyrical on the subject at another time, I could not take any pleasure in it now. It was all too predictable, and I reacted rather coldly and asked him what his point was.

"Well, whether you like it or not, the Reverend talked about you too," he said at last. "He said he'd never met a person who needed saving more than you do."

Feeling uncomfortable, I laughed. My first impulse was to ask him why, but then I remembered how the Reverend's wife had asked me why I was "fretting so" and was worried that Daniel would make some connection with Robert's death or make some general observation, so I let it go and instead tried to brush it aside.

"We'd do better to work out what's up with you."

He did not answer, and I did not press the point.

"Apart from the fact that he must have had far better candidates for the title than me," I said, making no effort to hide my scorn. "If not here, then perhaps on another continent, among savages in the jungle, if there are any left."

"I'm afraid not."

"Among the godless and the heathen."

"To be honest, I don't think anywhere in the world," he said. "You're one of the few he still regrets not having had any success with."

For me the conversation was all the more ridiculous because neither of us had ever mentioned that he had let himself be saved, although the event itself, such as it was, had been described to me by Judith in all its details soon after it happened. I had, of course, noticed him asking about her as soon as he arrived, although he did so very casually, giving the impression that he was not especially bothered about my answer. Even so, it was the first time he had mentioned her, he had not asked about her on any of his previous visits, and whenever I did tell him something of what I had heard, he either passed over it in silence or made a meaningless remark and ensured that we changed the subject. This time was different too because she had recently come back to the school to complete her probationary year and he had worked out that she was teaching under my supervision for a few weeks. So his question was about how she was getting on, about which I tried to fob him off with an all-purpose answer, saying that he knew her and knew how, whenever she decided to do something, she would do it properly and so I had no cause for complaint. He acknowledged the truth of this with a laugh, and when he then said that he just found it sobering that she of all people should become a teacher, a cowardly decision considering the dreams she had had, his arrogance annoyed me but I restrained myself from rebuking him for it.

It was also hard to put up with because, as she had told it to me, he had not cut a very fine figure in the story of his salvation and should have had every reason to treat her with more respect. She and I had gone out for dinner in her very first week of teaching, and of course we had talked about old times and about what had happened the night she had stayed out by the river with the two boys. I had seen her a few times at the end of the summer, then quickly lost sight of her and only occasionally had news of her, always third- or fourth-hand. I knew for example that her child was being brought up by her parents, and when she came to visit every other week I sometimes heard she had come but never saw her. Our relationship was not one in which I could expect her to find the time to get in touch with me, and so for me she was still half the girl she had once been, half a stranger to me, and I found it hard to believe that she was the first person to tell me about that night.

I had asked the head to recommend a restaurant and had reserved a table there, but although he had praised it to the skies we were the only diners. I was nervous because I was not sure how we would handle the situation together, but if I infected her with my nervousness at the outset she quickly defused it, and nothing in our behaviour would have led a bystander to think we had once been teacher and student. It was not really autumn yet, the evening was balmy, and she had on the same sort of plain dress she had worn at school, a white strap dress with blue dots and lace hem, but her hair, which she tied back for teaching, was loose and when she moved her head the ends swung back and forth over her shoulders in a slightly delayed action. She had put her cigarettes on the table but she didn't smoke, just once, and then again later, took one out, put it unlit between her lips for a few moments, then put it back in the pack. She radiated something oddly innocent with this gesture, and laughed as if she was laughing at herself, pushed the pack far away from her and for a while just looked at me, elbows on the table, chin in her hands.

"I don't understand why Daniel's never told you anything about it," she said. "Why do you think I called him Jesus?"

Up till then our conversation had been calm and straightforward, but I suddenly had the impression that she could hardly hide her agitation, and the mere memory of the night-time scene seemed to be filling her with revulsion as she went on, saying that Daniel had unquestioningly gone along with the whole rigmarole.

"He knelt down in the darkness and repeated everything the Reverend said to him, starting with the fact that he believed in Jesus Christ and the Bible. The only thing that was missing was that he didn't shuffle down to the river on his knees to be baptised. Then I started to have a really strong, almost physical feeling of what he meant about daring to do anything with divine blessing."

She was talking softly, and although she had been gesticulating as she spoke she now put her hands side by side on the table, giving her a slightly official look.

"He stretched out in his sleeping bag next to me and began reciting the Song of Songs, till Christoph stepped in and put himself between us."

I had not had a chance to respond because all this poured out of her in such a stream, so I tried to take her hand, but she pulled it away.

"That surprises you," I said. "He was in love with you."

"I'd prefer to say he was crazy."

I couldn't help noticing her gently folding her arms.

"Anyway, suddenly he was a different person," she said. "Some people might find it romantic, but I thought it was really creepy."

It had been my impression that there had not been anything between them for a long time, but then she told me that he had started calling her in the middle of the night again.

"It's not the first time, and whenever I make the mistake of picking up the phone he immediately starts on his old tricks, which used to make me shudder right at the start, out by the river that summer."

"He recites the Song of Songs?"

"Yes," she said. "He calls me daughter of Jerusalem, daughter of Zion, then goes into raptures over the mountains of Lebanon."

"He can't mean it seriously."

"It's always the same sermon once he gets going, the same hoarse voice, the same feeling of threat," she said. "Every time it happens, I check that my doors and windows are locked and look out into the street to see if he's loitering somewhere between the buildings."

As she said it she looked at me with an expression I had never seen before, a combination of uncertainty and outrage that did not leave her face for the rest of the evening, and when she went on talking the bitterness in her voice was unmistakable.

"I go back to bed and I lie there and I can't get to sleep for a long time because I'm just imagining that he's standing there somewhere in the darkness, lying in wait for me."

It was her saying that she could do without that kind of infatuation that stayed in my memory, and in fact, until that moment, despite all the baggage of craziness and difficulties that Daniel carried around with him, impossible to ignore as it was, I had not guessed how desperate he felt and it was only as a result of her words that I really began to have any insight. Certainly he could not have been said to be the most skilful young man in his dealings with girls, but until then I had thought everything was being played out in his head and his imagination, and that that was exactly the problem – there was no counterpart in reality, and certainly not one as sickening as those calls were. In their school years Judith had not been his only paramour by any means, but she was the only one where it became obvious, and his dancing attendance on her only seemed possible because he had Christoph at his side and there was safety in numbers – a sort of parody of a rescue – if he ever feared rejection. He had sometimes mentioned other girls when he came to borrow or return books, but not one of them knew or guessed anything about his attraction. I remembered a brunette with pigtails in the same year whom he had fixed on for a few weeks, the daughter of a colleague, of whom he spoke the way one might speak about a being from another planet after he bumped into her just once at the swimming baths; a girl he didn't know whom he had become aware of on consecutive days on the Hauptplatz after school – he turned up at the same spot at the same time for weeks on end without ever seeing her again. All it took was for him to intercept a look that might not even be intended for him, or hear a word addressed directly to him, which he would then turn over for days on end to examine its deeper meaning, or a well-meaning laugh that he felt related to him, and I had to listen to how he was going to bring about a chance meeting and what ploy or trick he was going to use to approach her, without it ever coming to anything. I was supposed to offer him tips, to tell him whether he should compliment them or whether that was silly, whether he should invite them to the cinema or suggest going for a walk or, if he did that, whether he would immediately be suspected of being a stalker, while his own ideas of how to go about it were bizarre. Rather than initiating a contact in any other way, he would happily have ridden up on a white horse or thrown himself at the feet of his chosen one with a bouquet of red roses, which is why I was hardly surprised that it had had to be at least the Song of Songs for Judith and the creepy late-night calls. The thing is that for a long time I failed to understand that for him all these purely imaginary relationships actually existed, so I did not think it could do any harm if he let me participate in his daydreams about his girlfriends, in which he made them the protagonists of his stories and flights of fancy, and in which there was no difference between princesses and fallen women when he strode onto the stage and took them by storm.

Nor had I ever considered whether I too was part of his phantasmagoria, but when he finally said to me the day we had our conversation about the Reverend that he, the Reverend, had always been convinced that we had had a relationship and that perhaps that completely explained the Reverend's fixation with me, I could no longer be in any doubt.

"There are smuttier ways of describing what we've had together," I said as casually as I could. "I hope that isn't a threat."

On his previous visits we had almost always got round to talking about the summer by the river but this was the first time I had the feeling that he was reproaching me for something. The nostalgic way he usually recalled it was replaced by a burning desire to provoke, and if he had talked about himself the night before as if the future was wide open for him, now he gave the impression that he could not stop rummaging in his past and looking for a reason there, without being able to say for what exactly. He attempted a smile, but it fell flat and I wondered whether they were really the same person — the eighteen-year-old who would have made fun of any suspicion that there might be something between us, and the young man sitting opposite me who did not even appear to know that he only need go one tiny step further and it would be the beginning of blackmailing me.

"Of course I'm not saying that," he said. "I'd just like to hear from you what you wanted from me then."

"For heaven's sake, Daniel." At a stroke, his outspokenness had changed everything. "We spent time together."

The way he laughed — he had to know that he was putting himself on the same side as the hikers who had watched us from the mill's boundary and whom, when he mentioned them, he still referred to as insufferable gawpers.

"We spent time together," he said, separating each syllable. "Is that all?"

"Yes," I said. "What else do you want to hear?"

"There must have been a reason."

"That I can gladly tell you."

I let him feel my disappointment.

"We spent time together because it was good," I said. "I don't know what's suddenly wrong with that."

Then I asked him if he needed money, but he shook his head, and when he enquired whether I had read his manuscript I said no, although a moment before I had been wanting to talk to him about it and it was becoming increasingly obvious that I was pussyfooting around it. I could see that he did not believe me, but I stuck to my story and went on sticking to it, so that later, on the few occasions when he came to visit, I turned a deaf ear to his questions until I had the feeling that my sheer disregard must have buried his scribblings for good. There was, however, a moment when I almost let the cat out of the bag, and it happened because I could not get out of my head the passage in his manuscript where he had written that I had sometimes stared at him that summer as though I saw my brother in him.

I had also expected him to ask me about that part of the book all along, and in fact had been worried about him asking. For a second I was careless, and was on the point of enquiring which book he had imagined the daughter of the American family throwing into Robert's grave. After all, he had described the scene thoroughly, but had not specified the title. It was a striking omission in a narrative in which he had dealt very freely with facts he did not, and could not, know, and I was grateful that he had held back in this instance, although I kept coming back to the thought of which book it might have been. But in the end it was idle speculation on my part, and he did not need to know anything about it, and it was a good thing I did not investigate any further.

The ill-humour between us continued until he left. He was standing by the door when I asked him what he wanted to do with the manuscript and he repeated the phrase he had used once before, to become world-famous and rich and a hit with all women, an ambition whose irony he had no need to elaborate. I laughed, and when I asked how many copies there were he said three, one for him, one for me, and one for the world, as he put it. Perhaps I was wrong, but I again had the feeling that his answer came with a hint of threat and when I wished him the best of luck it sounded, quite unintentionally, like the opposite. His smile, in any case, left no doubt that that was the way he took it, and although it hurt me, when he finally ambled away I was, for the first time ever, happy that he was out of the house.

Third Part

DOWN BY THE RIVER

1

TODAY I SOMETIMES ASK MYSELF WHETHER I HAD REALLY NEEDED the photo in the newspaper to make me think about Daniel. Perhaps it's the other way round, and I started to think of him as soon as I heard about the bomb threat and so thought I recognised him on the anything but clear picture. Was I surprised when the head said that there were people who were connecting him with it? I don't think so, or if I was, it was probably because of a defensive filter, behind which I could see myself as more innocent than I was in reality. I was cross at my own naivety when I left the head's office, and even more at his invitation to call him later, which he had made as though he had some evidence against me and wanted to suggest that I come clean to him. Which might only be a particularly odd way of proving his trust in me, but to be sure that I had not overlooked something the first time, I made up my mind to read Daniel's manuscript again for hidden clues when I got home.

The discussion about Camus reminded me of a discussion I had had with a colleague in one of my first weeks at the Austrian School in Istanbul. I knew that there were limits in the classroom when it came to political matters, which I had been prepared for when I took up my post, but, pleading innocence, I had asked my colleague what would happen if I put Franz Werfel's *The Forty Days of Musa Dagh* on my reading list. The subject it dealt with, the genocide of the Armenians, was one of the most sensitive issues there was for the Turkish state, but I was curious to hear his assessment. I remember him instantly motioning me to lower my voice. Whispering, he said it would be taken as a declaration of war and the school threatened with immediate closure, and that as a matter of self-protection he would have to report my question to the joint head, so as not to get into trouble should it come out at some later date that he had spoken to me about it. He told me the story of a teacher from another year who had merely uttered the word "Kurdistan" and been sent on leave until further notice, and made me promise not to say one word about our conversation to anyone. I had two Armenian students in my class, and although they knew nothing about any of this, I thought about it every time I asked one of them to speak or come up to the blackboard. I could tell myself as often as I liked that it was nonsense for me to feel guilty towards them in this vague way that was nothing more than complacency, but it was to no avail: I was powerless against the uneasiness I felt when I saw them. My cowardice did not consist in my having let myself be intimidated, so much as in my treating them preferentially – an all too transparent way of salving my conscience, as though I could somehow make things better by giving them better marks or just being a bit friendlier towards them. It was later in the school year when, once or twice a week, I used to pause at the small Armenian church that stands behind a metre-high fence in a side street close to the always overcrowded Istiklal Street, and for a long time it did not occur to me that there, too, I was actually apologising into a void that gave nothing to anyone except myself. I used to stop and stand for a few moments in front of it, touched and untouched, and that was it, and then would continue my stroll or, wearing one of my suits that were as if tailored for these excursions, go to have tea at the Pera Palas or sit on the roof terrace in the Büyük Londra and let the hours go by without once thinking of what had just moved me so much.

I have already said it was not me who suggested *The Just* for the theatre group, but Daniel. He was very keen on Camus, just as Robert had been keen on him, and also thought he was pleasing me by his choice. To tell the truth, I didn't like the play, but I stuck with it, despite seeing after the first rehearsals that its overblown freight of ideas would only become more conspicuous when it was dramatised by school-age actors. My chief reason for persisting was that I did not want to give in to pressure from the Parents' Association. The charge made by its incensed representatives was that it was all about communist machinations and was an incitement to violence, which was so laughable it became a badge of pride for me. We rehearsed in the gym, but glued-on moustaches and furious expressions failed to turn Daniel or Christoph into any sort of credible terrorists in Tsarist Russia, about to assassinate a Grand Duke, and nor did a wig and heavy make-up turn Judith into their companion who by the end was burning to throw a bomb herself. They had to say lines that were much too big for them, a non-stop bluster of truth and truthfulness about freedom and justice, and only when I drove them home later in the evening did they come back down to their previous relationships a little. They called each other braggarts and impostors and tossed quotes at each other as if they themselves were the authors of their lines and had not spoken them in their respective roles. Judith sat in the front, Daniel and Christoph behind, and I usually took the long way round to extend the drive, delivering the boys first, then the girl. She had repeated a year and so was in their class, and at this point they had not exchanged more than a few words with each other when they found themselves uttering the noblest ideals to each other. As they did so, I was able to watch from the very first moments as the two boys fell in love with Judith and she conversely became increasingly mocking and skittish because she ruthlessly understood how little they were growing into the characters they were supposed to portray. This sometimes led to her going off-script whenever one of the boys succumbed to the pathos in their lines, retorting drily that it was all well and good and she understood that he was doing his best, but he should puff himself up a bit less and please be a bit less theatrical and make a bit less ado about nothing. With her thumb cocked she would extend her index finger towards the object of her derision and say, "Bang!" and that was enough of his self-righteous nonsense, he was dead now, and if he failed to take her hint it was "Bang! Bang! Bang!" all over again. Occasionally she would just sit down mid-speech and silently let the world know that she did not want to do it anymore.

In any case the head must remember how much he had defended me against the Parents' Association on that occasion. He had asked me to draft a letter and merely cast his eye over it before signing it, and then I was invited to dinner again, where he asked me to explain to him what exactly the play was about. He heard me out, saying from time to time that he could not see what the problem was, while cleaning the fingernails first of his left and then his right with his thumbnail. He reacted with irritation when his wife said I shouldn't let myself be bullied, youth must be allowed to think revolutionary thoughts, but then reluctantly went along with her and expressly recommended that I should not give way to the protests and should proceed entirely according to my own discretion.

I was still standing outside his office when I recalled all this, and did not want to think that after so many years he could have changed his mind. At that time I had reassured him that in any case we were unlikely to get beyond the preliminaries and it would probably stay at the rehearsal stage, but he insisted that after all the effort there should be at least one try-out in front of an audience.

He had seen on his visit to Istanbul the performance of an Oriental drama in which the actors had played behind a screen illuminated by a floodlight, and was still so enthusiastic about it that he suggested to me that we fall back on that if there was no other way. At first I was against it, but then with several rolls of white wrapping paper I stretched a screen across the stage and it actually helped if you only saw the shadows: that way the whole play was shifted into an in-between world in which ideal beings full of inspiration could trumpet ideal phrases that in reality no person would ever speak.

I went from the head's office to the staffroom, and having already suspected that my encounter with Frau Pfeifer had been accidentally on purpose, it now felt like a threat to find Herr Bleichert sitting at his table again, nodding at me as though he was expecting me. I may have been imagining it, but I thought I detected a trace of mockery in his expression. I sat with my back to him and looked out onto the sports field, where in the penalty area of the nearer goal a group of girls was practising the high jump, one after another peeling off from the waiting queue, taking a few springing steps of run-up and flying with a curved back onto the mat. Although the staffroom windows were closed I could clearly hear their shrieks, but I could not order my thoughts because I could feel Herr Bleichert behind me. That I had snubbed him by my behaviour did not bother me. Our dealings with each other had become increasingly surly over the years, and when there was no-one watching us it had happened more than once that we had walked past each other without saying hello. Since Dr Prager had retired, Herr Bleichert was the only teacher who always had one or two students he was trying to win over for himself in his pushy missionary way, and in addition he had for some time also been popping into the head's house, and whoever mentioned this always put on a knowing smile in referring to the chaplain as the keeper of the soul of the head's wife, who had given herself up totally to the clutches of the Church.

"I can imagine what you've been talking about with the old man," Herr Bleichert said. "You must be asking yourself where he got hold of Daniel's manuscript."

His voice sounded smug with satisfaction.

"The boy gave it to me only a day after you."

He had got to his feet and walked around the table between us and sat down next to me. I tried very hard not to show any emotion.

"So Herr Aschberner got it from you?"

I looked out onto the sports field again as he moved closer and followed my gaze and in doing so leant so far forward that he touched the window with his forehead.

"There's nothing in it that compromises you," he said. "The boy's sometimes a bit outspoken, but I read it as a sign of his devotion to you."

He seemed undecided whether to laugh or not.

"There's an intensity to it that makes you forget you're reading a novel. To be honest I didn't think he was capable of it. He really is full of surprises."

I had never taken part in the competition for Daniel that he and Dr Prager had fought out for so many years in the staffroom, and did not want to be dragged into it now, but it was already done.

"Do you still see him?" I asked, sounding more wistful than I wanted to. "I thought that after that summer you'd had no further contact with him."

I had not finished speaking when I saw his triumphant expression and heard him breathe in with a smacking sound between his teeth.

"Why shouldn't I have had any further contact with him?"

He pushed his head so obtrusively into my field of vision that I could not look past him any longer, and I was again amazed by that face of his, an indecisive assembly of unmatched parts, a tiny nose on which sat rimless glasses, blue, zeal-filled eyes, the red cheeks of a well-fed farm boy. The mouth was in constant motion, and made me think of a carnivorous plant. The sun seemed to irritate him, and he made a movement as if a fly had settled on his brow and he wanted to flick it away.

"I know that he was completely and utterly devoted to you then," he said. "For a long time what would become of him was in your hands, but that doesn't mean he wouldn't have been in good hands with me too."

He had come out to the river twice that summer, both times because of Daniel. For a while he behaved as though he had merely happened to be in the vicinity and was having a look around. He walked around with his hands clasped behind his back, all round the mill, picking up an object here and there and peering literally into every corner. Then we had a long conversation about this and that, before he finally asked about Daniel. Everything pointed to the two hammocks having only just been vacated and the two boys having kept themselves hidden somewhere close by, but he just nodded when I said that I had not seen either of them that day. Undeterred, he had strolled down to the water, and while they escaped him the first time, the second time they ran straight into him. They only had trunks on, and he looked from me to them and back again as he started talking insistently to Daniel.

I was a long way off, but the wind carried every word to me and there was no mistaking the pressure he was putting on him. It was not the first time he had tried to bring him round, but it was the first time I had overheard it. He said that he would rather have met him in a different place, but because he had clearly been hiding from him, he had come to talk to him again about what he wanted to do in the autumn. That was when he put his hand on his shoulder and waited for Daniel, whose eyes were lowered, to look him in the eye. Then he asked Daniel if he still remembered the morning at the Dead Sea, when he had rushed into his room, and what he had confided to him there.

"Don't worry, no-one's forcing you, but if it's true that you heard the call then in the desert, you shouldn't hesitate to follow Him with all your heart," he said. "It's all down to you, whether you want to save your life or lose it."

It is true that he was not wearing a cassock and had no cross in his hand, but as he stood stiffly upright in front of the scantily clad boys, it could have been a scene in the jungle, a parody of something that had possibly happened in the dim and distant past but could not possibly happen now.

"Tell me, do you still pray?"

I had never seen Daniel so full of unease. He stood with drooping shoulders and eyes lowered again as he said yes, but he did not think anyone heard him. It looked as though he was squirming under Herr Bleichert's hand, but Herr Bleichert seemed only to tighten his grip until Daniel at last managed to wrest himself away and run back to the house. I walked towards him and threw him a towel, and he was already through the door by the time Herr Bleichert followed him. I offered the chaplain a coffee but he refused, saying that he was in a hurry. Then he looked around him again and asked, already half-turned to leave, but as though it was directly connected to the exchange he had just had with Daniel, if we had heard about the incident on the railway line.

"There was one casualty," he said, as if it was just a word, and for a moment I did not grasp what he meant. "It happened a bit further downstream. A man lay down in front of a train."

We had been down at the river all morning, and had seen the train standing on the far bank. It had taken the curve at walking speed, after which it had been visible as it halted and then went on for 100 or 150 metres before finally coming to a complete stop. We had often seen the trains make brief stops there, but when after a quarter of an hour the carriages were still standing in the bright sunshine, as if parked there for good, we walked out onto the gravel bar and sat on the rocks. It took some time for the first people to get off the train and come down through the bushes to the bank on their side, but soon more and more doors were opening until finally the whole stretch of river bank was lined with stranded passengers. We obviously tried to guess what the cause of the delay could be, but our shouted exchanges only revealed that no-one seemed to know anything, and in the end it just turned into a kind of dappled picture of a harmless summer scene until, less than an hour later, everyone got back on the train and it jerked into motion and disappeared between the trees.

Afterwards, however, an unreal atmosphere persisted, as though a window in time had opened before our eyes and then closed again, and I was still under this spell when I looked at Herr Bleichert. He was gazing across at the far bank, where nothing at all indicated anything out of the ordinary and where a stranger to the area would hardly even have guessed a railway line ran between the trees at the top of the embankment. Then he started looking around him again with his rude, intrusive look, and his gaze settled on the remains of lunch, which were scattered around the fireplace. We had warmed up some ravioli and eaten it with plastic spoons straight from the tin, and I could not help noticing that he seemed to be staring disgustedly at the sight. Next to the dead wine bottles and crumpled paper cups lay the books Daniel and Christoph had been reading, and he bent over, picked one up and put it back down again with a shake of his head, as soon as he had identified the author's name and its title.

He finally left, and it was the utter impropriety and presumption of his visit that day that were responsible for our having hardly exchanged more than a few words since then and that made me feel throughout our conversation in the staffroom as if he was doing it all over again. At the time I had not felt that the episode out by the river had been so laden with symbols as it presented itself in retrospect, but now I could have sworn he was thinking about it and alluding to it intentionally. In any case I could not pretend, and it was definitely directed at me when he kept repeating what a good boy Daniel was and what possibilities he could have had if he had been pointed in the right direction at the right time.

"The old man is convinced that you led him into bad ways of thinking," he said. "There's no dissuading him that it was your books that turned his head."

I could have retorted that Daniel had not got all that crap about the desert from me, but I was fed up with defending myself and I let him go on talking.

"He wanted to expel him from the school after his article about Israel. He didn't have quite enough to go on then. If he had, there's no doubt that he wouldn't have hesitated."

"Instead of which, he put him under observation and behaved as if he didn't exist," I said. "The question is, why is he digging around in the old stories again now?" I hadn't wanted to show my irritation, but I was showing it. "Perhaps he overestimates the influence we have. What are we really able to do? We can possibly strengthen something that's already there in a pupil, or weaken it, but we can't do any more than that."

Herr Bleichert shook his head vehemently. I didn't like talking like this – hearing myself sounding like some time-serving teacher who believed what he was saying – but to have it pointed out to me by Herr Bleichert was something else. He said he felt that that was too pessimistic, which obviously he was bound to say, because he had a boy in practically every class to whom he preached so doggedly that by the end of the year the student had either become unrecognisable or sought his salvation in flight.

"We have our ways," he said, no longer concealing his cynicism. "There's no reason for us to hide our light under a bushel."

He got to his feet and leant against the window again, but paid no attention to what was going on in the sports field, where the girls were still jumping amid their audible shrieks. He looked me up and down.

"How does Pascal put it?" He spread his arms wide and parodied himself. "Man is neither angel nor beast, and the misfortune is that he who would act the angel acts the beast."

I had had enough of this game, and when he then started singing the praises of the pedagogical Eros, I told him so. He could not know that I had overheard the whole conversation he had had with Daniel out at the river, but he must have thought me particularly naïve if he imagined that he, of all people, could pull the wool over my eyes. Wanting what was good, regardless of the consequences, was his job, and in my mind's eye I saw again how splendidly he had choreographed his exit that day. He had strode away, stiffly erect, hands once again clasped behind his back, as he used to whenever he wanted to underline his status, and at the memory of how even in defeat he had gone on playing the victor I had to laugh.

I had never talked to Herr Bleichert about the Reverend, but if he hadn't found out for himself it would have given me immense satisfaction to tell him how, only a few days later, Daniel had allowed himself to be saved by him. It didn't take much imagination to connect that utterly grotesque event with Herr Bleichert's own utter flop with Daniel. For a long time I had not been able to put it into words, but now I felt that Daniel must have done it to spite him and, in a sort of travesty, given to the Reverend what he had refused to Herr Bleichert, in order to eliminate the possibility of Herr Bleichert saving him, but at the same time to succumb to temptation and bask in the publicity of his salvation.

The subsequent course of our conversation was all the more absurd, although I refused to let the allusions he kept making annoy me. I just wondered if he was utterly blind to his own role and how much further he would dare go when he began to say that he hardly needed to tell me that there had always been stories about what I did with the boys out at the river. It was the same worn-out old record, and I was relieved to hear the bell ring for break and hastily got to my feet almost as soon as the first of my colleagues crowded in and I could make my escape in the mêlée.

I should have taught for another hour, but decided to cancel the class. It would have been the same class in which I had talked about the bomb threat, and the words rang in my head again. I had actually said that it was sometimes the longing for innocence and purity that could make a person take guilt upon themselves, and at the picture of how that must have gone down at the lunch table in the homes of one or two students, I couldn't help but feel a certain satisfaction. It was a mistake, but I didn't sign out. I should have said I felt unwell and I would have been excused, but instead I just walked out and didn't give it another thought. I was sure I was being watched as I strolled down the street outside the school. Most of the classrooms faced that way, and although the blinds had been lowered almost the whole length of the façade and I couldn't see behind them, I had a clear image of the first curious faces surging towards the window and how steadily the word would spread that I had left just like that.

The feeling was familiar: a sensation of irresponsibility, the completely weightless sensation of having been relieved of everything. For the first few months after I came back from Istanbul, basically for the whole first year, I felt I had not really come back. They say you need exactly as long to come back as you spent away, but that's no more than a nice saying, and not one I believe. After lessons at the Austrian School I occasionally used to go and stand with a group of tourists near the Galata Tower. When I recognised by their voices that they were compatriots, each time I felt a shiver of happiness, completely irrational, at not having to be counted and being able to walk away at any moment, at not being one of them. I don't know whether I had not had an ear for it before, or whether it was an early signifier of a new and aggressive political climate, but after I got back people were suddenly talking about "home" everywhere, and we teachers were evidently urged to do the same with our pupils. We were supposed to give them so-called "pointers" on the subject, and that led to my first confrontation with the Parents' Association. I had said that home was where what you trusted was painful and what was painful was trustworthy, and apart from the fact that it sounds a bit *bon mot*-ish, I still believe it. People had asked me to express myself more precisely, and I had expressed myself, and now I had to think about it again. A raging longing for Istanbul, or perhaps just for being away had seized hold of me, and at that moment I could also have said that home was where you didn't understand the language. I had arrived in the country without a word of Turkish, and when I left my knowledge of the language could at best be called rudimentary, but I had a smattering of phrases at my command that lent themselves very well to saying nothing.

2

I HAD SEEN THE RELATIONSHIP BETWEEN DANIEL AND ME TOO
little from his point of view. I was the older one, I was the teacher
who had to put up with the question of what I wanted from him,
and actually it was Herr Bleichert who first led me to consider the
other side more. I could not get his phrase – that he had read
Daniel's manuscript as a sign of his devotion to me – out of my
head. Maybe I had underestimated the boy from the beginning by
assuming there was something calculating in his asking me for book
recommendations so often. For a long time I felt that he was only
doing it to dazzle me, that he was asking me what he should read
in order to impress me, the way he had impressed Dr Prager with
his maths and Herr Bleichert by quoting from the Bible, and that
if he read, he wasn't reading because it interested him but because
he wanted me to see him doing it. I only had to remember the
conversations we had sometimes had when he brought back books
he had borrowed. I had often felt them to be tedious and staged,
exactly as though he were submitting himself to a test and wanted
me to look on admiringly.

On rereading his manuscript, I wondered how I had been able
to overlook his side of the story. Had he not written how much he
enjoyed, in the evenings, the anticipation of going out to the river
again the next day? Apart from which, right from the start it had
been the boys turning up there of their own accord; I hadn't invited
them, on the contrary I had made it clear to them that I preferred

to be alone, and they had kept coming anyway. If what Daniel had written was to be taken seriously, he had been observing me whenever I sat outside the house and dozed off in the afternoon sun with a book in my lap. He watched me when I went down to the water and swam a few strokes. Either he stayed where he was or he wondered whether he should follow me, and came after me with quick steps, strolling at my side and diving into one of the pools at the edge that were separated from the main stream of the river and only filled up when it flooded. The deepest were hardly a metre deep, but he managed with a shallow dive to glide smoothly over the bottom without hurting himself and then stood waiting in the muddy pool, over which the air buzzed with insects, and held his hands out to me. In the sun the water droplets glistened on his skin and I remember that I stopped every time, looked at him and waited until he dropped his arms again before I even dipped a foot in. The laughter on his face at those moments was at first him laughing with childlike joy, then laughing at me for acting so squeamishly.

I had thought I was hardly ever alone with him, but it was not true. Of course Christoph was usually there, but there were also moments when he was somewhere else and out of sight and earshot, and on one occasion Daniel came out to the river entirely without him. I forget what reason he gave, but I remember thinking that he felt the need to justify himself and I remember too his shyness that day and the way he said, as he lay stretched out, that I had no choice but to make do with his company, but looked as though he might rush off at any moment. This was three days after I had run in after him and hugged him, and I admit that I didn't know how to deal with him anymore. We sat for a long time in silence in the sun, talking, if at all, only about trivial things, and the mere fact that he was so taciturn and failed to grasp the opportunity to start one of his conversations with me, the way he almost always did whenever Christoph happened not to be around, shows how peculiar the situation was. On another occasion he would have changed the subject just like that, whatever it had been, and without blinking asked me where and in what time I would have liked to live, or whether I would have preferred not to be born at all, or started an over-excited discussion about whether I believed as others did that the Second Law of Thermodynamics was sufficient to prove the necessary finitude of the world and thus the non-existence of God, or gone as far as asserting that according to strict logic all that followed from it was that so far everyone who had lived had died, not that he too would die.

I didn't take any notes, sadly, but given his restlessness our conversations could only have been about the big issues, and they were adventurous flights that he took off on. I often had the impression that he would have liked to submit a list of subjects to work through with me and not waste time bothering with trivialities, and that was his favourite word too — "trivial", a word mathematicians use when everything is clear and there is nothing to prove. What was striking was his fitful faith in reality, his doubts about whether he would find a place in it, or more specifically whether it was worth finding one or even wanting to find one, whether it wouldn't be wiser to escape from the outset. This apparently only applied to what he should do after the summer, but he took the greatest care to ensure that every opportunity he could think of should be judged to be impossible. To study? At some point to have a job, a wife and perhaps children? To go to work in the mornings and come home in the evenings, as in a pre-prime-time soap? Wasn't the desert better? Discussions followed which he instigated purely for the sake of discussion, naïve and pretentious conversations in which he behaved as if he were the first to hit upon any of the ideas. It was normal at his age to have such thoughts; he was in good company. In almost every class there were the *Steppenwolf*-readers and *Siddhartha*-readers, who in the search for themselves had no firm ground beneath their feet for a while, and of whom some, even years later, took themselves off on pilgrimages to India, and if Daniel stood out from them it was perhaps only because India played no part in his world, and that paradise lost and the promised land were one and the same for him.

The turning point came with him abandoning his studies. He had finally decided to study maths. I can still hear him saying, with the mix of pathos and irony that was his trademark, that maths was the language of God and if he wanted to understand how everything was held together, then there was no end to understanding it. In fact it was probably more his preference for the abstract that drew him to it, plus perhaps a promise of truth with which he could counter the dissolution of all certainties, so the crisis, when it finally came, seemed all the greater. It was a weekday when he rang my bell, and as I opened the door, surprised to see him, he walked past me without a word, sat down in the living room and without preamble started to talk about it. He was wearing a sports jacket with his tracksuit bottoms and was unshaven and made a confusing impression as he sprawled in an armchair in a way that was utterly out of character, his legs wide apart, and would not let me get a word in edgeways.

"None of it makes any sense," he said. "Wherever I look I see people with empty, wasted lives, occupying themselves doing meaningless things, having empty, meaningless conversations, just waiting to be released from the whole nonsense and die."

It could have been any one of our discussions, had it not been for his note of despair, but I knew that it was different this time and so just looked at him expectantly as he went on, saying that he had to get away from everything. He dumped his backpack full of books on the carpet as if they were clear evidence of the futility he was talking about and declared that they all belonged to me; he had forgotten to give them back. I told him I had not missed any of them, but he insisted and handed them to me one after the other, and I took each one without looking and put it on the low table next to the sofa.

"Away from everything," I said finally. "Where do you want to go?"

He did not hesitate before answering.

"Somewhere there's meaning."

No sooner were the words out of his mouth than he seemed to find them funny. I can't say what was going through his mind from one minute to the next, but where a few seconds earlier he had looked brooding and agonised, his mood now suddenly brightened. It was as if he could no longer bear the sound of his own lamentation and was hurriedly sweeping it away.

"Oh shit, forget meaning. There's no such place. But if I could go to your house for a few days, that would be a start."

He sounded happy at the thought, whether it had just occurred to him or whether it was what he had been aiming for all along.

"I could hunt and fish."

"How would you do that?" I asked, surprised by his unexpected lightness, not trusting it. "With a bow and arrow?"

He had always had a thing about, had always boasted of having two left hands, and I could not imagine him knowing how to use a rifle, quite apart from where he might get one.

"And winter's just around the corner."

I said it very casually, but he instantly woke up.

"Winter doesn't bother me," he said. "It's my favourite season. For as long as I can remember I've loved being out in the snow. I was born in winter."

I knew that he was as unreasonably as he was groundlessly proud of the story of his birth, whether it was true or just part of his private mythology. He had once told me that he had come into the world in an avalanche in the middle of the night in the middle of nowhere, and that feeling for extreme circumstances was probably what lay behind the euphoria that now overtook him. He talked about what it would be like to spend the whole day out in the open, how he would follow animal tracks or lie in wait in the forest or cut a hole in the ice when the river froze. He could set traps and find out what had happened to the supplies that he and Christoph had put by that summer. One day, somewhere behind the house, they had buried a few dozen cans with "best before" dates sometime in the next millennium, not because they thought they might need them one day but because they liked the idea of such schemes and their hiding place would only be a real hide-away if they sealed themselves off from the outside world, at least in their imagination. Even back then I had thought that it was not the wilderness that put him in such a state of excitement, but his idea of wilderness, and the same thought occurred to me again as I listened to him.

"I'm not sure you have any idea what it's like there when it starts snowing," I said. "The paths aren't cleared for days on end, and not a soul ventures out there."

"Even better," he said. "I want to be alone."

I looked at him, shaking my head.

"Do you know how cold it gets by the river?"

It may sound crazy, but everything I said to deter him only attracted him all the more. His eyes were shining as he said that he loved the cold and that in any case there was a fireplace in the house too that they had put there precisely for such an even-tuality, and two weeks later, with the first snowfall, he appeared determined to give it a try. He came to my door unannounced, carrying a new backpack – he had bought a sleeping bag and a gas stove, both best quality though I had no idea where he had got the money from – and insisted that I take him out to the river. I didn't know where he had been staying till then, but he looked like an adventurer from a catalogue about to set off on a well-planned expedition, perfectly equipped in anorak, windproof trousers and ski cap, and more determined to get going than a novice would ever have been.

Only a week before, however, I had witnessed an outburst of his that made me concerned for his state of mind. We had been sitting in the cinema when an advert he didn't like had suddenly offended him so much that he started criticising it in a loud voice, shouting at the screen until I had to take him out of the auditorium. The advert in question featured a young woman in front of a black-board, wearing a short black skirt and with her breasts pushed up as in a dirndl, showing her teeth when she smiled and with a pair of glasses in her hair, asking her adult and clearly older pupils how to spell the word "success". Using the baton in her hand to point at two of them, she listened to their obvious and correct answers while condescendingly shaking her head; she then drew a large "D" and "O" on the board, enunciating the letters as she did so, the way she might have done if she was dealing with hearing-impaired or special needs students. She hadn't finished her lesson before Daniel jumped to his feet and started noisily abusing her. I had the sense that he felt she meant him personally, and he swore furiously back at her in the same personal way, calling her a sleazy, dumb nothing who would soon see where her crappy talk got her when she found out what life was really like and she had to come up with something else besides her ignorant babbling and shoving her tits in people's faces.

Of all the peculiarities I had noticed in him, this was the first time he was openly aggressive, and on the drive out to the river I reflected how little I knew him, in spite of the summer we had spent together and the connection we had kept up since then. I remembered how he had asked me more than once if I would take him in if he was ever guilty of something, whether I would be there for him if he fell through all life's safety nets, whether I would stand by him if the police were looking for him because he had robbed a bank or run over a pedestrian in a hit-and-run accident or was suspected of having murdered a woman. He connected the house with that sort of state of emergency, seeing something secret and other-worldly in it that filled him with a chilly pleasure, imagining that he could retreat there and it would keep him safe when he had turned everything in his world into chaos, and now we were driving out there in silence and so, somewhat pointlessly, I made a point of reminding him that happily nothing of that sort had happened. Among the books he had left with me I had come across a piece of paper I wanted to talk to him about but didn't manage to, because his air of good humour overwhelmed everything else. It had a heading handwritten in block capitals and was intended to be a list of things he hated, but it was empty and I wondered if he had planted it intentionally. Meanwhile he sat beside me in the front passenger seat and twiddled the radio knob until he found a music station, and whenever I addressed a word to him he went on humming and unconcernedly watching the passing scenery as though we were just out on an excursion, the way we had been on other occasions, and would be back again that evening.

It still seems utterly unreal to me that three days later I made the same trip with his mother. She had heard he was out by the river and wanted me to drive her out to see him. I had only seen her with him once before. That had been on the football pitch after my return from Istanbul, when I was coaching and Daniel, before our first encounter at school, had turned up once or twice to training. She had picked him up and exchanged a few words with me as he stood sheepishly by her side, pushing away the hand she was stroking his hair with. He blushed and pulled her away when she asked me to be careful he didn't over-exert himself. She said that he had asthma, which was the first thing she talked about on this time too, although in her agitation she could only stammer and keep repeating over and over again that he was too weak for such escapades and that spending nights in the open air would kill him.

I hardly managed to say a word for the entire journey because she reproached me repeatedly all the way there, and on the way back she wept. We were still in the car park, sitting where I had just parked the car, when she lit a cigarette, and tears ran silently down her cheeks as she smoked. I had left her alone with Daniel and gone down to the water to wait, but he had refused to talk to her, and now she asked me to try to talk to him. She wound the window down on her side and waved the smoke out with both hands, and with the cold there came into the car the almost palpable silence that I had always thought I could find only by the river. She turned her face to me, and I saw it was already starting to lose its contours in the failing light.

"You're the only person who can still reach him," she said when she had calmed down a little but was still silently crying to herself. "He trusts you."

I doubted that she was right. I only needed to think how he had looked straight past me when I turned up at the house with her. He was sitting some distance from the veranda on the boulder I had struggled with so much during my early efforts to clean up the property, and he didn't move, but the hunched way he sat, as if he had been frozen in mid-movement, told me everything. When

I put my hand on his shoulder it seemed to me as though he had a reflex to play dead; his whole posture was defensive, as though I had betrayed him, and unsurprisingly he had refused to say a word to me.

So I held out little hope to his mother.

"The best we can do is wait a few days and see what happens," I said. "If we're lucky, everything will work out on its own."

She answered so abruptly that a second later she apologised, saying she had not meant to shout at me, then almost tonelessly went on,

"It's too long. What's supposed to happen?"

"We see if he comes back on his own."

"I don't believe he will," she said. "I'm scared."

She had dropped back into her harder tone.

"I'm scared," she repeated, and I could hear a tremor in her voice that she was trying and failing to control. "He was peculiar as a child, but I've never known him like this."

She started talking about his aloofness and coldness, but I don't remember how she got from there to saying I was like a father to him. For a while I had only been half-listening, and when she said it I was startled. We were still in the car park and I looked at the isolated lights of the village in the distance and, closer to us, those of the new housing estate, trying not to show how inappropriate I thought her comment was.

"He's always praised his father to the skies," I said finally. "I have no ambition to take over from him."

If I had known what I was stirring up, I would have approached the subject more carefully.

"What has he told you about his father?"

"Nothing but good things."

"Did he tell you he's dead?"

"No," I said. "That is the first I've heard of it."

"Did he tell you he was a bon viveur?"

"That's one way of putting it."

"That he lived in Paris and London for a time?"

"I think so, yes."

"That he loved women? That he owned a sports car? That he once had a winning lottery ticket but he left it in a restaurant and never regretted it afterwards?"

"Yes," I said. "But why are you asking me?"

"It's a pack of lies," she said. "I brought him up on my own and he never knew his father."

I had deflected one deeply tricky subject, taking myself out of the equation, only immediately to let myself in for another, into which she plunged no less eagerly, the story of the absent father, which had long since displaced that of the prodigal son in the legendary canon. I started the engine and began driving without speaking, feeling I needed to put a couple of kilometres between me and this conversation, but she kept talking. The details have slipped my memory, but I am not doing her any injustice to say they were the same as they always are and made no difference to me. It seemed entirely predictable, the rationalising about who had left whom and whose fault it was, and while she was losing herself in details and looking for one reason after another as to why Daniel had become the way he had, I was thinking all the time that he was not sitting in the forest at minus ten degrees attempting to prove to himself that he could do without human contact simply because one misfortune inevitably followed on from another.

It didn't surprise me greatly in the circumstances that after this scene she didn't appear in person again. She phoned from time to time, but it was enough for her to hear me say that Daniel was fit and well, she didn't really want to know any more than that. I told her that he came to the apartment to have a shower, that he was going to the library to borrow books and would sometimes spend a few hours sitting in a café; I let her in on what we talked about, even if in fact we didn't often talk, and in doing it I developed such persuasive powers that it really sounded like a proper life. The first few times I mentioned that he was still out by the river, but eventually I didn't bother and it stayed unspoken between us, without my being able to know for sure whether the fact had taken root in her head or evaporated.

Daniel's manuscript contained none of this. For a long time I had felt that he must have started it in his two winter months at the house, but he wrote only about our summer and when I came to read it again, I could find no sign that betrayed anything about his exposed state. I failed to find the slightest clue – unless I wanted to interpret his positively voluptuous dwelling on the humidity and heat of those days as a compensation for the bleakness and cold in which he had deliberately immersed himself. It would have been obvious for him to make a connection about thinking over his situation and at least mentioning that he was back at the same place again where years before he had spent a few weeks, albeit under different circumstances, but there was nothing, not a word, and nothing to be read between the lines either. He disregarded it completely, and the winter simply didn't seem to exist for him when he recalled our time out by the river.

I don't know what I was expecting, as one day led to another and he made no move to break off his experiment and resume his old life. Maybe I would have reacted differently and tried harder to talk him out of it if I had known at the start that it would go on for two whole months. He didn't give the impression that he was unhappy, and when he came to the apartment to have a shower the most I can say is that the calm he radiated, the nonchalance with which he turned up in the early afternoon and left again as it began to get dark, was disconcerting. Unlike before, he never seemed very talkative on these visits, and I got used to not asking him questions. If he talked at all, it was about his days by the river. They were basic observations, what tracks he had found on the bank, or that a deer had come to the house and stared at him at close range for several seconds, or that in the mornings, when it was very still, he sometimes thought he heard a sound whose source he couldn't identify. Occurrences, as small-scale as possible, one after the other, inconsequential and unconnected. He was not really a hello-trees, hello-sky sort of nature-lover, and was either forcing himself to be like that or was expressing what was happening to him. He had tried to explain the continuum hypothesis to me a few months earlier, juggling around with infinities of different cardinality until he had my head spinning, but now he suddenly seemed to want to renounce all argumentation and to be all amazement, reverence and living in the moment. I can't believe this happened voluntarily. He didn't talk about it, but I suspect that he had over-extended himself – a sort of altitude sickness of thinking was how I thought of it – which compelled him to focus on the very simplest things. At the time, I hadn't quite worked this out, but it was as if he had finally discovered in his thinking the simplicity that for a long time he had been proclaiming in many other things and in which he had actually been living since his first visit to Israel.

Of course I was alarmed. He had been my best student, and now he seemed to have metamorphosed overnight into a not merely materially but also intellectually undemanding and permanently smiling simpleton. In his final year he had written essays in which his love of complex reasoning was more than just to be sensed – his thoroughness fully visible, always looking at a thing from one side and then another, then explaining how all sides were inadequate, sometimes footnoting almost every sentence to show where something came from and where it might go – and now he would probably have swept it all aside as vain delusion. I didn't know what he was reading when he went to the library, but I couldn't imagine they were books celebrating a new simplicity. He had always seen that as posturing and said that such self-restraint and modesty of perception, with its admiration of the small and esoteric, its frugality that wants to find paradise in a little corner of the world, yes, that all that understatement was, in its covert push- iness, just a pose by which people made themselves more visible, a swindling less of the needy than of the simple-minded; and now, all of a sudden, he was going along with them. He had never been able to tell the difference between one tree and another and now he knew their names, pronounced them as if pronunciation was an act of creation that each time attested afresh that in the beginning was the Word. He had carved himself a walking stick and decorated the felt hat he usually wore with a cock's feather or a fir twig. He could pick up a pebble at the side of the road and turn it over and over until he was in ecstasy. The new moon was like a never-seen star to him when he stopped in mid-step to contemplate a cloud formation, and it would not have surprised me to see him setting off into the twilight singing a song like a wayfarer from a hundred years ago, full of the proverbial joys of spring.

I don't know if you can learn unworldliness, if you can decide from one day to the next to take on the eccentricities of some old-fogeyish nobody, but that seemed to be the drift of his plan; unworldliness as intimacy-with-the-world, although he would doubtless have denied having any plan at all. At the time I was not so aware of this, and in fact it has really only crystallised in retrospect. I think I invited him to stay overnight every single time he came to the apartment, but he refused to be tempted. He sat in the living room and every time I thought that this time he might make an exception and let himself be persuaded, but he would look at the clock and say he had to go. Mostly he refused to be driven too, and whenever I went with him part of the way I wasn't sure whether he wanted me to or whether he would have preferred to be alone. Usually he made no comment, but once he asked me if I could go with him halfway and although it was probably pure chance that he made such an exact request, it stuck in my mind, as though he had meant it very precisely and was thus making sure that I didn't go a single step too far with him.

3

MY INTERVIEW WITH THE HEAD AND SUBSEQUENT ENCOUNTER with Herr Bleichert in the staffroom had taken place on a Wednesday, and until Sunday nothing else happened. I went to school as usual the following day, and contrary to my expectations no-one raised the subject of my disappearance the day before. I didn't think much about it, but perhaps the silence ought to have made me more suspicious than if I had been called to account. On Friday I again taught the class in which I had talked about the bomb threat and then skipped the next lesson, telling the students that the head's secretary had probably forgotten to pass on the information that I had to be away from school on a matter that could not be postponed. As reasons go it sounded about as false as it really was, and the students' bored looks let me know that I could tell them whatever I liked. When one of them asked me to explain more precisely what I had meant about it being sometimes just the longing for innocence and purity that motivated a person to take guilt upon themselves, it was an open challenge. It came from one of the usual suspects, and I was about to decline it but then decided to go for it, replying that it was a question of where you stood in relation to the law. I said that the law was not everything and it would not take a person long to come up with examples in which the evil consisted not in violating the law but in strictly adhering to it. I actually used the word "evil", adding that there could indeed be an appeal in trying something evil if you weren't getting anywhere with the good, or you saw that good was being corrupted everywhere. It was both pretentious and unforgivably woolly on my part, and in the way I expressed it, and I imagined the agitation it would cause when the Parents' Association got hold of it. Here I half-turned away from the class and looked out of the window at the empty sports field, but when I looked back at the rows of students it wasn't the anticipated consternation that struck me but blankness, rejection, perhaps even pity, that ghastly pity of the young for the old that is an early-warning signal for a teacher that one day he will be able to say whatever he likes and it won't make any difference, and of course somewhere there'll also be someone who's laughing.

I had hoped to bump into Judith in my free hour on Thursday, but she called in sick, as she had done the day before. Whenever we could, we used to take advantage of the opportunity to spend the hour together, and it was the first time since the start of the school year that she had not been there. I badly wanted to talk to her about everything that had been preoccupying me since I had seen the picture in the paper, and how I had suddenly been taken back to the summer with Daniel and Christoph out by the river. I had a short conversation with Frau Pfeifer in the staffroom instead, from which it turned out that the head was in fact waiting for me to go to his office. Frau Pfeifer said nothing straight out, but the way she spoke made it sound as though unanswered questions remained between us, and I must see his request as a summons. Frau Pfeifer had no qualms about letting me know that she had a finger in every pie, and I made sure not to say any more than was necessary to her before taking my leave as quickly as possible. I had bumped into the head in the corridor earlier, and greeted him and passed by without haste. I had felt him gazing after me, and even when I was on the stairs and long out of view I had thought, with a kind of prickly discomfort, that he might call after me. For a while I considered knocking on his door and getting it over with, but it made me feel the way I had when I was a child and had had to go to confession without feeling any sense of wrongdoing or having any sins. I would have been compelled, as I was then, to make up a story or perhaps even a whole confession, just so that he would be satisfied. I would have admitted that in my lesson I had done everything to lead the students away from the right path and added, with obviously malicious laughter, that I had given them the wrong books to read and that, with the things I told them, I was planting a seed that would only need to grow in a sufficient number of their heads for the world to detonate in an almighty explosion.

I know how absurd outbursts of omnipotence are when they come from a powerless person, and there was none of it left on Sunday afternoon when I finally phoned the head at home. Talking to him about things outside school would take away the feeling that I was supposed to go and report to him, and of course I was trading on our old friendship and the kindness he had shown towards me since Robert's death. I had, in addition, been going over the story all day Saturday and Sunday morning, to the point where it had begun to sound ridiculous. None of the ingredients had much to recommend them, but for my own amusement I blew them up and stirred them together into a crude plot. In it there was an apocalyptic preacher who sought out the crash sites of American bombers in the Second World War all over the country and in each place proclaimed the coming of the Last Judgement. There was a group that had called itself after Camus' play *The Just* and years later emerged to make bomb threats in exactly the same places, which they dressed up in biblical language. It had an ascetic and charismatic leader who called himself Jesus, and naturally there had to be a connection with Israel, because messianic prophecies are fulfilled in the Holy Land. I didn't bother about how little it all had to do with the starting point, and the more I distanced myself from the facts and the more audacious and hair-raising my scenario was, the more certain I was that it must have been in a novel long ago. I went on elaborating the story for so long that in the end I couldn't tell the difference between what was probable and what was improbable, and had no powers of judgement left to say what was possible and what not. It ended with me jumbling up all the elements so much that I almost reached the point of thinking that the mere fact that something sounded like a bad invention was a strong indication that it must be deeply rooted in reality.

The head was not at home, and so it was from his wife that I found out about the letter that had arrived at the newspaper on Saturday. Allegedly it had contained a sheet of paper, again with letters of different sizes glued to it, saying, "Woe to you, Chorazin! Woe to you, Bethsaida!" and another sheet with a detailed guide to how to build a bomb. The head's wife said that her husband had tried to reach me about it; he had just gone out, but would be back at any moment. For the first time her calling him Karl did not make me pause.

"He says the boy must be behind it, the one you were with that time out by the river," she said. "I remember how enthusiastically you talked about him."

I hadn't left the house all day Saturday, and hadn't looked at the T.V. or listened to the radio. The phone had rung a few times, but I hadn't picked it up. Yet I couldn't believe a piece of news like that would not have reached me somehow, even through the walls.

"'Woe to you, Chorazin! Woe to you, Bethsaida!'" I repeated, trying not to let my agitation show. "It's from the Bible."

"From the New Testament."

"But it sounds completely different. Doesn't it sound more like the wrathful God of Abraham, Isaac and Jacob, who is having another quarrel with His children or inciting them against their enemies? The punishment is bound to be terrible."

On matters of religion I had for a long time been of Stendhal's view, that God's only excuse is that He doesn't exist. There was not much to be added, in my opinion, and I couldn't help using irony to defend myself against the absurdity of even having to discuss it. At the same time I was predictably thinking about the report Daniel had written after his trip to Israel, which must also have been in the head's wife's mind. In it he had talked about the God of the Jews, who was to be opposed by an entirely different God, and I alluded to this, without bothering to conceal my sarcasm.

"The New Testament God is a loving God, though."

"Definitely," she said. "He is." She hesitated for a moment. "But the New Testament is full of mysteries, and you can't assume that the love in it is only ever expressed as love."

To me, it all sounded like a tacky continuation of the ludicrous plot I had conceived. She mentioned the exact source of the quotation, Matthew 11:21, and I repeated it, although to begin with my absolute intention had been not to get involved in any discussion at all. Then, despite myself, I asked whether she had a Bible and could read me the text in context.

"I don't need a Bible," she said. "Jesus is pronouncing judgement on both places in Galilee. Some of His best-known miracles were performed around Chorazin and Bethsaida. He becomes dissatisfied with them because they don't want to repent. Do you want to hear it?"

I said yes, and she recited the verses. Perhaps she had only just reread it herself, but perhaps she could also quote it at will. After all, Herr Bleichert had been taking her under his wing for some time, and it was exactly the sort of thing he would have regurgitated to her. Her tone was gentle and threatening at the same time. When she finished, she waited in silence, and although I knew there was absolutely no point, I felt myself getting worked up about it.

"What a lot of crazy shit," I said. "Repent what?"

She was about to respond, but I interrupted her.

"Repent that they weren't sufficiently impressed? He threatens them with a fate worse than Sodom's because they won't wear sackcloth and ashes and at the end still portrays Himself as the God of gentleness. Repent that they didn't fall for his magic tricks?"

For a moment there was silence, and I thought she might have hung up, but then her voice came back on, quietly and as if from a great distance.

"I know it's not very satisfying for someone living in our world," she said, as if it was her fault and not the way of the world. "But that's what's written."

Then she started talking about Daniel again.

"Why would he do something like sending that letter? Apparently he was a good boy. He went to the Holy Land with Herr Bleichert and wrote about it. Didn't he even study theology later?"

I said goodbye at that point, and it was only when I called her Frau Aschberner that I became aware that she had used her unmarried name when she answered the phone. On another occasion it would have struck me more forcefully, and I would have added at least a few personal words, asked her how she was or suggested that I might be coming over soon, but at that moment I just wanted to be on my own as fast as possible and to reflect calmly. I said I would call again later when her husband was home. The first thing I thought when I put down the receiver was that not only did the biblical threat seem absurd, but the bomb-making instructions that apparently accompanied it were too. Either they were ridiculous or they were a particularly cynical clue as to how easy it was, if only you wanted to. Purely out of curiosity, after the first threat – and before Daniel ever came to mind – I had looked at a few sites on the internet and even if it was only approximately true, what could be discovered there with a few clicks showed that it wasn't much more than child's play. Half an hour was enough to provide me with all the information I needed to become your average amateur dynamiter. It looked to me as if you could find all that was required to start the process in your kitchen or bathroom, if you happened not to possess a school chemistry set, or you could buy it at the chemist's, and then all it took was a little technical skill and you'd be ready to build yourself a modest infernal contraption. When I thought about it closely, I couldn't quite believe it. I told myself there had to be a catch somewhere, and what I found truly perplexing was why something didn't blow up every few days when it looked so out-and-out simple and there were so many crazies who, we were led to believe, had nothing in their heads besides making the world go up in flames.

I had never been to Bruckner's on a Sunday before, and there were different faces from my regular days, a different atmosphere. When I opened the door, all the noise stopped and through the smoke-filled room the first person I saw was Herr Frischmann, the newspaper proprietor, who was standing in a group of men at the bar and who paused mid-sentence. He was an athletic man of fifty with a few strands of hair combed carelessly across his forehead, and although at that moment he was prancing lightly in front of the other men as if they were his sparring partners, there was no question that he too had noticed me instantly. He beckoned me over, and my first impulse was to go straight over to him, like a good schoolboy, but I just about managed to veer off and stand slightly away to one side. We had never exchanged a word with each other and I wondered how he knew me. But there could be no mistake about what he had just been discussing with his listeners.

"Here comes his former teacher," he said, a cigarette in one hand, glass of wine in the other, still looking as though he wanted to embrace the other men. "If you still don't believe me, that none of that's important, ask him. He knows the boy better than anyone. He can tell you that he would never build a bomb, even though he might have written the letter, assuming that the letter didn't come from someone else altogether."

I knew most of the men only by sight. There were one or two brewery workers, one from the law firm newly set up in the Hauptplatz, and the others were faces from the football ground. They looked over at me now as if they were, quite seriously, expecting an explanation. I had noticed, after my conversation with Herr Bleichert at school, that some of my colleagues had started talking behind my back, even though no-one had said anything to me, and Herr Bleichert had promptly reverted to his usual distant manner. For them I sensed it was more because they had no idea what was going on than for any other reason, but when I looked at the heated faces in Bruckner's I didn't feel an explanation tripping off my tongue quite so easily. As a teacher you would swiftly find yourself mocked if you kept the wrong sort of company, and more than once it had been flagged up to me that the way I was behaving was all very well but was far from being a proper life. Here, however, such subtleties were out of the question. I'm fairly certain that what I felt was genuine hostility. I said nothing, just looked back at them, and would have preferred to leave there and then, but I felt myself grabbed by my sleeve from behind and pulled backwards.

"For heaven's sake, leave him alone."

It was Agata, who went on holding on to me as if she wanted to make sure I didn't do anything stupid. She then informed the men, in her combination of friendliness and firmness, that they were in her house under her rules, and led me away, under her protection. She had spotted the stand-off immediately and, half-turning away from them so that no-one heard her, told me what lay behind it.

"Herr Aschberner was here just now and he told them about your house by the river. They wanted to drive out there immediately to check it out."

"The head was here?" I said, astonished, because this was the last place I could have imagined him. "What was he doing at Bruckner's?"

"He comes every Sunday."

"And he told them about the house?"

"Yes," she said, again making sure that only I could hear her. "If that horrible newspaper man hadn't restrained them, they'd be on their way there right now."

Just then I overheard Herr Frischmann saying that he hoped Chorazin and Bethsaida weren't Jewish communities, otherwise he'd have to steel himself for another call from Vienna if he was going to dismiss the incident as harmless in the newspaper. Which was exactly what he intended to do, because he refused to be part of whipping up any hysteria and would instead insist that it was a stupid prank that he found unappealing only because it placed the Church in a bad light in which it didn't belong. He could not repeat often enough that the bomb outlined in the instructions was no more a bomb than the famous picture of a pipe by Magritte was a pipe, and anyone who didn't grasp that only had to imagine what would happen to a robber who walked up to a bank counter brandishing a water pistol and started demanding cash.

"The Jewish religious community are bound to see it differently yet again," he said. "If they get wind of it, they'll no doubt turn it into an affair of state."

It hadn't escaped his attention that I was listening, and he looked at me triumphantly over the men's heads. For a couple of seconds he held up his hand, holding the cigarette in front of his mouth, giving the upper half of his face a smug expression. Then he took a long drag and, as he blew out the smoke, addressed me directly.

"What do you think about it, Herr teacher?"

I pretended that he had caught me unawares.

"What do I think?"

"Yes. What's your reaction, Herr teacher?" he said. "You've been to university. I'm sure you can explain to us why it regularly sets off an earthquake in Vienna when someone here shifts something by a few millimetres without permission from on high."

His tone was full of mockery, and I was annoyed that I had replied instead of saying nothing and letting him talk, which had been my intention since I arrived.

"I don't know what you mean," I said evasively, yet at the same time so timidly that I felt pathetic. "I've only just heard about it all, and until I know the facts more precisely it's better if I say nothing."

The men were still looking at me as if they were all set to rush me on a word of command, and the thought that they might pile out of the pub all together on some vague mission to the river gave me goose bumps. I listened with half an ear as Herr Frischmann went on explaining to them that it had not yet been ascertained that the bomb-making instructions would work, and the police had to check that out, and then I turned back to Agata, who had poured me a glass of wine and a sip for herself too. It was unusual for her to drink with a customer and I understood instantly that she had done it in order to prise me free from the conversation. She went on standing beside me, even when someone called her from somewhere else in the pub, and carried on her conversation with me for everyone to see, asking me where I had been on Thursday and looking around again as I replied that I had needed to think in peace and so had stayed at home.

"It's all been building up here since Thursday," she said. "People have been going around saying that the picture in the newspaper could be Daniel, and after the letter yesterday the mood was like lynch law."

"But absolutely nothing's happened."

"You can look at it how you like. In any case the men were dead set on making a search of the area by the river to put a stop to it. And the only thing they have to go on is what Herr Aschberner told them."

I had obviously already thought of the house, but then rejected it as being too simple.

"They don't seriously think Daniel's there."

I remember how Agata looked at me when I said this. It was the look she usually reserved for her roughest regulars whenever they started wanting to set her straight about how their messy lives could take a turn for the better and have a happy ending and as soon as that happened they wouldn't be coming into Bruckner's again, because they would be spending their old age in the south or somewhere similar, or how they had found a new woman and were back in the game and getting the better of the Devil and the good Lord with yet another bite of the cherry. She responded to me with about as much enthusiasm as she responded to the worst of those bores, saying, with the lassitude and resistance born of years of pointless conversations, that she needed to look after her other customers, before unexpectedly gripping my sleeve again.

"Just so you know, for the last few days the inspector has been here every evening quietly digging around. Don't turn around. He's sitting right behind you, watching us."

I couldn't help looking, even though, as she swiftly moved away, she told me not to; and there was Inspector Hule sitting at one of the back tables that were mostly empty the rest of the time, letting his gaze wander between the group around Herr Frischmann and me, and then back again. He was in plain clothes, with a big glass of beer in front of him, and raised his glass in my direction when he realised I had seen him. I hesitated when he pulled the nearest chair closer and suggested I join him by patting the seat as if he was patting an animal lying there or trying soothingly to hold it back. I had spent some time thinking about our conversation on Tuesday night and was no longer so sure that he hadn't been playing cat and mouse with me. Perhaps he had already had a suspicion and only played down the first bomb threat to get me to talk, and his breeziness had made me fall into the trap without knowing it. His reasoning about what constituted a normal life, his sceptical view about how hard it could be if you had nothing you were ready to die for, even his initially monosyllabic speech, all seemed like a lure to me now, tailored to gain my confidence, either because his knowledge of human nature had told him that was what would draw me in or because it was a strategy he had learnt in his text-book. I didn't want to be so naïve anymore and chat to a police officer in a friendly careless way, as if I wasn't giving him informa-tion with every bland sentence I uttered, and so I stayed where I was as he, annoyingly, went on stubbornly patting: a gesture that gets more urgent and reluctant the longer you do it. I let a full minute tick by, and when I finally got to my feet and went over to him I felt I was prepared only to encounter a player who was shrewder than I would have given him credit for.

"Surprised?"

His very first word was intended to draw me out of my reserve. He leant back on his chair and couldn't hide a self-satisfied expression as I sat down next to him. I had nothing to hide, but as he looked at me I could feel the corners of my mouth quivering and all my equilibrium had vanished.

"Why should I be surprised?"

"Well, everyone seems to think it's a former pupil of yours that's behind this," he said. "I'm not nearly so sure, but these things don't happen every day. Or is there something you didn't tell me on Tuesday night, and you thought so too? Dorothea says, for what it's worth, that you looked extremely nervous to her."

When I started justifying myself, he laughed. He said there was nothing to get excited about, and that to start with I should have a drink, before I talked myself into trouble. Ignoring my refusal, he ordered two glasses of schnapps and waited until they arrived before picking up the conversation again.

"Can you imagine him being the one?"

I wanted to say no, but just shrugged my shoulders.

"Let's assume for a moment that he was the one," he went on, my reaction not having produced any effect on him. "Why would he do such a thing?"

"If only I knew," I said. "You tell me."

"There are no demands, apart from this biblical call to repentance. That makes him either a fantasist we don't need to take seriously, or genuinely crazy and dangerous. Even the most frustrated little loser will come up with something to distract the world from the fact that it's just about him and his own pitifulness."

I had never seen him so sarcastic before, and I felt increasingly that he only needed me there to help him develop his thoughts out loud. He had apparently done his homework about Daniel, and as soon as he was done with these general remarks he started to talk about him, speaking first loudly and then softly, as if he couldn't make up his mind whether he wanted the men at the bar to hear what he was saying or whether it was just something between him and me.

"An obsessive reader, from what I hear," he said, sounding as though this alone might prove something. "What can you tell me about that?"

"You know that I teach German. What can I tell you, apart from the fact that he was a good pupil? For me it's the most normal thing in the world if someone reads a lot."

"But the question is, why?"

"I don't know," I said. "I don't need a reason."

"Reading as a means of escaping from the truth?"

"Maybe that too," I said. "But if it is that, why not? Ultimately it doesn't hurt anybody. Besides which, what truth?"

"You're not seriously asking me that. The truth that everything is what it is, and no more. That it's meaningless to ask for meaning. You can call it reality too, if you like."

When I said, mockingly, that the world had lost a true philosopher in him, he looked at me with a sorrowful expression but went on, undeterred.

"It becomes a problem only when you're also a truth fanatic who believes that the truth has to be told in all circumstances, because otherwise the world will no longer be a healthy place," he said. "A logical thinker who wants to reduce everything to true or false can never escape their opposite."

He asked what Daniel had studied, then held up a hand to silence me.

"Don't tell me. Let me guess. I'd put my money on something scientific. Perhaps even mathematics."

When I nodded, he puffed himself up with satisfaction.

"You see, even that fits the picture almost too well."

None of this was any more than conjecture, but he merely shook his head when I pointed this out and said that he had studied such cases and the patterns were always the same, even down to the religious quirk of his "Repent!" and his "Woe to you, Chorazin! Woe to you, Bethsaida!"

"In the olden days people like that would have gone to a monastery. It would have been enough for them to renounce the world. Today they're determined to avenge themselves on it, they think they have to smash it to pieces just because it's all a bit much for them. They're lonely and angry without knowing exactly what about."

I must have looked at him as if I was wondering how a provincial police inspector of all people could arrive at such theories. Because he felt the need to explain that he had once wanted to do something different with his life from handing out parking tickets?

"Do you remember our conversation on Tuesday?"

"Of course," I said. "What about it?"

"We talked about normal life and you asked me, 'Since when had that been part of the police's job?' Do you remember what I said to you?"

I looked at him, and because I still didn't know where he was going with it, I asked him, half-joking and half-serious, if he was trying to say that he would have preferred to enter a monastery himself because normal life was too demanding for him.

"Not exactly that," he said, laughing. "But given the opportunities that normal life offers most people, I have to admit to having a sneaking sympathy for people who take refuge in the impossible. I went to Umbria last year for two weeks. There isn't a single hill there that hasn't produced its own saint. I'm not trying to say that today they'd all have been bombers, but the thing just isn't that simple either."

He didn't react when I asked him whether he wasn't in the wrong job with views like his, just looked absently into space before adding, apparently unrelatedly, that you didn't have to be particularly religious to find yourself making the sign of the cross sometimes in the old churches in the south. He was ignoring the men who were still standing around Herr Frischmann at the bar and looking over at him, and without his cap on, leaning forward, with his forearms on the table, there was something humble about his demeanour and he obviously not only knew it but intended it to be that way. His own loquaciousness suddenly seemed to sit uneasily with him, although it didn't stop him from going on to say that he had studied psychology for a couple of semesters and that creating a perpetrator profile had to some extent been a hobby-horse of his since then and I must excuse him if he sometimes got carried away with his enthusiasm. Then he said that, whoever it was who was behind the two threats, he would bet his right hand that we were dealing with a notorious loner, a young man, definitely under thirty, pathologically shy, who hated social situations and very likely had a serious problem with the opposite sex.

I reflected that this description almost certainly applied to a large number of the crazies who thought about making a bomb, and let him carry on talking. It was one of those shots in the dark that ultimately sound as if they come straight out of the manual, and I was glad as he moved further and further away from his starting point and drifted off into generalities again. So I didn't answer when he asked me whether his characterisation sounded like someone I knew, and when he then asked me if I could picture Daniel being at the house by the river, I said no. A police car was probably already on its way there to check anyway, and he didn't need my opinion. He looked at me for a moment, as if he couldn't decide whether it was even worth carrying on talking to me, and then he asked me all the usual questions as though he wasn't at all interested in my answers because he knew them already, and was just working his way dutifully through the interrogation. When was the last time Daniel was with me? Was it true that I had given him money? Had it been a large amount? Did I know what he needed the money for and where he was staying? Was I sure it couldn't be anywhere nearby?

I tried not to display any weakness, but when he asked whether Daniel had blackmailed me I snapped at him, demanding to know what had made him think that. He looked simultaneously shocked and amused at the outburst and told me that people were saying so, and when I wanted to know what exactly people were saying, he seemed to weigh his words as he said that I shouldn't set any store by it because people have always got an opinion even when they know nothing, and then he spoke more frankly, saying that it was being said that I was very close to the boy. I was unable to detect any ambivalence in his expression, but he seemed to be waiting for an explanation and when I didn't say anything he said that if I didn't want to talk about it now we could easily do it on another occasion, and he would be very happy if I dropped in to see him at the police station again soon.

To leave the pub I had to walk past the group at the bar. The men looked at me as if at least now I ought to justify myself to them, while Herr Frischmann stood in the middle of them, tapping himself nervously on his chest with his clenched fists. No-one said anything as I came up to them, and they actually fell back to make room for me, although as I studied their expressions I still more than half-expected them to pile into me. I had already reached the door when Agata came hurrying after me and asked if I was going to come back later, so we could talk undisturbed. She no longer seemed to mind that people could hear her and said, glancing around, that she would be closing at ten, but it was Sunday after all and if the gentlemen decided to go home soon she would try to close earlier.

Outside I looked for a phone box. I still didn't own a mobile, and I had to walk halfway across town before I found one that wasn't broken or out of order. I had decided that I should call the head, at least to show goodwill, and as long as I did it before they settled down for the early evening news on T.V. I wouldn't give them a fright. The city looked utterly deserted again, and as I walked down the high street, the only living soul in sight, I heard my own footsteps, weirdly, like those of someone else. I didn't dare stop because I was afraid that that would only make them more audible, and as I walked I kept turning around, although there was clearly no-one there except me.

4

ALTHOUGH I HAD REGISTERED THE AGGRESSIVE MOOD AT
Bruckner's from the moment I set foot in there, I was startled to
hear from Agata how the discussion at the bar had flared up again
after I left. The men were apparently positive that I knew more,
and had taken my long conversation with Inspector Hule as confirmation that I was under suspicion, or that at any rate the police
believed I could help them with their enquiries. They suddenly
remembered that there had been stories going around the summer
I had spent with the two boys out by the river, although what the
stories were exactly, and whether or not they were justified, not to
mention the fact that the summer was very nearly ten years ago
now, had been practically ignored. Basically it seemed obvious in
any case: what was a teacher going to do with two of his students,
for a few weeks in the middle of nowhere in a house that hardly
deserved to be called a house, if not "something kinky"? Either
he was "playing for the other team" and got too close to them,
or he was "off his rocker" and indoctrinating them with his views
which, because of their obsessiveness, kept bringing him into conflict with the Parents' Association and his colleagues. It surprised
me that they also knew about my having given Daniel money, and
of course the amount was much bigger, in the tens of thousands,
and had allowed him to hatch his sick fantasies in peace and lead
an underground life (a view with which I had some sympathy if
you took the hair-raising things I sometimes told even ten- and

twelve-year-olds in the classroom as an indicator). The fact that
no-one else was being mentioned in connection with the bomb
threats was a foregone conclusion to them, and there was no point
waiting to see if the madman was still inclined to play games next
time around, or whether he had had enough of games and wanted
to show he was capable of more than that. No sooner had I stepped
out of the door, apparently, than they began arguing that I should
not have been allowed to leave without explaining myself, and it
was only Herr Frischmann who mollified them again when a few of
the most fired-up of them made moves to go after me, by urging
them not to read any more into the story than they knew.

I went back to Bruckner's for the first time at nine, for the
second time at half past, and when, at nine forty-five, Agata still
wasn't on her own I waited on the other side of the street and
kept the entrance in view. I had phoned the head. It had turned
out to be a short conversation, in which he repeated several times
that now the shit had really hit the fan, which as expressions go
wasn't really one of his trademark phrases, and then he suddenly
switched to asking if I knew something I had been keeping from
him. Waiting outside Bruckner's, I could not get out of my head
the impatient, hectoring tone he had used when he said we would
talk about it again at school, but then at that point I didn't yet
know how worked up the men at the bar were as a result of his
having told them about the house by the river as a potential
refuge. I nevertheless instinctively stepped back behind the wall
where I had been standing as the first of them came out into the
street. I could hear their voices, but nothing to suggest they had
just been talking about me. Inspector Hule was not with them,
he must have left earlier, but Herr Frischmann was one of the
last. He stood outside the door for a while, smoking, as though
he wanted to make sure that everyone was going home peace-

fully, then walked briskly away with both hands in his pockets, whistling.

I thought Agata was over-reacting. I stayed where I was for a few more moments as the last customer finally left and she turned the lights out in the pub. She came to the door and looked up and down the street, and when I walked in seconds later she was so impatient that she grabbed me playfully by the lapels and shook me, as though she could somehow make me come in more quickly. She had left a lamp on at one of the tables at the back of the pub, which was hardly visible from the street, and she led me to it as she asked me if I had been out to the river and I answered, in a roundabout way, that I hadn't had any reason to yet, and looked at her with a pained expression.

"If I understand you correctly, you too believe it's clear that Daniel's behind this," I said. "Do you really think it's that simple?"

"I'd love to say no, but when you have to listen to all that talk for a whole evening you can start to go crazy. Anyway, you started it. You were the one who thought you recognised him in the paper."

She had sat down next to me, but now she got to her feet and started rummaging behind the bar. She said she'd like to have another look at the picture and I told her I didn't have the cutting with me. She looked at me as if somehow the last piece of evidence had been lost that might perhaps prove that everything really was different from the way it seemed.

"Nobody can be sure they recognise him, but actually it's not necessary," she said. "The stories about him speak for themselves, and when you think about who might come up with a really dumb idea like that you don't have to wait long for him to come to mind."

I don't know what I expected, but not that she would have caved in so quickly. We had talked about Daniel so much and she had always been on his side, defending his most outlandish behaviour whenever people reported some new monstrous thing, or even something piffling, that he'd done, and saying people should give him time, sooner or later he'd get a grip on himself. I remembered the two occasions I had slept at her place that summer, both of which had been preceded by an encounter with the Reverend. The first time was after he had spoken to me at the service area and I, infuriated, had run to her and she had scooped me up like a distressed child. The second time was after he came out to the river: on that occasion I remember telling her that the two boys and Judith were spending the night there together and how, as if going straight to the heart of the story, she had retorted that Judith was pregnant and she could imagine Daniel losing it completely when he found out. I recalled the matter-of-factness with which she said this, and how I had irritated her by saying that we weren't living in the Middle Ages anymore and there was no need to make a song and dance about it. Now we had spent the whole night talking, and the early dawn was just making itself felt in the vague half-light of her room. I looked at her face, but there wasn't enough light to see her expression. Probably it was full of the certainty I always felt I detected in her when she talked about Daniel.

"I'm surprised to find you suddenly giving up on him," I said. "You've never let anyone prejudge him before."

I knew myself that the evidence didn't speak in his favour, and basically the only argument I could muster was that he would not be stupid enough as to act so clumsily that all traces pointed to him. I asked Agata to consider whether he was really likely to threaten with the idea of a bomb, or whatever you wanted to call the bomb-making instructions, from which you couldn't even tell whether they would work or not, rather than with a bomb itself. I asked her whether he would choose, of all places, the town he went to school in, and as I did so I not only remembered that I had already asked the head the same question but also thought, to my consternation, that actually Daniel probably would do just that.

"I agree that he's capable of anything," I said, trying not to sound too placatory. "But one has to assume that whatever craziness he was involved in, he would at least take some precautions to deflect suspicion away from himself."

It didn't sound particularly convincing, and when I stopped talking she looked at me like someone flogging a lost cause and making it more lost with every word.

"I'm not nearly so sure," she said, as if underlining that I couldn't pull the wool over her eyes. "Doesn't he have a long history of doing exactly what people least expect him to do?"

Then she went back to all the things she'd had to hear in the course of the evening, but when she mentioned that she had defended me to the death I thought I had to have misheard her.

"Me?"

At last I saw how weary she was. I didn't know when she had started work that day, but ten years of running around Bruckner's must have left its mark, even if standing behind the bar and chatting with the regulars or listening to their silence was possibly even more strenuous. The light from the lamp fell on her face, and I remembered how I had suggested to her after the second night at her place that we should go away together for a few days. By then Daniel was only coming out to the river from time to time, and Christoph not at all anymore, and I had told myself I could save myself the disappointment of waiting for them and go to Istanbul with her for a long weekend instead. It had been an illusion, of course, because she could never get away in the middle of summer, but in any case she reacted as though I had suddenly crossed a line, and for weeks into the autumn she treated me as if I was one of her diehards, the ones beyond salvage, who brooded to themselves for weeks and even after the second or third rebuff came back with yet another proposal. I didn't know whether she had ever thought about that time since, but I made an oblique reference to it as I gave expression to my amazement.

"Why should you defend me?"

I laughed uncomfortably when she asked whether I'd have preferred her to say nothing when I was attacked, and still couldn't quite believe that she meant me.

"You shouldn't have let yourself be intimidated by those guys. They'd have got the message. The truth is, you've coped with much less gentlemanly customers."

"No, but you should have heard the way they talked," she said. "You can't imagine. It wasn't just about the two bomb threats. They talked about that summer too, and the part you must have played in it."

I was expecting all the old stories – all the unsavoury stuff about a man and two boys by the river, all the uptight rumour-mongering that went on and on, as though no name existed for it until, with mathematical precision, it suddenly found the filthiest – but even if there had been an echo of that, it was not what had got them worked up.

"According to their spokesmen, you led the boys on proper para-military exercises out there," she said. "You supposedly showed them how to survive in the forest. You went for days without eating, stayed by the river, crawled around in the jungle. Made them swim in icy water to toughen them up and I don't know what else – oh yes, it was also alleged that you shot at passing trains on the opposite bank with bows and arrows. And it seems that the rafters going down the river were warned that when they passed your camp, they shouldn't venture too close."

"That is crazy," I said. "Paramilitary exercises? I assume that they aren't your words. But how on earth am I supposed to have shown the boys how to survive in the forest? I don't even know myself."

"I know," she said. "You don't have to tell me. But I remember you telling me about the hikers who came out to the river to look at you as if you were animals in the zoo. I think everything comes from them."

"The hikers, ah yes, the hikers."

I put all my contempt into the word, wanting to delineate their every feature as I remembered them, how on Sundays there had often been genuine processions of them, come to survey the marvel that a man and two boys wearing only swimming costumes were lying on the river bank and reading, but she interrupted me.

"They supposedly felt threatened."

I repeated her sentence, word for word. "Who felt threatened?"

"You know, the hikers," she said. "The boys are supposed to have insulted them, and once even to have put up a barrier across the path and not let them through."

"If anyone had a reason to feel threatened it was us, not those pathetic gossip-mongers," I said. "You know what? To them, the mere fact that we were out there together, by the river, having a good time, that was the scandal."

I could not believe that this situation could have been smouldering all these years and had now suddenly erupted. I remembered joking with Daniel and Christoph about what people would think about the two of them aiming arrows across the river, although obviously not at passing trains, leaving aside what possible harm their blunt, hand-carved wooden arrows could have done to a train and that the very idea they might pose any threat was ridiculous. They had either used tree trunks as targets or not bothered with any, because it was only about getting the arrows to fly across the water, the other part of the game being to collect the arrows up again in the evening. For that they had had to ride their moped six or seven kilometres upriver and then on the far side follow the railway line back down along the bank again, and that part of it they did just for the hell of it, just to use up their energy.

It was the same with the secret supply store they started to organise one day. Behind the house they dug a big hole in the ground, lined it with rough boards and what was left of the board they had used for the roof, and put two big aluminium boxes in the hole – who knows where they had got hold of them from. They quickly filled them with tinned food and water bottles and whatever else they thought was absolutely essential, vitamin pills, if I remember rightly, matches, aspirins and bandages, and in the end there was room for a few bottles of wine too. It had been a matter of honour for them to collect all this stuff together on their own, and what that meant I only found out after they had shovelled the earth back over it and as good as removed all trace of their digging. The truth was that most of it had been shoplifted, but when I said they would only have had to ask me and I would have given them the money for it, they looked at me as though I was from another planet and replied that, if it was just a question of buying them-selves something, they didn't need the house at all, they didn't need the summer, and could just as well have stayed in town, gone to the pool and met friends, or found some other way to kill time.

I tried hard to tell Agata all this the way I have written it down here, and I remember how she asked me whether I wasn't present-ing it as more harmless than it actually was; after all, there had been the business with the fire too, and I could hardly blame people for finding it hard to overlook that. It was true, the two boys had, on one of their stealing sprees, thieved ten or so old car tyres from outside a petrol station, including a couple of tractor tyres that were more than head height. They had used Christoph's father's flatbed truck to bring them out to the river, where they had hauled them to the far end of the gravel bar and stacked them one on top of another on the flat rock. Then from the forest they had collected branches and twigs and piled them around them before dousing the giant stack with a can of petrol in the gathering dusk and setting fire to it. I can still visualise how it only took a single match to set the whole thing ablaze, with an oddly tame hissing sound, and how surprised they had been at the suddenness of the flames shooting into the sky. True, I had let them get on with it, although I had suspected it would cause a stir and for a while had been worried that flying sparks might set the dry wood on the bank alight, but I found it extremely hard to imagine, ten years later, that it was even worth talking about. I pointed out that neither the police nor the fire brigade had turned up, as if that somehow proved the harmlessness of the whole incident, and I remember Agata's mixed reaction of astonishment and dismay.

"But Anton," she said, "you must know that they were both on standby, and the only reason they didn't intervene was out of consideration for you. There were more than enough voices raised to say that none of you should have been allowed to get away with it, and it was only because of the story about your brother that you were."

"Because of the story about my brother?"

"Yes," she said. "Don't you remember?"

I looked at her, shaking my head.

"You were only left alone because Herr Aschberner held back the deployment. He put in a good word for you, saying that he would take responsibility and asking them not to get you into any more trouble than you were in already."

"The head?"

"Don't you remember, he was in the fire brigade? They were on the spot almost instantly with a fire engine and they wouldn't have wasted a second if there had been the slightest outbreak in the forest. Didn't he ever tell you that?"

I genuinely knew nothing about this, nor did I have any idea that the head had afterwards intervened to keep the story of the stolen tyres out of the courts, which is why this is the point at which I start to doubt the whole story, or at least my version of it, each time I go through it. There's no reason to think that Agata wasn't telling the truth, and when I look for explanations of how it could be that I hadn't seen the fire engine, or hadn't actually remembered that it had been there, I'm groping in the dark. I only had eyes for the fire, and the two boys were so close to it as the heat exploded, dashing forwards a few quick steps then withdrawing immediately and carrying on pouring petrol on the flames, that neither they nor I were paying any attention to what was going on behind our backs. Yet that hardly justifies our not noticing that less than a hundred metres away from us a fire crew was taking up position. I suddenly have every reason to doubt my memory's reliability, and although this is the only place where reality appears so seriously awry from what I have in my head, I wonder whether I'm not twisting or repressing much more of the story, or whether I just haven't properly perceived the facts. It's also striking that the head has never spoken to me about it, and when I think about that I tell myself that, if it was because he cared about me, then I'd be better off doing without his care and knowing exactly what happened.

To Agata I pretended that everything was gradually coming back to me. She had begun to look at me so suspiciously that I couldn't go on contradicting her any longer. She didn't really seem to believe me, and when she added that the fire was another reason that people had thought anything could happen she stared at me as if she was no longer entirely convinced that I was right in the head.

"It reached the point where the guys at the bar started speculating whether the bomb-making instructions didn't originate from that time," she said. "Think about what sort of a fire it was."

"Small it was not," I admitted. "Does that change something?"

"Flames shooting high into the sky, and burning late into the night too, not to mention that it was in the middle of the forest."

"What's that got to do with bomb-making instructions?"

"You'll have to ask them that yourself," she said. "Anyhow, in the end they even brought up the Reverend to explain why everything went quiet for so long before suddenly, after ten years, these two threats came along."

I had told her, on the first of my two nights at her place, how repelled I had been by my conversation with the Reverend at the service area, by his insistence on knowing what had brought me out to the river and how he had not been satisfied with any of my answers because he wanted to see me as a disciple who could make his own ideas a reality and renounced everything, a seeker after God, not just someone who had decided to spend a few weeks surrounded by nature. His phrase suddenly came to mind again, about how we had to leave the world behind us like a blazing ship and go into the forest, and besides the fact that the image was somewhat wide of the mark, I didn't want to return to it.

"Do we really have to talk about the Reverend?"

"He's supposed to have said that this year is the year."

"But Agata," I said. "What year?"

I waited, but she didn't react.

"What year is this year supposed to be?"

"You should know better than me," she said finally, looking at me as if I was the one who was wrong to insist. "I've never spoken to him. The year his prophecies will be fulfilled? The year the Messiah's supposed to come back down among us? The year the world ends? I assume that that figures somewhere on his spectrum."

I asked her to stop. She had been starting to work herself into a real state, but now she laughed at the absurdity of it all. I said it was inconceivable that someone seriously believed in all this stuff, yet she was right – the mood only had to switch and people became receptive to the most irrational arguments. Whenever she had spoken about the Reverend it had always been scornfully, and the contempt she felt for his religious activities was mirrored in her anti-American feelings. If you needed any proof that there was something fundamentally wrong there, it was to be found in the success that figures such as the Reverend enjoyed in their own country, and it was a simple calculation for her that the more of these wretched god-botherers there were in a country, and the more spiritual poverty they spread, the more they were the devil's work, always seeking out the axis of evil somewhere else while they called themselves the land of the free or whatever. I remembered how disappointed she had been when I told her that Daniel had let himself be saved by the Reverend and what that meant. I'm not saying that she went into mourning, although she had retorted that she couldn't imagine it and it had to be a joke – Daniel was far too smart to fall for a soul-catcher as narrow-minded as that awful old war veteran. Even when he had gone to Israel at the end of that summer and met the Reverend in Jerusalem, she maintained that it had to be a misunderstanding, and when I mentioned his later visit to him in America she simply denied that it had happened. She was immovable: I could show her photos, bring her people who could confirm it, or supply other evidence, she just wouldn't believe it because she didn't want to believe it, preferring to preserve the image she had of Daniel, even though it might be wrong.

Something of this inconsistency, her odd way of turning a blind eye, also resonated in the irony with which she then talked about the Reverend. I refused to react to it, but then somehow got drawn into her world when she once again mentioned Robert, saying – and this was the exact way she put it – that he had martyred himself. I interrupted her sharply, wanting to know what she meant by it, and she apologised and said that it was the word the men at the bar had used.

"Why would Robert martyr himself?"

"I know it sounds horrible, Anton, but it's only talk," she said. "Don't get fixated on the stuff people come out with when they don't know anything."

But I had also rejected it because it was exactly what I myself had thought when I heard about the altar that Robert had supposedly constructed down by the river, before he put the barrel of the rifle in his mouth and pulled the trigger. It was precisely the word that had come to my mind, and I shuddered at the thought of the archaic world it represented. I had pushed it far away from me in order not to have to reflect on it, and I was shocked it had caught up with me again.

"Why would he martyr himself, for Christ's sake?"

"I don't know, Anton," she said. "Calm down."

"They really said he martyred himself?"

"Anton, why are you tormenting yourself?"

"I just want to know what they said," I said, and if I had until then managed to give, at least to myself, the impression of staying calm, I now stopped trying to restrain myself. "When they said he had martyred himself, did they say what or who for, or is it just something you do out of sheer boredom or in a bad mood?"

I did not care that I was unjust in my sarcasm. She couldn't do anything about it, but my helplessness made me angry. That was why I didn't know if I should nod or shake my head when she said that the men at the bar had only come up with the idea of this word in relation to Robert because of the connection with the Reverend, and the biblical "Woe to you, Chorazin! Woe to you, Bethsaida!" message.

"They were saying that all the religious crap has got to end some time," she said. "That it was unacceptable for your brother's death to be followed by another accident as a result of it."

Then she was silent, and I didn't say anything else either. It was after eleven, nearly eleven-thirty, and when a passer-by knocked on the door – he must have seen our light – Agata went and made an unmistakable sign through the window that the pub was closed. She saw me watching her. She had this way of looking down at herself, as if there was something wrong with her, and when she looked up again her expression was a mixture of mockery and provocation. On one of the two nights I'd spent at her place I had asked her to read to me a few lines in Hungarian, and I had first noticed this affectation of hers then – a playful affectation that, with each sentence she read, contained more self-confidence and pride. On the bedside table in her sparsely furnished maid's room there were two or three books, and she had sat up and picked one of them seemingly at random and started to read. I didn't understand a word, obviously, but that was doubtless also why it was one of the moments I found myself in love with her – an almost required combination for me of a foreign woman with a foreign language, nothing but melodiousness in comparison with my unsuccessful and ever rarer attempts with the women of our small town and their ordinariness and lack of mystery. I had asked Agata not to stop when she made a move to put the book down after barely a page, and she had hesitated briefly, before going on with an ironic nuance to her voice. I wondered now whether I should remind her

of the occasion, but I shied away from the sentimentality of it and
let it go. Instead I waited until she sat down again and, to cover up
the embarrassment that had come between us, asked her whether
she had still the same room and realised that I had reached the
point of mere small talk when she answered yes, as though nothing
further lay behind the question.

It was time to go, but when, apparently on a whim, Agata suggested we could drive out to the river "just to make sure", I balked.
I had no urge to go, partly because it was the middle of the night,
but also because it meant giving too much space to the possibility
that Daniel could really be in the house. I said that if we did it at
all we should do it in daylight, to do it in the dark was crazy, and
who knew, there might even be police there, prowling around like
ghosts, to whom we would then have to explain our presence. She
waved the suggestion away, saying it was just a thought, but then
acted as though somehow I had let her down and was curt with
me, saying no more than was necessary until we parted company.

I walked with her part of the way, and when I got back home I
looked for my copy of the book from which she had read to me.
It was a novel, *Without Me* by Miroslav Krleža, a Croatian author
who, along with Agata's grandfather, had attended the Military
Academy in Budapest at the beginning of the last century, and she
had given not just me but Daniel too a copy of the German translation, both signed, to me with a dry dedication, to him with the
wish for "A thousand and one lives, from your A". It had become
one of Daniel's favourite books, if not his favourite. When I found
my badly dog-eared copy I started leafing through its pages,
although I must have read it at least half a dozen times before and
knew every twist of the plot. I have never really understood what
attracted Daniel to the story of a man who manages, in the space
of two or three sentences uttered at an evening party, to torpedo

his middle-class life so utterly that he lands up in prison and the madhouse and nevertheless still takes pleasure in it. The wretched man might have been telling the truth when he calls the business-man who employs him a murderer, but it was hard to identify with him because he pursues his misfortune quite deliberately, and I did not want to believe that it might be exactly that that Daniel had been interested in. I remembered him saying that the way the odds were stacked against the hero after his perfectly justified accusation demonstrated the best thing of all, that man is a man to man, as it says somewhere in the book, and it sounded as though it came from an excess of bitter life-experience, which he could not have had at his age.

5

I REALISED THAT SOMETHING OF THE GENERAL TENSION HAD
affected even Agata when I went straight back to Bruckner's after
school and brought up the subject of Krleža. I told her I had reread
parts of it that night, and when I asked her where she had got the
idea of giving both me and Daniel that book, of all books, she
looked at me with a surprised expression. Because of her grandfather, she said, I knew that, and she repeated that he had worshipped
Krleža, the way you still could worship a writer in those days, and
then she stopped and wanted to know, with mistrust in her voice,
why I was asking her.

"Well," I said, "if everyone's so sure Daniel's behind the bomb
threats, and they start asking where he got the idea from, perhaps
it'll give them another lead."

I had intended it as a joke but she reacted defensively, seeming
to take everything I said about it subsequently as a personal attack
on her.

"The book's subtitle encapsulates the whole thing very neatly.
Isn't it called *A Lonely Revolution*? That might be a subject for
debate, to start with."

"What are you trying to say?"

"Anyone reading it who has a bit of intelligence might very
quickly conclude that they're not going to put up with having a
boss over them or any of the other lies that hold our business
world together."

"Anton, just listen to yourself. 'The lies that hold our business world together.' Maybe a fourteen-year-old can get away with talk like that and dream that there won't be any more wars and everyone will love each other, but not you. Not every boss is a murderer. Start applying the morals you get from books to the real world and business will grind to a halt really quickly. It's ridiculous."

"That may be true, but it may just as easily not be," I said. "All you have to do is try it properly and see what happens when people start telling the truth and stop pretending."

"It's not just ridiculous, it's totally crazy. Have you got any idea what you're saying? Refusing to put up with a boss over you and making a bomb are, with all due respect, two completely different things."

I had mainly kept this conversation going for the pleasure of arguing and because I was enjoying her excitement, but when I said that I wasn't so sure and that actually I thought they were sometimes just two different ways of expressing one and the same malaise, she retorted that there was no sense in talking about it anymore if I was just going to say whatever barmy thing came into my head, and left me standing at the bar. At school that morning I had already registered a similar tense atmosphere, in which I would have been happier making myself invisible. The murmur in the staffroom had fallen to zero as I entered, my colleagues either staring at me or doing their best in an all too obvious way not to. I hastened to take the books I needed from my shelf and disappear again before anyone could engage me in any kind of interrogation, and at break didn't even go back, making sure I avoided anyone I saw in the distance in the corridor. My students were attentive to a degree that they hardly ever were, as if for them I was a teacher who was under surveillance and could be relied on to wade even deeper into the quagmire into which he had got himself, if they just waited long enough. Here I refused to oblige them, talking in the first lesson about *Elective Affinities*, a book I didn't like and probably wouldn't like if I read it a hundred times, in the second I dealt with the era of Empress Maria Theresa; in the third organised a study period and not only allowed myself no distractions but fulfilled my role with the self-consciousness and applied professionalism of an animal-tamer at the circus managing a whole leap of panthers, which was ultimately the only way to gain their respect, no matter what the apostles of caution and their fellow experts who preached gentle handling said. The head said he was busy when I called on him and hardly looked up from his desk all the time I sat in front of him, which was his way of advertising his displeasure, and merely repeated what he had said the night before, that I should not conceal anything from him if I knew any more. I was about to get up and go when he informed me, with a maddening casualness, that the bomb-making instructions apparently worked, although without shedding any light on how he had come by this information so quickly. Then he asked me if I had heard that the Vienna newspapers would now be taking up our unfortunate story and wordlessly bent over his papers again.

I had stopped reading the Vienna papers years ago, and the so-called quality newspapers with their "how to stop smoking", their "how to stop eating unhealthily" and "how to stop seeing pushy people with bad manners you would have done better never to get involved with", and wonder of wonders, I didn't miss a thing. The only reason I happened to know already what the head had told me was because Barbara had phoned that morning, just as I was trying to leave the flat. I was still annoyed that in my surprise my first reaction had been to ask stupidly to what, after all this time, I owed the honour of her call, as if I were still offended that she had left that day, but fortunately we wasted no more words about it and she merely said that she had immediately thought of Daniel when she read about the bomb threats in our town. I noticed no triumph in her voice, no malice that she had always known something like this would happen, only concern, and faced by her concern, I abandoned my stance that it was in no way confirmed that he was behind them, the way I had defended him to everyone else, and talked about him as if I suddenly believed that he was. I felt a feeling of betrayal as I did so, but also relief not to have to fight against appearances yet again, at least for the duration of the call, and as Barbara asked if there was anything she could do I thought about how Daniel would react to my change of heart. I imagined him being able to hear us and how, listening to our restrained way of talking about him, he would burst into incredulous laughter and find some way to sabotage the exchange before every clear thought sank in a broth of goodwill and understanding.

Barbara's last question was whether I had been out to the river. I said no, and when she wanted to know whether I was scared to go, I said yes. It was the one moment when I thought that perhaps she was not just concerned and that, given the slightest encouragement, she would rapidly slip back into her old way of thinking, namely that Daniel was my downfall.

"Scared of what?" she asked, leaving a pointed silence before she went on. "That he might be there, or that he might not be there?"

I had often been conscious of similar dichotomies in my mind, but never with as much force as now. Obviously I knew that we were talking about Daniel, but suddenly it was the image of Robert cycling out to the river that urged itself on me. Not far from the place where he had put an end to his life, his bike had been discovered in the forest, from where he must have climbed down into the ravine, a hazardous descent, although what did hazardous mean in his situation? I saw him in my mind's eye, groping his way down a gully, the rifle on his back that I couldn't believe he could ever have turned on himself after making all that effort, and could not get rid of the illogical wish that he had fallen down there, because if he had he would not have done it. I had always resisted the thought that my clinging to Daniel could have had something to do with Robert, but what I was experiencing now were not thoughts but a trick my brain was playing on me.

"I'm probably scared of both."

"That he might be there and that he might not be there?"

"It may sound crazy, but that's the way it is."

These were no more than my own fancies, but as the plot and stories surrounding Daniel thickened and proliferated into absurdity, I could also see in them what Herr Bleichert told me. He buttonholed me outside school that day and forced me into conversation. I pretended to be in a hurry, but he refused to be shaken off, and the quicker I walked the more he stumbled along beside me, saying, between his "Woe to you, Chorazin! Woe to you, Bethsaida!", that he had been reminded of one thing he had thought he had forgotten. With that, he couldn't think of anything better to tell me than that there had already been something the matter with Daniel even before he wrote his report on Israel that could have developed into an incident, and which proved what fanaticism lay dormant in him.

"It happened while you were in Istanbul," he said. "I talked to his class about Savonarola, and when I asked the students to come up with suggestions for what we could do during Lent to limit our needs for a few days, he came up with the idea of staging a bonfire of the vanities."

"A bonfire of the vanities?"

"Like Savonarola's in Florence."

"But that was hundreds of years ago."

I looked at him disbelievingly.

"The manias of a fifteenth-century Dominican monk. What are we supposed to make of them today? He can't possibly have taken them as a model."

"You're right," he said. "But that's what he was like."

Then he explained what he meant.

"He wanted to go around the town with the other students, in pairs, and invite people to put out possessions that they would be happier without. It could be books of dubious content, all sorts of music, as well as jewellery, children's toys or whatever else struck them as being unnecessary trinkets. He would collect everything together and burn it at a public event, outside the school."

"You can't be serious," I said. "Aren't those the methods of the Taliban? And you're actually saying a twelve-year-old thought this up on his own? That's the purest invention."

"I'm trying to tell you, it didn't come to it," he said. "Obviously I talked him out of it, but whether you believe it or not, the intention was there."

I don't know why I found him disgusting at that moment, though it certainly had something to do with the fact that he had been both the initiator and the informer of this craziness. I was in Bruckner's by the time I thought about it again, amusing myself with the picture of Bleichert at last letting me go and hurrying away, almost bent double, as though he had finally worked out for himself what an appalling impression he had produced. His walk, like that of a bow-legged footballer, always seemed bizarre for a priest, and as soon as he had recovered a little and loosened up he looked, with every step he took, almost obscenely happy from the movement of his hips. I couldn't find any explanation for the story he had told me; it was hardly likely to have been mere scandal-mongering, but nor could he believe that it had any validity, and he must have been aiming for some other effect, even if it was only to make himself important yet again. I had not asked whether it was usual to talk about Savonarola to students of that age or whether it was just his idea, and in what light he had presented God's dictator and his tyranny of virtue. I had sometimes mentioned the subject myself in my history class, when I talked about the Renaissance and its excesses, but for him to do so in his religious studies class was a different matter and he was the last person who could accuse Daniel of false ideals, considering that he had been the one who had first implanted them in him, whenever he had the chance. I felt him to be a shifting contradiction, and as I watched him go with his rolling, weaving movements, it made me think that sin had perhaps really only come into the world via the law, as you can read in Paul's Epistle to the Romans – through the possibility of its transgression as well as by the possibility of its fulfilment and over-fulfilment.

Actually I had planned to drive out to the house straight after lunch, but now, on reflection, I changed my plan and decided to go and see Judith. She had not been at school again, having phoned in sick, although no-one knew what was wrong with her. I phoned her, and when no-one answered I tried again half an hour later, letting the phone ring for a long time, again without success, then decided that my unease was a good enough reason just to go to where she lived. Her apartment was in one of the blocks behind the football ground, and my way there took me past the police station. My first impulse was to skirt round behind it, but then I told myself that to do that would be to behave as if I were already guilty, so I strode straight past the entrance. As soon as you fall under suspicion all your behaviour feels like something you've seen on T.V. anyway, and you're unable to do anything either right or wrong and end up merely becoming the second-rate performer of your own life. I didn't know whether Inspector Hule was on duty, but suppressed the urge to go in and ask him for a coffee, as if it was the most natural thing in the world. I had nothing to tell him that I had not already told him, and conversely he would doubtless have seen it as most significant that I had come voluntarily to find out whether there were any new developments, which in turn would be a clear indication that my conscience was not clear.

I can't say what made me so sure that Judith was at home. As I came closer to the estate there was, as so often in our town, no-one to be seen, which once more triggered in me the illogical certainty that I was being observed. I walked across the empty children's playground, where toys lay strewn as though after a disaster, which reminded me of the blunder the regional bishop had committed a few years before, hardly worth mentioning in its absurdity, but in the small world in which we lived enough, nevertheless, to provoke a huff of indignation. What he had said was that high-rise buildings were evil, because they encouraged children to lie when their mothers called them from the sixth or seventh floor as they soon discovered that they could pretend with impunity that they hadn't heard. It was utterly trivial, an old man adding two and two together who doesn't understand the world anymore, and I found myself chuckling as I climbed the stairs and rang Judith's bell. I waited a while, then when nobody came to open the door, knocked, and when that too failed to produce a response, I hit upon the idea of writing a message on a piece of paper and pushing it under the door, which worked straight away.

Judith opened the door only enough for me to squeeze through and immediately pulled it to behind her once I was inside. She guided me along the narrow corridor into the living room, and as I glanced around she walked to the window, pulled the net curtains aside and looked down onto the forecourt. She had hardly said a word so far, but when she invited me to sit down she apologised and started clearing away the building blocks and picture books that were scattered all over the sofa and the two armchairs. She had lived here since she had come back to teach at the school and, probably because the estate didn't have the best reputation, for almost as long as she had been teaching she had been saying that it was only temporary and she would be looking for somewhere else soon. It was the first time I had visited her at home, and even if I had known nothing about it I would have been struck by its provisional look, given the length of time – at least four years – that she had been living there. In one corner there were a number of banana boxes piled up that looked as if they had been there for more than a few days, her bookshelves were made of fruit crates, and I tried hard not to let her see that I had noticed the carpet curling away from the wall in several places. The apartment needed dusting and the windows needed cleaning; at the moment they shaded it from the sun with a thick layer of dirt. None of it corresponded with the way Judith usually looked at school, in her carefully chosen secondhand clothes that were nevertheless of the best quality, and generally radiating an aura that made you wonder why, when she went away, she hadn't left our town for good. She owned a big old Mercedes, which with its chrome trim stood out among the mid-range and economy models in the school car park as the height of luxury, even though it was practically falling apart, and sometimes on Saturdays when lessons were finished she packed it full of students from the senior classes and drove them into the country, without caring in the slightest about the rumours she caused among many colleagues.

I need hardly stress that there was little of that faintly decadent sheen left in the Judith standing in the living room with me. She was alone; her son, of whom there were pictures on every wall, was being looked after by his grandparents. I knew the stories, that he was nearly ten now but like a four- or five-year-old, although Judith herself never dropped any hints about him. Almost none of her colleagues had ever seen him, but that only made him all the more present, as he was here in the apartment, a laughing, almost painfully open face in all the photos, with his wide-apart eyes and the serene expression of a little innocent. I studied the pictures one by one and was aware of Judith following my gaze. I got the impression that she appreciated my attentiveness, but just as I thought she was going to say something she fixed me with a stare that seemed to want to make it clear that the social part of my visit had gone on long enough.

"You've come about Daniel, haven't you?"

She was still standing by the window, a thin cardigan over the pyjamas she was wearing, and she laughed when I said I had been concerned because no-one at school knew what was the matter with her.

"Now you know," she said, and her glance shifted to the wine bottle on the glass table in front of me, nearly empty apart from a tiny amount left at the bottom. "Would you like something to drink?"

I nodded. On her way to the kitchen she stopped behind me and put her hands on my shoulders and her voice was very close to my ear, in a way that was simultaneously soft and hoarse, so that I hardly recognised it.

"You didn't expect that from your Judith, did you? So many years at school, and never any unpleasantness, never the slightest cause for complaint. A nice colleague you can chat to once a week about the important things in life, without knowing anything else about her. You thought, she's a good girl, and now you feel let down."

I did not turn around. I waited for her to laugh – that sarcastic laugh of hers from before, that seemed to say that everyone was free to do what they pleased with their life – but she didn't. I still felt her hands on my shoulders after she had let go, and did not know what to do but shut my eyes, although I would have preferred to shut my ears. I heard her moving noisily around in the kitchen, and when she came back with two glasses and a new bottle I was glad her voice was her own again and she was talking about Daniel as if her emotional outage of a few moments before had not happened.

"I was expecting you to come," she said. "You want to talk about him. All right, let's do it, let's get it over with as quickly as possible. Tell me what you want to know."

At that moment I could have done nothing more stupid than to ask her whether he had got in touch with her, yet I did. I was still so irritated by what she had said that I probably wasn't paying attention. Yet I should have known how difficult it would be for her. I only had to think about Daniel's repeated intrusions into her life, which she had told me about years before, to sense what it meant for her, the night-time phone calls out of nowhere, in which he recited the Song of Songs to her and which even then felt like a threat to her, and then there was the grotesque appearance he had made at her wedding that still produced universal head-shaking whenever it was talked about. She had invited him in the hope of being able to control him, and even had the idea of making him her witness, and he had thanked her by setting out to destroy the whole festive occasion with his impossible behaviour. Every time she looked as though she was about to dance, he came up to her and insisted that actually it was his turn and refused to be put off, threatening her that it was a matter of life and death, they would never see each other again if she didn't instantly grant him his wish, and in the end actually lapsed into the lunacy of saying that either he was given the next dance or he would run down to the petrol station, douse himself in petrol and set himself on fire. I was standing nearby and heard him, and what in other circumstances might have been dismissed as the boorish and out-of-control gallantry of a drunk became, because of his insistence, an utterly misjudged blunder. She had kept on repeating to him, "That's enough," but when I thought back to how she had looked at him, it was exactly the same expression that was reflected in her face now, and there were no soothing words for it, no placatory gestures. She was scared.

"Has he been in touch with me?"

I wanted to apologise, but it was too late. She had dropped into one of the armchairs, stood up again, and then, as if beaten with a blunt instrument, sank back down again, asking me what I meant by the question. I realised then that that was the only reason she was not at school, the only reason she had not answered her phone or opened her door, so that Daniel couldn't get to her. As I launched into an explanation, she waved me away, laughing, and said that his "Repent!" had been enough for her, but with his "Woe to you, Chorazin! Woe to you, Bethsaida!" she had finally got the message and did not want to wait until something happened and everyone was wise again after the event, saying they should have known it earlier and it was incomprehensible why no-one had done anything.

"I've always been scared of that religious mania of his," she said. "Do you know what he called my son?"

Horrifying as it is, I knew before she said it.

"He called him a judgement from God."

I only had to raise my eyes slightly to see, on the wall facing me, one of the photos of the boy. It looked like a picture of him running off a jetty and jumping into the water, eyes shut, arms raised as high as he could, fingers stretched up to the sky, and in the background on the shore a figure could dimly be made out, behind whom Judith was probably concealed, watching him. It was said that her husband had left because of the boy. I was annoyed with myself for thinking about it. He was a sales representative, whom she had magicked out of nowhere a few months before their wedding, looking exactly like someone out of a lonely hearts ad, and a few months later she had let him vanish again, without any special tricks. He worked away from home more and more often, sometimes he was away for a week at a time, and at some point it was said that he had moved to Vienna and she was planning to follow him as soon as possible, but I had known it would never happen. I would, however, have given a lot to think of a meaningful sentence at that moment, to erase Daniel's appalling verdict from our conversation. It went on echoing in my brain but I did not know what to say and in my helplessness could not stop staring at the boy and his white, skinny chest with its almost non-existent shoulders, his little pot belly and his crooked knee.

"Why should he be a judgement from God?"

I turned back to Judith, who had begun to cry softly but now sat up in her armchair and said angrily that Daniel saying something like that was him being crazy, but she did not want to hear anything about it from me, not even as a rhetorical question.

"I can't stand it anymore," she said. "It starts with the words. A judgement from God? Where exactly are we living? A judgement on me because I didn't go to a nunnery? And at the same time he tells me I could have saved him."

"Your son?"

"No, him. That's what's absurd. How would that have gone? As if that fucking Jesus hadn't already asked to be saved by the Reverend."

It had been a long time since I had heard her call Daniel that, and now her nickname not only rang with the mockery it had had that summer when she first christened him, out by the river. She called him that as she left, as though she was saying goodbye for ever, and it rang with revulsion and contempt. I remembered how she had ridden away on her bike back then as I kept my gaze fixed on her face and she dabbed her cheeks with the backs of her hands. She had already been pregnant then, in the early stages, and thinking about how Daniel talked about her, I realised he almost certainly could not have known.

"You're right, it is absurd," I said, as if to bring the subject to a conclusion. "But perhaps there is something in it."

Of course I immediately knew that I should not have said that either, but the vehemence of her reaction still came as a surprise.

"In what?" she gasped. "Be careful what you say."

"That you could have saved him."

"I could have saved him?" she said, jumping up and starting to pace up and down in front of me. "What are you talking about?"

"You know," I replied. "A life can go off in a completely different direction, just because of one tiny decision."

"I don't know and I don't want to know either," she said, becoming even more upset. "What decision? That I could have saved him the way a woman can save a serial killer before he turns into a serial killer? If you think that, first, it's complete nonsense and secondly, it's just hideous."

It didn't matter that I was trying to reassure her. She walked across to the window again, pulled back the net curtain and stared down at the forecourt as if I wasn't there, saying that anyhow it was all down to a single misunderstanding, if you thought about the real Jesus. She was the last person I expected to make such a reference, and although she suddenly lowered her voice and started to speak as if to herself, I made out every word.

"That's precisely the joke about him – he didn't let himself be saved. Anyone with an ounce of pride left after being called Jesus ought at least to know that. The joke about him is that he turned himself into a martyr."

It wasn't just the word that made me shiver. Judith could not know anything of my conversation with Agata about Robert or how he and his death had been discussed at Bruckner's, but I obviously made the connection immediately and then thought about the story of Abraham and Isaac and what a perversion it was, even though the old man had succeeded in saving his son from God, who Himself famously allowed His own son to be nailed up on the cross. I was silent and looked at her, and as she stayed standing at the window, her hair falling over her face, there was nothing to hint at what she had just said. With her arms folded across her chest, she leant, seemingly indifferently, against the wall, and I took it as an invitation to leave. I had not touched the wine she had poured me, and her own glass still sat on the table, full, as though to underline our failure of communication. I got to my feet and said goodbye, and it was only when I was outside that I understood what had upset me so much. I had imagined, despite my closeness to Daniel and despite his weirdness, that I lived in a completely secular world, and now found myself having to accept how little it took for the religious hangover we still possessed to start encroaching. I had taken the head's wife's keenness on board – some people were like that; where Herr Bleichert was concerned, blindness went with the territory and he would always find a coachful of people to go on a pilgrimage to Jerusalem with him; but Inspector Hule, a policeman of all people, blustering on about there being potentially no very great difference between a terrorist and a saint, had undermined my certainty, and now Judith was using the very same vocabulary that previously had always repelled her. My head full of such thoughts, I crossed the forecourt of the high-rise blocks, not needing to turn around to know she was watching me because I could feel her eyes on my back.

I don't understand why all this weighed on me so much. I had thought of Judith as a woman whom life couldn't harm, even though, as I write this down, I have to admit that of all the stupid things I could say that's one of the stupidest. Back then she had been among the first to put her name down for the theatre group, even before Daniel and Christoph, and when I thought back to how we had met twice a week in the gym for rehearsals it seemed half an eternity ago. The sweat from the last session of circuit training still hung in the air and the space we marked off with blocks, bars and a balancing beam to make a stage had something deliberately avant-garde about it, a mixture of modern torture chamber – with the rings that dangled over our heads – and unfinished ballet hall in which her every move looked as graceful as it did archaic. The springboards on the floor could have been either catapults to heaven or trapdoors to the abyss, but when she ran with two or three steps to one of them and launched herself from it, the next instant froze into a still life in which she hung gracefully in the air. The grunt of her landings resounded in your ears for a time afterwards like the clicking shutter of an oversized camera, by which time she was already leaning against a horse and staring back at the spot, as though she could see a shadow of herself there. As long as it was still warm that autumn she came to our meetings in dreamy long dresses in bright, girlish colours which came from her mother's youth and which in the previous months she had mostly put on in front of her mother's mirror but now wore like the uniform of a secret sisterhood that counted loose living among its precepts. I saw it all again, so clearly, in my mind's eye that I didn't want to connect it with the woman who was living as if imprisoned in her apartment. I had asked Judith then what she would do later, and I still remember her laugh and her saying what an honour it was that I should come out with that line to her too, but I really didn't need to worry. I looked at her, uncomprehending, and I remember how she hesitated and half-tried to disguise it as a joke, going on to say that it was well known that I'd prefer it if none of my students ever left school because I was so afraid for them.

"Obviously first I'll go and have a look at the world, before I do anything else," she said. "I'll travel for a year, then see what I think, and not let anything or anyone tie me down."

This conversation took place on one of the evenings when I drove her and the two boys home, after I had dropped off Daniel and Christoph and we found ourselves alone in the car. It was the day we had invited a writer to the rehearsals, an author who, it was said, had met Camus in Paris in the 1950s. It had been heavy-going, because with every sentence he uttered the old man had only reinforced the impression that in his life he had done pretty much everything wrong that he could have done wrong, and was now attempting to deal with it by carrying on doing more wrong, even as he clung laboriously to the stories he trotted out about his own greatness, which only made him less and less great with each telling. People had wanted to rescue him from his foolishness, and some of the sadness he had radiated was still hanging in the air. The most likeable thing about him was that what he had to say about Camus was confined to the fact that he had once seen him cross the street with a woman and that at that moment he had not envied him his books but the woman, his fame, his expensive suit and the nonchalance with which he had stopped and stood with her in a doorway to light a cigarette. Apart from this story, he had entirely failed to fool the students. Daniel and Christoph had just been amusing themselves in the car joking about him and all his blether about meaning, but it was Judith who, after they had gone, started imitating him in all his pomposity.

"Did you hear him say that if he hadn't become a writer he would either have strung himself up from the nearest tree with the first clear thought he had, or ended up as a criminal or a terrorist?"

This was before the turn of the millennium, when you could say such things without blushing or wanting the ground to swallow you up out of embarrassment, when at least there were writers, perhaps not the cleverest, who flirted with such ideas, but she dismissed them all. She had been against our theatre group staging *The Just* from the beginning, but had been overruled. She said she would prefer anything else, *A Midsummer Night's Dream*, *The Winter's Tale*, but something light, not this ghastly play about a bunch of terrorists in a dark time that said nothing to her about her life. She liked Camus, but she liked him in other ways, and even if it possibly sounded superficial at first hearing, something in her verdict hit home when she said that in the clash between Camus and Sartre, you only had to look at photos of them to know that Camus had been right, or at least to want him to have been right. She had listened, bored, to my remarks about the historical background of the play, sat, equally bored, through the speech on tyrannicide that I had given to Christoph, and then come across as far more credible in her role than either Daniel or him. I personally felt she was the only one who was really capable of throwing a bomb, so much rage did she evoke in her character, while the boys' speeches stayed on the page and their earnestness produced exactly the opposite effect, making them unintentionally funny and turning their play into a drama for children, ultimately without any ill consequences, where everyone who had died during it would come alive again at the end. So in a way I understood her rage at the perhaps slightly too glibly delivered lines of the writer as well.

"That's making it too easy for himself," she said. "Criminal or terrorist. He really would have been better off stringing himself up from the nearest tree, no-one would have missed him. I find it creepy."

"It's just stupid talk. It's so easy to see through that it's not worth wasting your breath on. He's a harmless dreamer, let him keep his romantic relationship with himself."

"Oh sure, let him. But if I tell you I'd like to be happy that probably sounds naïve, but only because posers like him would rather smash everything to bits than admit they've got it wrong. That whole negation of the world thing makes me sick."

"I'm not sure why you're even comparing yourself to him," I said. "You're a young woman, he's an old man, and that's the end of it."

I had been so sure that Judith would stick to her guns, but less than three years after this conversation in the car, in which she had finished by saying that she really did not know what she would do later except that she wanted to get away from the town, she was pushing a buggy through its streets. At her side was the dubious boyfriend who had made life so hard for both Daniel and Christoph, a perfectly nice boy, a bit colourless in his appearance, yet I couldn't help thinking that he had ruined her. He joked around uneasily when you met him, while she carried herself very determinedly, if I can put it like that, although I couldn't banish the feeling that she was avoiding me or at least making sure that no conversation went beyond saying hello and small talk. I saw her once or twice at the football ground, where she walked the length of the stands with her son just before kick-off, as if she wanted to be seen and to put a stop to the gossip about him that was already going around. Afterwards I only had occasional news of her, and by the time she came back to our school to teach there, she had long since joined the gallery of former students whose images slowly faded in my memory.

My visit had so unsettled me that I went for a walk to give me a chance to consider what I should do next. I had reached Bruckner's before I decided that I would not go in, because I suddenly knew I mustn't postpone my trip out to the river any longer. As so often I procrastinated madly as though it might buy me some time, and only didn't go via the service area because I decided to stop off there afterwards instead. For a while I had the feeling I was being followed, but as soon as I tested my suspicions by pulling into a lay-by to let the car behind me pass, my fears turned out to be groundless. When I reached the house my expectations were disappointed too. Someone had obviously been there, looking around – you could tell by the trampled-down grass and a piece of a page from the previous weekend's newspaper – but even the padlock looked untouched: it was all a long way from being a designated crime scene, which was one possibility I had entertained. I stayed at the property for a while, even going down to the river where I found an empty cigarette packet, but it turned out that I had been wrong to imagine there might still be someone loitering in the area. At least, when I called out, no-one answered and when I finally strolled back to the mill and unlocked the door my first glance told me that no-one had been there since my last visit. Everything was as it had been then, and I stopped for a moment in the doorway before sitting down at the table where I had played cards with Daniel and Christoph whenever a downpour had driven us indoors. I found a bottle of wine dating back to our summer, and opened it but didn't drink it. The thing that I most needed was to be clear about my feelings, and it would be a lie if I did not admit that, mingled with the relief I felt, there was also a trace of disappointment.

I don't know if it had something to do with it, but on the way back I spent a while at the service area looking at a display of photographs of the region on the walls of the stairs down to the toilets. They were all of rural idylls from the first half of the last century, purporting to be indictments of the modern world and testimonies to what had been lost, but they were neither one thing nor the other, just yet more lies in black and white. I had stopped bothering to think about this sort of fakery long before, but on this occasion it pained me to look at such dead-end folklore, in which even the attempt to criticise it legitimised the same folklore. I felt it all as an affront, a kind of mockery and self-mockery, as though this was always how it went now when you attempted to depict a once supposedly whole world, and I was about to leave when I saw a picture that reconciled me to everything. I had completely missed it at first, because the girl in the foreground, with her plaits and gap-toothed smile, perfectly fitted the formula, but now I saw, in the background, the Au and then, on a second and third look, very small in the distant fields but actually gigantic, the crash-landed bomber. The little girl could have been my mother but was not, perhaps she was a friend of hers, perhaps a stranger, not from the village at all, and I decided to find out. I looked into her face and, whether I idealise or not, everything suddenly changed for me; suddenly her shining eyes were no longer part of the whole fraud, no longer the shining eyes of all those black-and-white films about "home", but instead sparkled back at me with her happiness at the Americans descending like angels from the heavens and all the good things they would bring.

It was a mood in which, in other circumstances, I would have gone to the cemetery to visit my grandparents and all the other non-emigrants who had lived their lives honestly and meekly and literally by the sweat of their brow until death, like a travesty of their dreams of leaving and advancement, overtook them without warning. But I didn't go. I stopped at the crossroads where my grandfather had died and had the same thought I always had, about how in the 1950s, six years before I was born, he had managed to get himself run over by a motorcycle there, where even now sometimes minutes went by without a single car passing. It was never mentioned in the family, and when my uncle walked into the river the silence deepened, becoming a full-blown taboo after Robert put the barrel of the rifle in his mouth and pulled the trigger. It produces an approximately equilateral triangle, if you add to the two points where Robert and my grandfather died the place where my uncle was last seen alive, an equilateral triangle with sides just a few kilometres in length, and within whose boundary lie my house by the river, the meadows of the Au that once belonged to my family and in which the American bomber crash-landed, a triangle that is basically the whole piece of land on which, apart from a few odd runaways who left to be happy or unhappy in the wider world, the lives of my family on my mother's side have played out for generations. I don't know why I thought about all this with such intensity while I hung on at the crossroads, not two hundred metres from the village, and looked out at the fields, or why I abruptly thought, which I had never thought before, that I belonged here and simultaneously resisted the thought with all my might. I looked at the single outline of the mountain in the distance and told myself that perhaps it was enough if the earth revolved underneath the sky and if the sky above this piece of earth was perhaps not exactly the sky above New York, not exactly the sky above Rio de Janeiro, but possibly the sky above a settlement in Brazil which had fallen out of time and in which my grandparents lived, in the deepest jungle. I had sat down on the verge and I carried on sitting there for a while, and when I finally got up and walked to my car an expectant silence was hanging over the countryside and evening was coming on.

6

THE TIME THAT FOLLOWED COULD BE DESCRIBED IN DIFFERENT ways, depending on my mood. On the one hand I had the feeling that the excitement in the town after the second bomb threat dissipated as quickly as it had after the first, on the other hand I could not ignore the signs that the tension, for me all too palpable in Bruckner's on that Sunday night, persisted. I was admittedly a poor authority on what was truly going on, because I had only a few observations to go on. I felt that Herr Frischmann, in his editorial which appeared in the middle of that week, was over-simplifying things when he again wheeled out the trite verdict that it was a childish prank, writing that the internet was full of bomb-making instructions, functioning and non-functioning, and that life nevertheless still went on and if anyone was really determined to be worried, there were a thousand other things to worry about. It was not quite adequate, and yet I too was disinclined to be hysterical or to let myself be intimidated like Judith, who no longer dared to go outside. Three days after my first visit, I drove out to the river once more and again everything was unchanged at the house, even though on the way back I bumped into two policemen who were certainly not roaming around there by accident and who took careful note of my presence. I avoided Bruckner's, where I would have had the best chance of discovering something new, because I didn't want to get into another situation where I felt threatened, and at school I steered clear of all conversations about Daniel and forbade myself to get drawn into the affair, in particular where Herr Bleichert was concerned, who suddenly started putting on conspiratorial airs and greeting me as if we were members of some secret society. The head sulked. When he bumped into me in the corridor he looked at me as if to say that after all the trust he had put in me he had expected something better, but he said nothing, and just when I started thinking that I must be imagining it, it was Frau Pfeifer who convinced me of the contrary, advising me that I should take care to clear up the discord between us. The students for their part were well behaved and remarkably quiet, and it would be going too far to say that for precisely that reason I suspected them of cooking something up and it was only a matter of time before they would work out how they could use the story against me. But I received several anonymous phone calls that made me think they might be behind them, and when the phone finally rang again at an unusual hour and I, jolted out of sleep and without thinking, said as I picked it up, "Daniel, is that you?" I thought I heard muffled laughter in the background and could not think of anyone else who would find it funny, apart from a bunch of thirteen- or fourteen-year-olds.

It was clearly not by chance that I found myself outside the gate of Christoph's house the following weekend. I always had a bad feeling when I thought about him and how that summer, after the Reverend appeared, he had vanished from my life without ever showing his face again. It is true that from the outset I had been less interested in him than in Daniel and had simply accepted him as his friend, as though for all his stolidity I felt that he was rather a lightweight. Then afterwards I felt snubbed that he, of all people, behaved, whenever we bumped into each other, as if I had got too close to him. He never said anything, but his reaction was unambiguous, a bashfulness that really amounted to impertinence, of him not wanting to be seen with me, or at any rate wanting to distance himself as much as possible from all the rumours that were circulating about us, or which might do, and for that reason I kept out of his way as much as he kept out of mine.

He had studied architecture after leaving school, and since qualifying had not only worked in the planning office of Herr Oswald, the then mayor who had just started campaigning for a second term, but had married his daughter, Manon, with whom, as they say, I had form. She was also a former student, and in year six I had flunked her, which was actually no big thing but turned into a drama as a result of her father intervening and my making it a decision to stop her going up to the next year in any circumstances. Dr Prager had not retired at the time, and I had a strong ally in him because he nursed an almost pathological aversion to those doted-on sons and daughters for whom, if there was ever a problem, Daddy would always fix it and who then clogged everything up, taking away not only the places but the lives of others, believing they deserved better and that their correctly awarded results failed to reflect their worth, even when they had been proven incapable. He had once almost been sued for going so far in class as to say that basically such spoilt children should be sent away for a year or locked up on a diet of bread and water before they were let loose on the world — one of those diatribes that Dr Prager's generation still thought they could get away with. It had thus not taken much to get him on my side. It had been enough to tell him how Herr Oswald had appeared at my consultation hour and alternately tried to flatter and intimidate me until I no longer knew whether he was going to offer me money or start bellowing at me the way some violence-prone overlord would bellow at his serfs, for whom such obstinacy could cost them their neck.

It also became a sort of line in the sand for me, because he kept saying that his daughter was going to lose a year just because of her bad grade in German, that she was going to have to repeat a year just because of that, and I could not stop thinking how self-indulgent he was, and what did he know about losing a year, and how many years Robert had already lost by then, because he had already been dead then for as many years. I had looked at him disbelievingly, but he had utterly failed to notice the contempt I felt for his complaints. He was one of those dialect-speakers who spoke dialect the way others drove their oversized 4×4s, aggressively barging other traffic out of the way, which doubtless in his position cast him as a man of the people; that someone like him should presume to find German irrelevant was bound to infuriate me. I let him talk, however, and kept my thoughts to myself. I had a dim view of the high society of our small town, whose privileges included coarse looks and bad manners and who held their showy backwoodsmanlike airs and graces to be a virtue, and he was no exception. Although I would have liked to put him in his place, I calmed him down by saying I wanted to think it over, and when I was called to the head's office a little later and the head asked me if I couldn't turn a blind eye, I found myself laughing and at the same time as firm in my resolve as I had been from the start. The head pointed out that it was for the good of the school too and rebuked me, saying that it was not about principles and if I thought that making the mayor's daughter's life difficult was in some way a revolutionary act and the beginning of an overthrow of the status quo, then I was suffering from a great delusion that only showed I still had no grasp whatsoever of how the world worked.

I had passed the gate many times without ever ringing the bell, and even now it cost me an effort to overcome my resistance. I almost turned around when I heard Manon's voice through the intercom, inviting me in. The grille slid back noiselessly and I walked up the gravel path to the two houses, the Oswalds' villa, a plain functional building from the outside, and the old house right next to it, where Christoph and Manon lived. It was a huge property, a park-like garden in the middle of the city, behind a two-metre wall and with a lily pond, a summer house and an unused swimming pool. When the grille closed, the traffic noise died away as if it had been switched off, and as soon as I started walking my shoes seemed to crunch more and more loudly on the gravel with every step. The two buildings stood on a small rise, with a view over the wall, and I didn't take the direct way, up a broad staircase with a landing every few steps, but chose the bombastically proportioned double flight, veritable infinity loops that a part of me hoped would prove to be the entrance to a labyrinth into which I might disappear, still undiscovered.

I had not seen Manon since school and was unsure how she would react to seeing me. She had been a rather nondescript girl, tending to podginess, with a grotesque conceit about her origins and all the attitudes of a small-town beauty, a dreamy Erich Fried reader who smoked hand-rolled cigarettes in order to watch herself smoking and being dreamy, and I had a hard time connecting her with the woman who greeted me at the entrance to the house, sitting in one of the wicker chairs that were arranged around a massive wooden table in front of it. She was slim, in that pinched American way, wearing tennis clothes, white shirt, light blue skirt, white sneakers, and no longer embodying the adolescent denial with which she had once held the world at arm's length, entrenching herself behind a cold aloofness. Anyone who ever pronounced her name in the French way had been brusquely corrected, as though she did not want any unnecessary subtleties to develop, and at the memory of her insistence and her underlying pride about what was true and authentic, both expressed in the most surly possible manner, I shuddered. Her way had been to say no to everything first time around, even if the statement in question was necessarily or logically true, but as soon as I saw her I realised that she no longer bothered to do this, because at some point she had learnt that politeness was a far better weapon.

"You'll excuse me," she said, before I had even had time to consider whether to mention school to her or not. "Unfortunately I have a prior engagement and will have to leave you alone. My husband, however, is entirely at your disposal. I assume you've come on his account, haven't you?"

She disappeared without another word, and I don't know if it was her opening that determined the course of the subsequent conversation with Christoph, but in any event I felt as if I were in a bad movie with this entrance, or rather exit, of the lady of the house, which any clever director would have cut as a cheap imitation of a cheap imitation, and I wondered whether I shouldn't just slip away. I remembered how, in the year when I had flunked her and it was already clear that it was going to happen, she had once stopped me at breaktime. She had stood squarely in front of me and asked why I didn't like girls, looking at me as though she had some kind of hold over me. I walked past her without replying, but something of the unconscious anxiety of being at someone's mercy that I had felt at the time crept over me again now. In front of me on the wooden table, as if placed there especially for me, was a book, a red doorstopper of a book, which I picked up and leafed through for a while. Now and again I looked up at the Oswald villa, the veranda of which had a perfect view of where I was sitting, so of course I felt observed and also felt, when Christoph finally appeared, that he must have been watching me for some time.

"I'm sorry Manon didn't offer you anything," he said. "I'm afraid she's still offended with you for making her repeat that year."

I looked at my shoes and did not react. He had a bottle of wine in his hand and uncorked it, performing the whole operation with, as it only became clear to me later, the same mixture of irony and resignation that characterised all his actions. I looked down at the flowerbeds next to the stairs and he followed my gaze, I looked over to the villa where one of their staff was washing Herr Oswald's car, looked across the ornamental shrubs to the far end of the garden where a folded table-tennis table stood in the sunshine, and all the time he kept his eyes glued to me.

"It's a nice place you've got here," I said finally, doing my best not to sound disparaging. "A bit bigger than our house out at the river."

"A bit, yes."

"You could almost forget that true beauty comes from the heart, when you look around you here and see that it's all good."

It was not that he looked as if he wanted to apologise after I had spoken, but he glanced at me quickly, to make sure of my goodwill, before laughing nervously.

"Still the same old teacher," he said, slightly put out. "But it's not as simple as you think."

I did not need to remind him how much he had rejected all this, back in the summer by the river, and didn't try to. He had sometimes gone even further in his ideas than Daniel when they talked about what they wanted to do the following autumn, and I still recalled how he had once said that the worst and basically the only impermissible failure was provincial success, and that was why they had to ban themselves from becoming, under any circumstances, part of the sordid, clannish society that ran our small town. He had taken immense pleasure in imitating their coarse dialect, deliberately emphasising its coarseness, and acting out impromptu sketches of them mutually recommending the dentist, gynaecologist or lawyer as "one of us, the best", and now he himself had the prospect of being, as an architect under Herr Oswald's thumb, one of those same "best" – a prospect I would have had too if I hadn't flunked Manon – of being "one of us" among the plebs, helping himself with a bish! bash! bosh! to positions of status and influence. There had been plenty of rowdy talk too that summer, about which I did not make the mistake of reminding him now, rather he did it himself, and his initial unease stemmed from it. He took a long time to relax, and although we talked about other things, I had the impression that all the time the subject was subliminally pushing its way towards the surface.

"You get accustomed to the few pleasant things that this life brings with it," he said finally. "But they can't save you in the end."

I couldn't fail to hear the word. I had already wondered, as I came to the gate and glimpsed the property for the first time, whether this was Christoph's way of saving himself, but now it struck me that there was no salvation and that the whole secret consisted in putting up with life, perhaps if necessary even with a house, a wife and in-laws within sight, and not fighting it. I did not say so, and wild horses could not have made me say it, but the thought, foreign though it was to me, made me forgive him. I had expected him to make things more difficult for me, after we had gone our separate ways for so many years, but he could not have been more open, and the only remarkable thing was how long we took to get to the point. It was as if we could not have picked a more absurd backdrop to the conversation we subsequently had, and because of that we shied away from starting it.

I had hardly mentioned Daniel myself when Christoph said he did not believe the story had even the slightest connection with him. He had finally sat down in one of the chairs opposite me, having previously remained standing, giving off a nervous restlessness, and he put all his emphasis into the sentence. He still radiated something boyishly winning when he looked at you, and he stared at me now across the wooden table as if he did not want there to be any doubt of his sincerity.

"You only need to look at the amateurish way it was done," he said. "Do you think Daniel, with all his perfectionism, would do it so bunglingly that everyone would treat it as a juvenile prank?"

He waved his own question away, although he was expressing exactly what I had thought, and said that in any case that was not the thing that made him so sure.

"I'm convinced he's not even in the country. You know he wanted to go to Israel. He came to see you to borrow money. I gave him a bit of money myself."

"Wasn't that six months ago?"

"Maybe so, but I heard from him three weeks ago," he said. "He was still there then and didn't give me the impression that he was coming back any time soon."

I refrained from saying that that hardly amounted to an alibi and would still have left him enough time to carry out both threats. To me, it even counted against him and was entirely in line with the "Repent!" and "Woe to you, Chorazin! Woe to you, Bethsaida!" nonsense. I had no idea where on earth he had been living in the months before his last visit to me, but the fact that he had wanted to go to Israel again, of all places, could not be a coincidence. He had not said what he needed the money I had given him for, and I now regretted that I had not been more curious.

"To be perfectly honest I'd find it surprising for him to be in Israel," I said. "Has it got something to do with the Reverend?"

I didn't expect the pitying expression with which Christoph responded. As if to gain time, he looked towards the gate, which opened and shut again, and kept his gaze fixed on the two girls who had come in and, talking and gesturing to each other, were walking up the path to the villa, both of them in bright summer dresses, fourteen or fifteen years old and oblivious to us observing them, so absorbed were they in their conversation. He said they were his nieces, and the way he emphasised it made it feel, from the hidden vantage point where we sat, like a foreign word and actually like something indecent, which only occurred in those self-important soft-core movies about the sexual awakening of young girls. Then he fell silent, and I thought he was going to ignore my question when he suddenly turned to me.

"With the Reverend?"

He looked at me with an ironically apprehensive look.

"What makes you think that?"

"Well," I said, "supposedly the Reverend thinks this is the year in which Israel's decisive struggle is imminent."

I was not sure why I uttered this nonsense at all and I felt embarrassed, even before he irritably demanded whether he should tell me everything else the Reverend believed. In doing so he put me in the position of interrogator, which I was not, and when I tried to point this out I made things worse. He interrupted me, saying that he could not see why he should have to grapple with such fantasies, and that it was best not to have anything to do with them.

"Let's just say," he said, "that you go along with some of what the Reverend believes. O.K., he believes that it is scientifically proven that a person can survive for three days in the belly of a whale. Obviously he believes in Adam and Eve, and that oral sex gives you cancer and makes your hair fall out. And he believes a whole bunch of other things, which you'd rather not hear about."

"I know," I said sheepishly, feeling that he had put me on the defensive. "Which makes it all the worse that the bomb threats breathe his spirit."

"Oh for God's sake," he said. "You don't need a Reverend for that 'Repent!' stuff. You'll find people everywhere who agree that the world can't go on like this and will inexorably come to an end if something fundamental doesn't change. You don't even have to express a specific unease. Who's going to tell you you're wrong?"

"But isn't a bomb threat a bit different?"

"What's different about it – at least one like this?"

"All the same, it's an announced fact. It says something's going to happen soon, and anticipates that happening. They're not just words anymore. Surely that's a difference."

"As long as it remains a threat, it's no more than what you can hear every day, at any bar," he said. "You only have to go to the right places and let yourself hear who deserves to be put up against a wall or whose head deserves to be stuck in a bucket of shit, not to mention the more refined suggestions on offer."

I had never known him so combative, and when he went back to saying that none of it had anything to do with Daniel, I was inclined to agree with him. He said that the Israel dimension should not be overestimated either: it was just his love for a country that had attracted him since he had first gone with Herr Bleichert, and all he had said was that if eventually there was no place for him in the world any longer, he could at least go back to the Holy Land or, as he curiously put it, to Judea or Samaria. When he had spent those few months in Jerusalem after our summer by the river, Christoph had visited him, and what he told me about his visit explained a lot. I had always considered Daniel's penchant for the desert to be an eccentricity, one of his efforts to make himself interesting, but now I was reminded that for him it was the place in the world where you could get furthest away from the world, where advancing in the chosen direction and going backwards were one.

The two of them had driven around the country for a fortnight, and Christoph told me how in the beginning Daniel had sought out the locations they visited according to their names and incidence in the Bible, and then had chosen, more and more frequently, destinations that had no name.

"If you go there with false expectations, there are hardly any more bleak and dreary places on earth than the places where Jesus performed His miracles," he said. "Do you know the joke about how the Second Coming's never going to happen because He had enough the first time and has no intention of making a second trip to such a godforsaken landscape?"

With the exception, perhaps, of the Crusaders, it was exactly what travellers to Palestine had complained of ever since such a category had existed, and although I didn't doubt the validity of his observations, I nonetheless hardly understood why he was getting so worked up about them.

"Even Nazareth. What do you think it's like today? A run-down, 100 per cent Arab city with a few grotesquely tasteless churches. Even Bethlehem."

I found this somewhat tedious and told him that such disenchantment occurred with every book, not just the Bible, if you tried to equate it with reality. I remembered the few letters that Robert had written from America and his underlying regret that he had found nothing in St Louis of the St Louis of his Indian stories and that not even the Mississippi, be it ever so long and ever so wide, could match up to the Mississippi of his childhood imagining. For me this required no explanation, it was the good fortune and misfortune of every reader.

"You're not trying to tell me that Daniel was driving round Israel with his head full of Christmas cribs and winter dreams?" I said, because I was cross that I had let myself in for this conversation in the first place. "He might have been naïve, but not quite that naïve."

"But he still had that longing."

"What longing, exactly?"

"The longing to be moved."

I laughed uneasily but Christoph did not react, just said evenly that in fact he had been moved, once, on a single occasion on the entire journey, in Hebron of all places, where he had absolutely had to visit the Cave of the Patriarchs.

"It could be just because memories of the massacre are still so live there, but it could also be because we had to identify ourselves at both entrances," he said. "I still remember Daniel saying to both the Jewish and the Muslim guards that he was a Christian, and how it was something simultaneously painful and solemn for him."

"And what about you?"

"I told them I was nothing. Neither Jew nor Muslim nor Christian, and nothing else either. It's not the worst thing to have a choice and reject it."

"Didn't they insist that you were something?"

"No," he said. "'Nothing' was good enough."

At first they had shared the Jewish prayer room with a school group, then found themselves in the mosque on their own, staring at the sombre cenotaphs in front of them, when an attendant approached them silently from behind.

"We hadn't noticed him when we came in, but when he pointed to the tomb on the right and said, 'Isaac' – with a clear break between the two 'a's – and then pointed to the tomb on the left and said, 'Rebecca', with his Arabic accent and then walked without another word back to his alcove, Daniel stood quite still, as if he had been struck by lightning."

"Struck by lightning?" I smiled ironically at Christoph. "I'd like to know how that feels."

"I saw the horror that initially came over him, followed immediately by joy," he said. "I'm sorry, I can't put it any other way."

I had already noticed in Daniel's essays after his first trip to Israel what a double-edged experience he had felt it to be, suddenly to be able, to some extent, to walk around in the Bible. On the one hand he assimilated it as something completely familiar, as if he had finally come home, because he knew the names, and as if "the children of Israel" actually also referred to him, the way the Reverend had later extravagantly claimed, and on the other hand he was disappointed. The unattainable had come within reach, and all of a sudden it was exactly that that seemed to be his problem. He could enter the walls of Jerusalem by the Jaffa Gate or the Damascus Gate, or through the Lion Gate, as Jesus had in his final hours. He could leave the old town and on his way to the Mount of Olives find himself only a few steps away from Mary's tomb here, the Garden of Gethsemane there, or, over there, the tomb of Absalom, the tombs of the prophets; he could walk over the Mount of Olives and be in Bethany, the home of Lazarus, or go into the Kidron Valley and the city of David. The Way of the Cross ran through the Muslim quarter, right through the middle of an Arab souk, and the Place of the Skull, Mount Zion and the ruined Temple of Solomon with its Wailing Wall were within comfortable walking distance of the Austrian Hospice. The Temple Mount was the origin of the world, the place where God took earth to create Adam, the place where Cain and Abel offered their sacrifice and Abraham wanted to bring Isaac, his son, for sacrifice, but also the place from where Mohammed ascended to heaven. Everything lay at his feet and he could run through several thousand years of history in a single day, could stroll through the Old and New Testaments and their myths and embrace little digressions into the Koran too, as if he were out for a harmless walk and not performing a constant balancing act on a blood-soaked highway of history.

I could not help suddenly having all this in my head again, however much I resisted it. It was miserable to be dragged into that world, miserable to see how little it took, how much of it was still in your bones if you had grown up with the Bible, and how strongly it emerged above all as destiny, as fate, and not as the promised land that had kept you on your toes from childhood upwards. Of course I recognised in this Daniel the Daniel of our summers together out by the river, but at the same time he was foreign to me in the way he deliberately detached himself from the world, and yes, I found his solipsism repellent. It was his second time in Israel, and for the second time he bothered little about reality, even if Christoph claimed differently and maintained that it was all much more complex. All at once it came to mind what trifles we had wrestled with for whole afternoons at a time, and I wondered even more than I had before how much of his detachment might come from me. To us the most elegant thing had always seemed to be to move, wherever possible, from one position through a labyrinth of thought to its opposite, without, obviously, even touching the ground of reality, as if this were the most self-evident way to get from one truth to another. I did not know whether via such sophistries you could really render someone unfit for a more robust purpose, but I was glad Christoph disagreed with me. He himself had arrived in the country a few days after an attack in which two suicide bombers had killed more than a dozen people in the largest market in Jerusalem, and he said I would be underestimating Daniel if I thought he had not reacted to it with the same dismay as everyone else.

"I know you blame yourself for the books you gave him to read," he said. "But I don't think he found anything in them that didn't already exist inside him. If you want to know why he turned out the way he did, you'll have to look somewhere else for the reasons. Have you talked to Judith?"

"Yes," I said. "Why?"

"Because she's where you're most likely to find an explanation."

"Judith?"

"Obviously she wasn't the only one. Did she tell you about his phone calls at night and how he recited the Song of Songs to her? He tried that shtick out on other people too."

I was surprised by the conversation's sudden turn and by how sure Christoph seemed to be that he had the definitive explanation. It chimed perfectly with Inspector Hule's diagnosis of a young man who hated social situations and was likely to have profound difficulties in relating to the opposite sex, and it was how I found out about the incident that had ultimately led to Daniel losing his job at the Austrian Hospice, although I guarded against attaching too much significance to it because the way Christoph told me the story left me with the feeling that he was making a complicated story all too simple.

"He would accost young women in the Church of the Resurrection, of all places, apparently attracted by their devoutness, and follow them right around the city," he said. "It led to complaints and finally, after a particularly dumb blunder, to his dismissal."

I let him talk, listening with half an ear. Admittedly it gave me another story connected with Israel, but it was a story I would have been too embarrassed to tell. Not a word about the continuing conflict in the country, not a word about the real story, instead the woes of an unforgivably naïve one-time altar-boy who was apparently putting considerable energy into escaping those woes. I would have preferred it if Christoph had told me about Daniel's love for a Palestinian girl, full of meaningful details, it would not have sounded any less sincere, far from it, and would at least have enabled me to build up some dramatic context, a connection to a terrorist group, a tangible motive for a bomb threat, and so on. Instead he offered me a clumsy late developer whom I associated with bitten fingernails and the smell of unwashed laundry, a pitiful figure from whom women rightly fled to safety.

I couldn't shake off the impression that I knew less about Daniel than ever. I obviously hadn't really thought that a political dimension would crop up that would make the two bomb threats seem less absurd, or at least absurd in a different way, but I would have preferred anything to this literal dissolution of a figure, this literal blurring of the story into the murkily religious, its vaporising and beclouding in tired fumes of incense. Then there was Israel. I could not make any secret of how much discomfort it caused me, as Christoph carried on talking about it. After all, I had taught him history, and I felt his blatant omissions as a kind of provocation. It was on the tip of my tongue to ask whether they had been to Yad Vashem, but I didn't. I didn't want to hear him, perhaps triumphantly, saying no, as though he had to prove conclusively that he had grown out of school, or saying yes with an exaggerated groan – the same groan that was never completely absent when the essay topic was given out, as if some students were tired of being given that subject for the hundredth or thousandth time, even if I'd never given it to them before. Christoph had been one of my most interested students, and even Daniel had not closed his eyes to how, when you travelled in a country, you were likely to make assumptions about it; as was his style, he had asked me for books and I had given him, first and foremost, Primo Levi, then Imre Kertész and Aleksandar Tišma, and had viewed his silence when he returned them to me as a sign of his shocked response.

On a sudden impulse I again picked up the book I had been leafing through before Christoph appeared. It had lain on the wooden table between us throughout our conversation, and its more than thousand pages weighed heavily in my hand. I had read the odd sentence here and there and felt it reminded me of something, but it was not until I picked it up again that I was sure of what. It was Ayn Rand's novel *Atlas Shrugged*, the same book I had found outside the Reverend's farmhouse when I had driven out there to prowl around it in the middle of the night. I had found it on the ground by the front door and taken it with me without thinking. I had left it in the car, and later mislaid it again in the apartment, and when I finally did think to look for it, strangely enough I couldn't find it. It had been an English edition, obviously, a book I had not thought about since that time, but now, holding the German edition in my hands, I looked at Christoph.

"Well, well, this is a surprise," I said, and held it up excitedly in front of him. "You won't believe where I once saw this."

I told him the story, but when, in an effort to make a connection, I asked whether he could imagine the Reverend of those days carrying his crazy views right into the mayor's own house, he waved me away with his hand.

"It's perfectly possible, but what's your point?"

"I wonder whether Herr Oswald got the book from him."

"I wouldn't have thought so," he said, as though he found it unpleasant to be faced with the idea. "Admittedly it's not an easy book to get hold of, but of course he has his channels."

I asked him if he had read it, but he shook his head and a melancholy expression came into his eyes.

"Manon's the one who knows about it. It circulates as a kind of Bible among her father's party friends, although none of them takes the time to really study it. So he's asked her to do it for him and to tell him what's in it."

"And?"

"It's complete and utter trash, in my view. A fundamentally dishonest black-and-white portrait that you'll only find in America, although the author, as far as I know, was originally from Russia. It's not even worth discussing."

"It is, it is," I said. "You've made me curious."

He looked at me irritably and seemed to be considering whether I was being serious or whether I was pulling his leg, but then decided to answer anyway.

"It's about a group of people who think things can't go on any longer as they are and decide to go on strike. They believe that society doesn't value their contribution sufficiently, so they pull out of every activity, convinced that if they abandon the world, it will rapidly come to an end."

"Punitive action, then," I said. "So where do they pull out to? The world is everywhere. To another star?"

"No," he said. "To somewhere in the mountains."

"And after them the deluge?"

"Yes. A great purifying."

"What sort of people?"

"The ones who keep it all going, or think they do," he said. "Entrepreneurs, chief executives, managers. That sort. What's the word?"

"The elite," I said wearily. "Is that who you mean?"

"I've got no idea who else is supposed to be in on it," he said, apparently amused by the thought. "But there's bound to be room for the odd T.V. chef too, the odd celebrity hairdresser, fitness trainer and wayward daughter."

I was about to say the word, but he got there before I did.

"'The best', in other words."

The way he said it, they might have been extra-terrestrials, mutants from a sci-fi movie, perhaps with human faces but with completely different antennae and circuitry from those of ordinary mortals. You could see how happy it made him, how he was relishing the idea, and where before he had been holding in his feelings, he now cast off all restraint, exploding with laughter and gasping for breath.

"Imagine! The 'best' withdrawing from everything. Leaving us poor suckers all alone in the world, and firing themselves at the moon."

He did not sound as if he was saved at all. He seemed to have swung abruptly into a nervously boisterous, even downright hysterical mood, and as he went on being amused I noticed that nearly every time he laughed he glanced across at the villa, only adding to my initial suspicion of being watched from there. His rebellion had something of the rebellion of a child who, intoxicated by the power of his own words, simultaneously fears being punished for them. I did not know what he was compensating for, but if I needed any confirmation that it was no easy task being the son-in-law of a "Pöschte", and prospering and multiplying under his nose, or even merely twiddling your thumbs, this was it. I said nothing, feeling an oppressive sensation of having gained an insight into his life that I had no wish whatsoever to have, which was perhaps why he also backpedalled then and suddenly said that I should not draw any false conclusions: all things considered, he was very happy and could not complain. I assured him that he need not worry, and when he then offered by way of explanation that he had only got carried away because he had remembered our summer together, and looked at me as apologetically as if he were talking about some unforgivable aberration, the distance between us that was there, and had always been there, re-established itself.

I had not expected to meet Herr Oswald himself. I had not seen him since his appearance at my consultation hour many years before, but as he bore down on us along the path from the villa it was too late to say my goodbyes and duck the encounter. In my memory he was a much bigger, more powerful man, which was probably partly because I had been sitting down and he had been standing over me as he talked at me. He was walking quickly as he approached, and took the last few steps at a run, extending his hand to me as he did so and sitting down uninvited. He obviously remembered me but greeted me briefly, as if he could not recall the circumstances under which we had met. Instead he bristled with bonhomie, although he spoke not the dialect he had tried to intimidate me with before, but the sing-song, servile waiter's or servant's German into which, in our part of the country, even the roughest males can slip from one moment to the next if they feel it opportune, and which because of its servility makes you wish they would just bluster away in their usual fashion. Practically every street corner on the way to the Oswald property had sported a billboard with his picture, and given the gloss and bright colours of these images it was probably unavoidable that the original seemed rather pale and dull. He was being advertised as "best for the town", and I only had to think about how Christoph had been making fun of him moments before to feel myself on the point of laughter.

For some time it was not clear to me what Herr Oswald's intention was. For a while it looked as if he had only come to make small talk, perhaps in view of the forthcoming elections, and when he finally started to talk about Daniel I at first thought it was nothing more than that, and was astonished when it then became clear that he had actually known him. The business with the boy was sad, he said, apparently in no doubt that Daniel was responsible for both bomb threats. As far as I was concerned, this was the usual reaction, as it was when Herr Oswald added what a pity it was, because Daniel had seemed a clever and open-minded boy to him and would definitely have had a great future, if only someone could have managed to disabuse him of his religious fantasies.

Then I thought I must have misheard him, as he said that it was no wonder his daughter had fallen in love with Daniel first. As he said it, he glanced at Christoph to reassure himself that he had not gone too far, but at the same time left no doubt that he was free to say what he liked on his own premises. He said it as if it was something that had to be said if he was going to be fair to Daniel.

I cannot claim to have felt sorry for Christoph, but I looked at him in dismay as Herr Oswald patted his arm and, still turned towards me, went on to say that that was just the way it was in life, that you opted for second best if you couldn't get the best. It was a moment I can still conjure precisely in my memory. He made no effort whatsoever to make it sound especially ironic – either that or his irony had all been used up, because it was not the first time he had played this game, and in fact he did not seem in any way aware of what a monstrous remark he had permitted himself.

"The boy definitely had something special," he repeated. "I remember him coming to me once and asking me what was the thing I most missed from my childhood."

I had forgotten that Daniel had also included him in his survey, but of course he had.

"He had just come back from Israel and he may have been a bit over-excited," I said. "What did you say?"

I forced myself not to look at Christoph and to pretend to be interested in Herr Oswald's reply, but he just laughed at my question.

"As you may remember, I was mayor at the time," he said, as though it was an answer. "You don't have much leeway in that position."

He did not stop patting Christoph's arm, all the while keeping his gaze fixed on me and going on talking, all affability.

"I could have said my teddy and everyone would have thought I was being self-serving. You know what? No-one can imagine that a politician is a person with feelings. I could have said my first nanny, who put her arms around me after I went tobogganing one winter, and I would have exposed myself to ridicule because it would have been construed as a male fantasy."

"So how did you deal with the question?"

"I said I missed myself as the boy I had been. I missed myself in my blue suit at my first communion, between my father in an identical blue suit and my mother in her blue suit. I said I missed everything I believed in."

This outburst of sentimentality caught me totally unaware. I did not know what to say and this time turned to look at Christoph again, who had finally freed his arm but continued to sit where he was, not batting an eyelid. He seemed to have heard Herr Oswald's speech before and he contemplated him with expressionless eyes before saying that his esteemed father-in-law was becoming a little whimsical in his old age, putting just enough irony into his words to make it indistinguishable from bitterness. Then he stood up and excused himself, saying that unfortunately he had to get back to work, but making no move to go until Herr Oswald also rose to his feet. For a while they both stood in front of me, as though it was now up to me to decide who had won their exchange of blows, but just as I thought there might be more to come, Christoph turned quickly away without saying a word.

In front of the villa the two girls had reappeared. They had seen us and waved across at us. For a moment we heard their laughter, the laughter of youth that always sounded as if it found something comical in the mere idea of older people. Then, arm in arm, they walked down to the gate, turned around to us again and in a moment had disappeared like two creatures of the air.

I was back out in the street when it struck me that I should have asked Herr Oswald about the book. I had had the chance when he shook my hand and said that he hoped he could count on my vote in the elections. It was still going through my mind that perhaps it was not mere coincidence that I had walked off with the same book at the Reverend's farmhouse, and the idea that the madman could have exerted some influence over Herr Oswald would not leave me, even though there was no proof. At home I looked for my copy of the novel again, but was unable to find it. I wondered whether it might be among the books I had put up in the loft a while before, but just as I reached the point of deciding to go up and look for it, I restrained myself. I shrank from opening the banana boxes I had packed the books in. I had had great difficulty separating myself from every single one, but then was soon glad not to have them around me, although it took me some time to admit it. I had also stopped asking myself, when I was reading, what Robert would have said about a book I found myself liking, and I knew that I would have to separate myself from many more of my books in the future, perhaps even from my whole library, if I finally wanted to make my peace with him.

My visit to Christoph left me with an empty feeling. I was no wiser than before, and I told myself it would have been better if I had not gone. I had never thought very much about how the two boys related to each other, leaving aside the basic certainty of their friendship and inseparability, but Herr Oswald's revelation that Manon had been in love with Daniel first, however jokingly meant, started me thinking again about what chance elements determine a life that outwardly appears preordained, as though there was never any possibility of choice. It went completely against the grain to think that Daniel might have been the one in Christoph's place, living in the house next to the Oswalds' villa, but the more I disbelieved it and wanted to disbelieve it, the more I found myself thinking about it. I forcibly placed him at Manon's side, pictured him with her on the house's veranda, a couple like a thousand others, and in such images could see nothing more than another form of evil. It would have been impossible for him to play his role as Christoph did, and when I tried to imagine how he would have behaved inside the gilded cage, the bomb threats retreated into the far distance, but I could not allow my mind games to extend beyond a certain point or they ended even more inevitably in death and destruction.

7

IT WAS THE WEEK BEFORE THE SUNDAY OF THE SACRED HEART
that the bomb exploded. I write it like that because the newspapers
made a point of it, not just the local papers, the nationals too, and
not because I observe feast days or because I found myself lumping
the two events together the following year. To be honest, I found
the religious tagging increasingly sinister as time went on. It was
typical of Herr Frischmann to get off on it, and reading the article
he wrote about it, you couldn't avoid getting the impression that
he did all he could to introduce the timing of the explosion into
his editorial as frequently as possible – Sacred Heart this, Sacred
Heart that, not to mention that the piece was also full of talk about
the fight for freedom against the French, which is where the tradition started, except that that was 200 years ago and there are no
French left for as far as the eye can see, besides a few stray tourists
now and then, so that you have to piece together for yourself what
he means by muttering on about how it wouldn't surprise him
if the bomb-maker saw himself engaged in a similar struggle for
freedom as the heroes of old, who dedicated their country's fate
to the Sacred Heart of Jesus. I mention this so that you have the
full picture, and even if you were used to all this stuff from Herr
Frischmann it was of course total madness and full of his tendency
to take flight into realms where the air was thick with grievances
and conspiracy theories. He wrote that the explosion was indeed
a sad event but likewise a time to reflect, then launched himself

into a wild muddle of values, ideals and everything that had supposedly been lost and the necessity of fighting to get it back again, however hopeless a struggle it might appear to be. There was also, incidentally, the tradition that our region maintained of lighting beacon fires to celebrate the feast, and it was not the first time that, during the preparations of the preceding week, an accident had happened when people insisted on playing with fire.

I was at school when I heard the news. The head's secretary came to my class and asked me to go with her, saying that there was an urgent call for me. This was highly unusual, and as I hurried after her I puzzled over who it could be. I couldn't think, but then I heard Agata's voice on the line and she only needed to say one word and I knew. I didn't let her finish but promised I would be with her within a few minutes and rushed out without explanation. Luckily I had the car with me that day, and when I arrived at Bruckner's she had already shooed the few early customers out and closed up. She didn't waste a second. When she got into the car I saw that her face was unnaturally pale and her lower lip was trembling continuously. The head's secretary had said that she had refused to be put off and behaved like a madwoman, but nothing could have been further from the Agata I saw. It was only her accent becoming noticeable that offered any sign of what an effort it cost her not to lose control.

"It's only just happened," she said. "It can't have been more than half an hour ago. One of the regulars called me. He happened to be near the place and heard about it first-hand."

I drove away, asking her where to go and only noticing later that, either by accident or instinctively, I took the right direction. Obviously it had to be in the village, and when her account confirmed it, then it had to be either at the farmhouse where the Reverend had lived with his family back then, or in the very near vicinity. Since the two bomb threats a number of weeks had passed and a part of me had not thought anymore about them, while another part of me had visualised what the worst-case scenario might look like, yet never considered it possible that it could actually end like that.

"A proper bomb?"

What little Agata knew was quickly told.

"No games this time?"

"Apparently not," she said, her face turned away as though she was ashamed of the truth or as if it would help if she didn't look. "It sounds like it made a real bang."

I wondered if I should go on the autobahn, then decided to take the shortest route, across country on a gravel back road that was actually closed to cars and on which the grass strip down the middle was knee-high or even higher in places, but I paid no attention. I don't recall whether Agata talked to me or whether I'm imagining it and she sat next to me and said nothing, but I remember distinctly that she flipped the sun visor down and studied herself thoroughly in its little mirror. I looked at her and she smiled and pressed her lips together, as if she had just put her lipstick on. It was an odd face to make and I had no idea what she intended it to mean, but I think now that it must have been something like a child's defensive magic, an involuntary gesture. I turned on the radio, but however hard I listened, hopping from one station to another, could find no announcements, and strangely this calmed me, as though actually nothing had happened yet or at least that everything would be reversible for as long as it had not hardened into a news item.

"A real bang?"

After this I have discontinuous memory of how we got there, only individual images that are razor-sharp. I can still see the hayricks that flew past us as if our slipstream would blow them to pieces and leave only heaps of wood behind us, the electricity pylons between which the cables sagged almost down to the ground, and somewhere there was a tractor rattling forlornly along. In the distance the clouds piled up in high towers on top of one another, and I was amazed at how distant and immeasurable the land locked between the mountains could be, if you only looked at it from a different perspective. As we passed close to where the bomber had crash-landed I think I pointed it out to Agata, but the word "bomber" was enough for her just to look at me uncomprehendingly and immediately turn to stare at the meadow, where obviously there was nothing left to show that the fields had not always lain there as peacefully as they did now. For a few hundred metres the track ran parallel to the autobahn and I expected to see emergency vehicles, firefighters and police, but there were just a few cars crawling wearily along. Summer had recently started with a vengeance; in the air there was a buzzing like a thousand cicadas, and through the open window I could smell, beneath the overpowering smell of hops from the nearby brewery and the heavy smell of fields and earth, the smell I loved most, of the very first cut grass of the year.

The farmhouse the Reverend had once rented stood in the sun, and I drove up to it slowly. I stopped outside the garden gate, where at first glance everything looked the way it had that summer. There was a "For Sale" sign back on the fence, which had once been blown away by the wind and weather, and in the flowerbed next to the front door was a shattered windowpane. You might have called the garden overgrown, with its widely spaced apple and pear trees, but it had been overgrown back then and it would not have surprised me now if the two girls had come tripping out of the house as if it were a doll's house to resume their badminton game. I still had the plop-plop of their shuttlecocks in my ears, which measured the seconds like a metronome and which, if you listened long enough, produced the secure feeling that there would always be another stroke and it could never come to an end. I was about to drive off when I spotted the flag on the second-floor balcony. It was a Turkish flag, not particularly big, perhaps one metre seventy-five by half a metre, but hung the way that squatters in the cities hang their flags and banners. I paid little attention to that at the time, but was reminded of it later, when it was to play a role in the progress of the investigation. The background was that the owners did not want to rent to Turks, so the farmhouse had stood empty for a long time, although in this area every dump found a buyer or a tenant sooner or later and there was actually hardly any property in the area that was not in Turkish hands.

The people in the street, who were all hurrying in one direction, showed us the way. It was another three or four hundred metres beyond the village, where there was a house that had not even existed ten years before. It was one of those detached houses that are put up in the most unlikely places in the countryside, with two or three guest rooms, ornate wooden balconies, gathered curtains and a garage that from the outside looks almost as big as the whole living area – houses that are built to be lived in unchanged for a lifetime but are sometimes up for sale after a few years because things have gone wrong and either money or love has run out, or both, and the only thing left is another awful story of yet another man and yet another woman, whose details you're better off not even knowing. It stood with its back wall facing a nearly vertical rock face and only a few metres between the two, which made you think that once upon a time it would certainly have been built into the mountainside. That it was beyond the village's boundary made no tangible difference, obviously, but perhaps it was one of those things that struck at the soul, when you had to pass the nameplate every day to get home, then had it underlined by another sign calling out "Goodbye" as you went. In the winter months it could only have got a few weeks of sun, and some of that coldness radiated from it now, with its painstakingly plastered and white-painted walls, its satellite dish, its bull's-eye windows to the left and right of the front door and the evergreen blackness of the firs, barely as tall as a man, which had been planted all round it.

We had left the car and immediately started running, but didn't get far because a policeman blocked our way. There was no barrier or cordon, just this uniformed man in the middle of the road, doing his level best to look grim and not let anyone through. I begged him to let us pass, and when he wanted to know if I was a relative I said a former teacher and saw him prick up his ears, even before I found myself startled by my own description. I corrected myself, saying that of course I couldn't know, but he looked at me in an even more astonished way. I then mentioned Inspector Hule, which finally led him to take out his phone and call him. He walked away a few steps and I could not hear what he said, but when he came back he nodded.

"Stay here," he said. "Someone's coming for you."

It was not the inspector, as I had thought it would be, but Dorothea who turned up very soon afterwards. I would not have recognised her because I had only seen her in silhouette when I went to the police station, but I knew it must be her by the way she walked up to me and looked me up and down. She was a small, amazingly delicate-looking woman whose police equipment swung wildly around her as she got closer, giving her appearance a very animated quality. She stood with her legs apart in front of me and the palms of both hands resting on her low-slung belt, looking surprised.

"Well, no flies on you then, are there?" she said, and her voice seemed to echo with a trace of habitual mockery. "How did you hear about it so quickly?"

I launched into an explanation, but she waved it away.

"You can tell me all that later, when there's more time. You'd better come with me now. You may be able to help us with the identification."

It did not occur to me to ask whether this was the established procedure, as she turned her gaze to Agata standing half-behind me.

"Girlfriend?"

A nod sufficed, and we were through, and I remember that was the moment I saw the helicopter circling over the house, its rotor blades sometimes coming dangerously close to the rock face, then curling away again. It was also when I suddenly smelt the odour that hung in the air – a sharp, scorched smell. I thought of gunpowder, I thought of sulphur and rotten eggs, I thought what you always think about such smells, just to distract me from my first thought, that it smelt of burning flesh. Three police cars, parked as if they had come to an uncontrolled halt at the roadside, two of them with the doors still open, one of them with its blue light silently flashing, attracted my attention. Then I saw the ambulance and fire engine, then the men in uniforms scattered across the area, perhaps a dozen of them, although I immediately had the word "a hundred" in my head, and only at that point did I notice the garage and its metal door, hanging askew on its hinges. In the middle of the steep drive lay a tarpaulin, and there were no two ways about it, beneath it I instantly recognised the outline of a body.

I can still remember how familiar the situation seemed to me, the obvious explanation being that I had seen it all before in the cinema, or on T.V., yet it doesn't seem quite that simple to me.

The thing is, it's easy to say that something is like the movies, yet when you're actually in that situation you aren't thinking about it, or you're focusing on exactly what isn't like that. It's nearer the truth to say that you notice the difference between the two, and my perception anyway was confined at first to a feeling that I was hovering over the scene as I took the two or three steps up to the tarpaulin.

Doing so, I had not noticed that Dorothea had grabbed me by the wrist, but when I reached the tarpaulin I felt her suddenly slowing me down. A policeman was kneeling on the ground beside it, and I knew that at a sign from her he would pull it back. I thought of a plaster being peeled off a wound as I felt her fingers individually on my skin, and the only question in my mind was whether it would be done with a jerk or slowly and carefully.

"Are you O.K. to have a look?"

I didn't say anything, and the policeman glanced at Dorothea for confirmation before he uncovered the face. I don't know what I expected, but there was no trace of violence to be seen, apart from a trickle of blood from the left side of the mouth, white cheeks that were perhaps already a bit waxy, eyes closed except for a tiny crack, and yet it was very distinctly not the picture of a sleeping body. I stared briefly at it and nodded to the policeman, and he replaced the tarpaulin. I had bent down to look, and as I straightened up I looked for Agata, who had stayed standing further back and followed everything from there without really seeing anything. I watched her cover her eyes with her hands and for several seconds keep her eyes and mouth, and then just her mouth, covered with them. I became aware that I was shaking my head; it was only from her reaction that I realised I was doing it. I waited for a moment and looked at Dorothea, who touched me on the forearm and dismissed her colleague with a gesture.

"I'm sorry, but that's not him," I said, with an illogical feeling that I was disowning the dead man. "It's the first time I've seen this person."

I had avoided saying Daniel's name up till then, and continued to avoid saying it. It was up to Inspector Hule to do that, when he finally appeared on the scene. I can't say how much time passed, perhaps a quarter of an hour or twenty minutes, while Agata and I sat and waited a little way away on the lawn. I had listened to Dorothea talking into her phone, saying, with a glance at me, "negative", then turning to face me and going on to ask me to wait a moment longer; the inspector was on his way. It was his day off, but when his car stopped a few metres away from us he behaved as if it had been remiss of him not to have been the first on the scene, jumping out and giving the impression that he wanted to be everywhere at once. He looked around, his head bobbing in all directions, and eventually, less determinedly than miming determination, he strode over to where Agata and I were sitting. I automatically wondered what activity he had just broken off from doing, so assiduous did he look. I had only ever experienced Inspector Hule as calm and collected, but in his far from new casual clothes and trainers he radiated a sense of nervous disorientation, which may have come from the fact that there was something almost caring about him, a desire to take Daniel under his protection.

"It was my first thought, that it wasn't him," he said as soon as he greeted us. "Whoever the credit for the two bomb threats must go to, he's not so stupid as to blow himself up."

I hadn't given any thought to whether the two things were connected, and I was surprised at how quickly he drew his conclusions.

"I'm certain that we're dealing with a completely different case here. Only the biggest idiots do our work for us *and* clear themselves out of the way. This one, in addition, doesn't seem to have had much time for schoolboy pranks. It doesn't look as if someone was just experimenting with a bit of gunpowder or a school chemistry set here. He may well have had access to professional explosives. I can't explain the damage any other way."

He looked over at the garage, and I followed his gaze.

"Without a doubt it was an accident. If he had done it intentionally, he would have chosen a different place. Probably underestimated the danger, wasn't paying attention. Often a bit of heat or a bit of friction is enough for it all to blow up in your face."

I could imagine that it had taken plenty of force to lift the heavy metal door half off its hinges. Until then I had not even looked inside the garage, but I saw that the back wall was piled with electrical goods, which were apparently stolen, according to what the newspapers reported later. It was mostly washing machines and T.V.s, some still in their boxes, piled on top of each other and looking astonishingly orderly, compared to the shambles in the foreground. There, in the pile of bits of plastic, metal and wood and the tangle of cables and plugs, I could see what had once been musical instruments, a guitar or two, a drum, saxophone, maybe a violin. It looked like a band had been using the garage as a rehearsal space, but when I said it would be odd if the bomb-maker was one of the musicians, the inspector laughed.

"I hope you're not one of those romantics who thinks that just because someone twangs around a bit on some instrument or other, he's exempt from doing any of the bad things in the world," he said mockingly. "And perhaps the whole shebang is only there as camouflage anyway. If it was one of the musicians, that seems to me to be another indication that we're not dealing with the one who is responsible for the two threats. I'll bet you any money you like that this one doesn't play in a band."

He was in his element again, analysing, speculating wildly to himself, and when I asked what made him think so, he said it was just a sort of feeling, but a feeling that didn't usually deceive him.

"Whoever is behind this, it's my feeling that his world is a world of silence, and music would represent far too much life for him."

He turned to me with a jerk.

"You know that I don't think it's your former student, but let's assume it was him," he said, with undisguised pleasure at the memory of having used the phrase to me before. "Would you say that music was important to him?"

I had immediately thought of Daniel and how little he cared for music, but I was reluctant to encourage the inspector in his swaggering performance.

"He's young," I said evasively and as if, at a pinch, that explained everything. "How could music not be important to him?"

I knew how unconvincing this must sound and was glad that he showed no reaction. It would certainly have flattered his vanity if I had told him how Daniel had once said that the tumult of emotions he experienced while reading was enough for him, so long as he could explain cause and effect to himself, and he did not need music's inscrutability on top of that, but I did not feel inclined to give the inspector that satisfaction and said nothing. He had been squatting in front of us while he was talking, but now he straightened up, stretched and yawned. The sun fell on his face and he blinked wearily, beginning to look around him again as though he had only just grasped that this was reality. Until then he had not even looked at the tarpaulin, but suddenly stared at it, shaking his head. Then he crouched down again, saying that the dead man could not harm anyone else now, and what bothered him was the other one. As he said it I heard his breathing change, as if the short conversation had exhausted him.

"I can't imagine that he won't see this as having some sort of meaning for himself," he said. "Either it will placate him or he'll feel called upon to make some sort of gesture, to prove he's still alive."

He left us alone, and we made sure we left as quickly as we could. I took Agata's hand and physically pulled her along behind me. A barrier had been erected and when we came to it I saw that a television crew was setting up and for a while a reporter with a microphone ran alongside us and refused to be shaken off, even though we didn't answer any of his questions and stared fixedly ahead as if he weren't there. I was glad to get back to the car and I suggested to Agata that we could still go out to the river, but all she wanted to do was drive back. As she said it, she seemed to be only half-there, and I knew straight away that it was best to take her home, despite her protesting that she had to open the pub again or at least inform her boss that she was no longer in a state to do so.

We took the autobahn, and although I tried to speak to her I could hardly get a word out of her all the way back. When she got out, she held my hand for longer than usual, looking at me with that familiar deep look of hers that made her look years older. For a moment she said nothing, and then finally said she had thought it was the end and now she didn't know if she should be relieved or really start worrying herself stupid. As she said it, she smiled at me, and when she asked me what I intended to do now I gave her a vague reply, to avoid having to answer the question properly, taking refuge in trivialities and thinking to myself that I would probably go home, perhaps watch a movie, read something or go for a walk, or just sleep because anything else would make me more tired.

It cannot have sounded convincing, but right at that moment I could not offer her anything better. We said goodbye to each other, and for the next few hours I drove around aimlessly and tried to organise my thoughts. I stopped at the service area to drink something and finally, when it was starting to get dark, my restlessness took me back to the village. I don't know what drew me to the house again; I probably would not have got past the police cordon anyway, but when I came across a group of teenagers outside the farmhouse where the Reverend and his family had lived I stopped and parked. I wound down the window on the passenger side, and two of them detached themselves from the fence they were leaning against and came closer. I had done all this without consideration – not even how I ought to speak to them – and I can only put it down to my nervousness that, like the stupidest of idiots who wanted to be provocative, I brought out my few phrases of Turkish. I regretted it instantly, as they failed to respond and looked at each other as if they wondered whether they were dealing with a madman. Then the taller of them stepped forward, leant so far in through the car window that almost his whole upper body was inside the car, and hissed at me, deliberately emphasising his accent and smoothing the ends of his words to a soft mumble,

"Are you from the police?"

I shook my head.

"Why are you talking Turkish to us?"

"I lived in Istanbul for two years," I said, as though that made me definitively incapable of doing anything wrong. "I learnt some Turkish while I was there."

"You lived in Istanbul for two years, and you think that gives you the right," he said. "And so you speak Turkish to us."

As he said it, he leant even further in.

"Where are we?"

I didn't answer. He prodded me.

"I asked you where we are."

"In Austria," I said. "I didn't mean anything."

"So we're in Austria," he said, as though at last the most important thing had been cleared up. "What do people speak in Austria?"

I couldn't think of anything more intelligent than to point to the flag over the second-floor balcony. It was, after all, the Turkish flag, I said, and having noticed it straight away I had only wanted to be friendly, but he retorted that it could have been a hundred Turkish flags, it was nothing to do with me. He did not look up as he said this, before reverting to his earlier script, like an automaton.

"Do people speak Turkish in Austria?"

"No," I said. "That would be absurd."

"So why are you speaking Turkish to us?"

I was fortunate that at that moment the second one intervened, telling his increasingly weirdly behaving friend to leave me alone, I was all right. He pushed him aside and stood at the passenger door himself. He apologised, saying that the tension from the bomb was getting on their nerves, and I asked him if they had known the dead man.

"We never spoke to him, but obviously we knew who he was," he said. "The last few weeks he used to drive past nearly every evening in his van."

"On the way to his garage?"

"It looks like it."

"Didn't you ask yourselves what he was doing there?"

"He was always friendly," he said. "He sometimes shouted things to us through his open window, or smiled and held up two fingers in a victory sign."

To me this sounded like pure cynicism, partly because I had always felt there was a threat in the gesture, a mischief that needed no camouflage because it was common currency. Just imagining the scene gave me goosebumps. Nearly every day a person had driven past here, secretly nursing their future horrible triumph. Again I saw the soft, almost girlish face of the dead man in my mind's eye.

"A victory sign, of all things?"

That afternoon I had learnt a number of details about the man, and a history of xenophobia, as people described it, was one of them. Although nothing was yet known about the related writings that would be found when his room in the town was searched, he had a reputation, and whoever I talked to, it amounted to the same story. Dropped out of school, unemployed, allegedly in trouble with the police on several occasions, his last job had been at the abandoned, then briefly restarted, quarry site close to the cement works upriver, which explained the relative ease with which he had procured explosives. He had rented the garage of the vacant house with friends several months earlier, as a rehearsal space, but in recent weeks had only gone there by himself. The facts all fitted, almost too well, and the puzzle's final pieces were assembled in the days that followed, completing the picture of a man who was a loose cannon, with paranoid ideas about a threat from without, which would not have come as much of a surprise to anyone who knew the country we lived in.

I remember how I left the teenagers that evening. A wind had got up, the sun was about to dip behind the mountains, and all of a sudden, as I looked across at the fence and saw them all standing in a line, I had a yearning for flat country again, a yearning to leave this godforsaken corner behind and go somewhere far away. The boy who had threatened me had retreated a few steps, and the other one was still leaning on the passenger door and seemed to be waiting until he couldn't be overheard. Then he asked me where I had lived in Istanbul, and when I told him he said that his grandparents were from Anatolia but he had an uncle there, a bit further up the Bosphorus, and had had an invitation to go there for a long time. He wanted to know if I liked the city. I nodded. I told him I had lived just a few minutes from the water and had often walked up to the first bridge, and he replied with a laugh that when it came down to it I was more Turkish than he was, because he only knew it from photos. I didn't tell him any of what I had discovered about the dead man, but I couldn't imagine that he hadn't heard anything, and wondered, with every phrase we exchanged, what sort of conversation we were having. He was an alert boy, and if on my part talking to him was mostly out of a feeling of guilt I nevertheless couldn't see why he would play along with me. He became more and more polite the longer our conversation went on, and seemed constantly ready with another question, almost as if he wanted to divert me and stop me from going back to the explosion. Eventually I held out my hand to say goodbye, and waved to the others, and I remember wondering for far too long afterwards what they had made of my visit and what they would say to each other about me after I had gone.

My sense of unease grew in the days that followed. I was amazed at how quickly people allowed themselves to be reassured. It seemed as if most were satisfied that they at last had a perpetrator with a clear motive, however repugnant, and not the unknown phantom with his "Repent!" and his "Woe to you, Chorazin! Woe to you, Bethsaida!" There was a corpse, which had atoned for its act, and no-one seemed to want to hear sceptical views, expressed not only by Inspector Hule, that one thing had nothing to do with the other and that the suspected author of the two bomb threats might still be up to mischief somewhere. It was Herr Frischmann, more than anyone, who wanted to bring the story to an end once and for all and who thus did not bother much about logic or consistency, as long as he could come to the conclusion that our town, after months of tension, could finally breathe again and revert to its normal routine. I'm not sure whether he didn't know better or just didn't want to know better, but whenever he turned up at Bruckner's around this time, which all of a sudden was practically every day, I couldn't help thinking that he was holding court there, letting himself be fêted for the fact that he had urged calm from the outset. Whenever he saw me he nodded at me from a distance, and I was unable to decide where he thought this understanding between us came from. I acted as if I had not seen him, or turned away and was glad that at least he did not try to start a conversation with me, because if he had I would have had to tell him that I did not share his views on so many subjects.

I had intended to spend the night before the Sunday of the Sacred Heart at home, but when it came I was too restless, and as dusk fell I went out. I can't say I had been feeling queasy exactly, or even that I was worried something might happen, but even so it felt different this time. In previous years I had always gone out, but without attaching any significance to doing so. This year, I could not get what Herr Frischmann had written about the liberation struggle against the French out of my head. It almost sounded like a hidden message, although you didn't have to be in on the secret to understand it, and as I glimpsed the first fires being lit on the slopes all around, I wondered if it was all not perhaps quite as harmless as it was made out to be, and whether the folklore might not at any moment turn serious if a stray spark were to land on the right fuse. I remembered that there was an especially good view of the valley from the service area and I made up my mind to drive out there after I had walked around the town for a while and debated whether I should go and have a beer at Bruckner's. It was completely dark when I arrived, a cloudy, moonless and starless sky, and my gaze immediately fixed on the lone mountain in the distance that, in the penultimate year of the war, the burning U.S.

bomber had circled before it crash-landed. At first there were only individual lights to be seen, scattered over a huge area, but they multiplied and gradually joined up to form letters, and I already knew what the result would be before, in the far distance, the letters "INRI" assembled themselves out of the single flickering points, in sparkling red on a black background. As a child I had not understood their meaning, "Jesus of Nazareth, King of the Jews", and I still did not know what had brought this inscription, supposedly fastened to the cross, to our hillside at night 2,000 years later. I murmured the words to myself, but they made no sense either as glorification or insult, and I immediately stopped thinking about it and confined myself to silent contemplation of the flickering in front of my eyes.

After everything

INTO THE
DEEPEST BLUE

I WAS GLAD THERE WERE ONLY TWO WEEKS' TEACHING LEFT AFTER this. I have always liked the last days of term, as a teacher and as a student, but this time a real euphoria overtook me and I did not even feel the usual need to make myself scarce as fast as I could. Even when I had no classes to teach I tended to stay on the premises, to read in the staffroom or sit down at the edge of the football pitch and watch one of the class' games. After the bomb blast, my colleagues all greeted me as if they had done me an injustice, an attitude that was made harder to understand because they simultaneously behaved as if I must know more about it than they did or than what had been written in the newspapers. To which I should add that none of them had ever behaved so badly towards me in the past that there was any reason to apologise. So I could easily imagine what they were saying behind my back in their exchanges about what had happened. Whatever else, their relief was obvious, and Herr Bleichert did go so far as to say sorry to me without being able to say exactly what for, then took refuge in a monologue about how the whole rigmarole with Daniel had made him feel like going to the Holy Land again. The head, on the other hand, did what he always did when he was pleased with me, and sometimes when he was not, and invited me to dinner. Our mutual reticence, however, was so great that we failed to find a date immediately but left it that it should be sometime over the summer. I had told him I would be going away and, not just because I believed it myself, went to a travel agent and armed myself with a pile of brochures, as if I needed to exclude all possible destinations as impossible before admitting to myself that I was going to stay at home.

Very soon it will be two months already that I have been going out to the river nearly every day, and if there were no new school year about to start, if the summer holidays were not about to end and I did not have to consider at some point what to do when they do, time could have been standing still. Just as I did ten years ago, I started driving out there in the last week of school, the only difference being that this time it was more deliberate, even if my intentions were not too clear to me in the first days. If it had been an escape once, an escape from routine, that was no longer the case; it was more of a homecoming, although obviously that's not exactly the right word either. I have made up my mind not to return to the school. About everything beyond that I am at best undecided, and have only got as far as thinking that I shall go out to the house until the weather breaks in the autumn or until it starts to snow. So far I have not spoken to anyone about my plans, but I imagine just not appearing on the first day of school and it not occurring to anyone that I am not there, a childish idea I know, but not particularly bad, just a thought that soothes me instantly whenever I start fretting. I know that people will say I'm secretly waiting for the day when Daniel will turn up again, the way he turned up together with Christoph back then. It's true, I can picture them so clearly in my mind's eye whenever I think about how they rode up on their moped – the slightest noise of an engine in the distance is enough to remind me – but things do not repeat themselves. When I am down by the water and I lose myself in thought, it sometimes flashes through my mind that all I have to do is turn around and he will be standing behind me, but of course I don't turn around. I have my daydreams, and nightmares at night. I still have not been down to the gorge, but I know I will go down there one day; I have lost my fear of it and I don't have to do it now, the knowledge that I could do it at any time is enough. I watch the rafters who still come, hordes of them sometimes, as young as they once were, as unworried as they once were, when they come level with where I am and slow down and call something or just raise a paddle in greeting, boisterous boys and girls rowdily flaunting their boisterousness and happiness. Two or three minutes, no more, and they will be at the spot that I no longer picture to myself as the mouth of the abyss but as an opening through which the rapids run out into a wide pool, and I watch them go, full of trust, until they are lost to sight.

I don't think Daniel's in Israel, but purely for his sake I have been following the news, and when I see how the situation there is coming to a head yet again, I cannot get the Reverend and his prophecy, that this year is the year, out of my head. Assuming that he's still alive, the events must seem like a confirmation to him, the promised calamity that precedes the coming of the Messiah, the time of trial before the dawning of heavenly peace. At first it was just Gaza, supposedly to free a kidnapped soldier and because rockets were being fired from there into towns and settlements close to the border, but the army has also been conducting operations in the north of the country for a long time. The newspapers talk of a second Lebanese war, and I am certain the Reverend could say exactly why it all had to be that way – he would know the precise stage at which the world finds itself on the way to eschatological salvation. I only have to remember his maxims for him to reappear in all his craziness. The less I take them seriously, the more they stay in my head, and every time I read about fresh atrocities I hear his voice in that same preaching tone, telling me that wars are a sign of imminent peace, crime is a sign of grace, bad times are good. I can't imagine that Daniel believes it, even if he himself was the one who pointed it all out to me, and yet there remains in his bond with the Reverend an uncertainty that continually revives my doubts and that makes his character slip out of reach every time I try to put his life into some sort of context.

Of course there's plenty of work, when I want to distract myself. On the first day there, I set about straightening out the most important things at the house. There was less to do this time than in his day because the door had been locked and no-one had tried to get in, and apart from the dust there was hardly anything that needed clearing up. I collected the newspapers that were still there from Daniel's winter stay, cleaned the two rooms thoroughly, and thought about sanding the wood floor but then left it as it was. I repaired the damaged areas of the roof and enjoyed the old pleasure of pottering around outdoors. Collecting up the rubbish, cutting back the bushes, everything I had done before and now did again with the same relish, the same naturalness and feeling of having all the time in the world. I bought supplies, at first only food and drink for a few days, then eventually even started to fill up Daniel and Christoph's excavated stock. The two aluminium boxes were where they had left them, and I filled them with tins and water bottles the way they had. It was when I was busy with the shears around the overgrown hole that I cut myself. I looked for a plaster in the small first-aid kit, also dating from that summer, and sat down on the sawn bench near the entrance in the shade. I sucked on my bleeding finger before applying the plaster, and still had the taste of blood in my mouth when I picked up a piece of paper and a pen and started to write down this story.

The hikers have been here again almost from day one, on Sundays obviously but on other days too, and for all their speculating throughout that distant summer about what a schoolteacher was getting up to in the forest with two of his pupils, for all their outrage and indignation when they saw us lying half-naked in the sun, which was not even an accurate description as far as I was concerned, now I was definitely just another old codger to them, a weirdo who had created his own space in the middle of nature, as if he had resigned from the human race. Whenever someone approaches, I put my pens away, pick up my pages from the table I have set up outside and carry them into the house before going to sit and read on the boulder, which has become my favourite place, or making myself look busy some other way, or running, concealed by the bushes, down to the gravel bar and playing the person who's not there and doesn't notice anything anyway. Sometimes I even go and talk to them, up on the edge of the property, where it is entirely up to me how the conversation develops and whether they feel trapped and want to take their leave as fast as they can or stand there for a while and chat, the way you would to a neighbour over the fence back in the civilised world. The head came once, worried just as he had been worried before when it had come to his notice that I was out by the river a good deal, but I reassured him that everything was fine with me and he withdrew, shaking his head. One day Herr Bleichert appeared too, wallowing in sentimental memories about how he had done his best to persuade Daniel, as if it had all been nothing more than a harmless little episode and not a bitter experience for them both.

The other thing is the police. Since I have been here, not a week has gone by in which someone in a police uniform has not made their presence felt around the house. They creep up on me in twos along the path, they struggle through the undergrowth, and once one of them came up from the river – perhaps he had landed from a boat, and had only just zipped up his flies with clumsy fingers before attempting in some textbook way to take me by surprise.

They make sure I notice their presence and then disappear again, and when I call after them and ask what they want, I get no answer. I have mentioned it to Inspector Hule. I talked to him the first time he came out here himself one Saturday afternoon, in civilian clothes, and he said it was all routine, although he then added that if Daniel hadn't been responsible for the two bomb threats, it might be worth considering whether I should become part of their investigations. He passed it off as a joke, but as he said it he looked at me as if the idea didn't seem so far-fetched, and since then I can't help considering this ridiculous state of being observed in the same light.

Afterwards, to my astonishment, the inspector came back a few times more. I won't go so far as to say that I found his company congenial, but at least the stress was a bit less each time I saw him. He would turn up towards evening, probably straight from work, or perhaps it was the last task of his working day. He would bring something with him each time, a few beers, a bottle of wine, once it was strawberries, and sit down with me. After the first time he hardly asked any more questions, or at least none that seemed to be directed towards the two bomb threats, but just sat. He wanted to know what it had been like with the two boys that summer, and the question sounded innocuous enough. I started to tell him about it and found myself thinking what luck I had had, what an incredible gift those weeks, so completely and utterly out of time, had become to me over the years. I asked the inspector if he had heard about us back then and he said no, he had been working somewhere else, but if something about a schoolteacher and two students who were living together in a house by the river were to come to his attention today, he would self-evidently get in his car and go out to check on them. Then he laughed, as if he had not meant it, and sat blinking forlornly at the sun. I had a strong feeling that at that moment he regretted having become a policeman. He was a lonely man, whose loneliness had got into his bones, and I felt his long periods of silence almost as a physical act, exactly as if he were about to hatch something, and that when he got to his feet an hour or two later I would find a black, fossilised egg on the ground under where he had been sitting. I can't work out what he expected from his visits. Perhaps he thought his presence would, out of sheer empathy, bring him new insights, but whenever I saw him sitting there with his legs outstretched and his arms resting on his thighs, his fingers interlaced with each other, he looked more than anything like a man who did not want to go home.

It was somehow logical, then, that it was him who caught me committing one of my greatest acts of foolishness. One evening I had swum further out into the river than I ever had before, and when I turned around, intending to come back, I realised I must be more than halfway out and so made up my mind to head for the far bank. Carried a long way downstream, I eventually crawled, at the end of my tether, naked and shivering, onto the bank. I had the choice of making for the bridge further downstream, without clothes, which was at least two hours' walk away, or waiting until I had rested and warmed up again and then recrossing the river in the other direction. It was pure madness, but my mind was made up. I walked upstream until I was back level with the house, and when I got there saw Inspector Hule at the outermost end of the gravel bar, watching me. I couldn't hear him but he had probably been watching me the whole time and he was waving his arms, clearly wanting to stop me trying to undertake the return journey. I laboured on along the bank regardless, for about as far as I would be carried downstream again, and he followed me on his side. I saw him start to strip off his clothes as I put my first foot in the water, then almost at once I was so preoccupied with struggling against the current that the next I saw of him was when he was right in front of me, having reached me somewhere around the middle of the river. I could hardly get my breath anymore, and he shouted that I should hold on to him. He was a strong swimmer, and it was enough to have him close to me for my breathing to calm down. I held his shoulder just briefly and then swam on, slightly to one side and behind him, trying not to let it show that, against my belief and everything I had imagined about such a situation, I was on the point of praying.

We were hardly on dry land when he asked me if I wanted to kill myself. He stood, panting, facing me, and I did not answer. Because we were both naked I thought, weirdly, that that justified everything and no explanations were needed. We had got out of the water exactly at the gravel bar, where he had put an arm around my waist and, pulling and pushing me, led me back to the house like a limp doll. There he placed me by the door in a last patch of sun. He found a couple of blankets, threw one to me and wrapped the other one around his own shoulders. He made a fire and boiled water for tea. Without paying any attention to me, he sat down at my side on a tree stump and for a long time stared down at the river, where I realised there had not been a single rafter that day. He had not said anything else since we reached the shore, and when he suddenly wanted to know what was the matter with me and whether I would have swum back if I had not seen him standing on the other side, it wasn't a question anymore and he just looked at me for a while, saying nothing and shaking his head. Then he laid his hand on my forearm and looked into my eyes, as if he absolutely had to tell me something else, but although he had already started to tell me with his gesture, he left it at that and just kept shaking his head.

That was the last of his visits, more or less midway through the summer. I waited a few days, then went to the police station, where I learnt from Dorothea that he had unexpectedly gone on leave and left for Umbria. I could not work out whether he had told her what had happened, or if she had just tried to figure it out for herself, but when she said that I must have given him a lot to think about, to judge by the way he had turned up to work the morning after the last time he had been with me, in a state of complete agitation, I thought she could not know anything. I felt happy as I stepped out into the street again, and for a while I strolled around the town, lost in thought. It was almost evening when I walked into the town's bookshop and started browsing in the section devoted to guide-books. I found an illustrated book about Umbria, and I bought it and took it to the nearest café to leaf through, and the result was, as I had foreseen, I could not get enough of those yellow hills that marched away into the distance.

It was also around this time that I stumbled on a little book about Francis of Assisi among the remnants of Daniel's winter stay at my house. I had not thought anymore of it, but as soon as I got back I went and dug it out. The pompous, hagiographic tone of Hermann Hesse's text was probably as intentionally fatuous as it was unintentional, and I found it quite unbearable, but I looked at the frescoes of Giotto with which it was illustrated and in which various life stages of the saint were discussed, his famous sermon to the birds among others. In the book's small format of course I only got a rough idea of the impact they must have had in the original, but it was enough. From then on I left the book on the table where I sat down every day to write, made sure that it was with me in the mornings when I took my things out and that, open at this picture or that one, it was always to hand next to my rapidly growing manuscript.

That was where it fell into Judith's hands too. At first she came out a couple of times by herself. She had looked for somewhere to sit in front of the house, and after a brief conversation I had left her in the sunshine with her thoughts and busied myself with other tasks. The second time she was so quiet that I did not hear her, and she must have been watching me writing for a good while before I noticed her. In any case I had no time to put my things away, and from then on I made no attempt to hide anything from her when she came again. Then I just carried on writing for a while longer, and she would wait until I put my pencil down and turned to her. I had never asked myself what her son did while she was visiting me, so I was taken by surprise when she mentioned him one day. It was one of those swelteringly hot afternoons of that summer, and she had taken off her dress and lay no more than three paces away on a blanket in her swimming costume, lit herself a cigarette and leafed through the little book about Francis of Assisi.

"Next time I could bring my son with me," she said dreamily, between two drags on her cigarette, watching the smoke rise that, almost without opening her mouth, she had exhaled. "He's named after Saint Francis."

I had been so buried in my manuscript that at first I did not understand her properly and was mildly shocked to hear her beating her religious drum again, the way she had shocked me when I had gone round to visit her.

"After Francis of Assisi?"

"You know what his name is."

"Yes, of course," I said, although in fact I wasn't sure whether I did know his name. "You can bring him with you, any time you like.'

Having issued the invitation, I regretted it almost immediately. The idea of having the boy around me aroused all sorts of feelings, but enthusiasm was not one of them.

"He loves nature, and the fresh air would do him good," she

said, full of enthusiasm. "You could be the man in his life. I'm sure he would like being outside here. You must just promise me something."

I did not say anything, and she blurted it out.

"Promise me you won't turn him into a bomb-maker."

"What makes you think that?"

"Promise me," she said. "No experiments."

I was so nonplussed that I could only look at her questioningly.

"No books that he absolutely has to read. No theories about the meaning and meaninglessness of life. No unnecessary complexities, when everything is basically simple."

It should have been funny, and I wanted to pay her the compliment of laughing, but I could not quite manage it because I could not overlook what she was saying about me. I ought to have objected, but I nodded. It also seemed absurd to talk to me in those terms, when her son could neither read nor write and had the mind of a five-year-old, although perhaps that had to be part of the joke she had allowed herself. She had stood up and was standing in front of me in her swimsuit, with one elbow supported in her other hand and holding her cigarette between her middle and ring fingers. She had smoked it down almost to the filter and with screwed-up eyes took a last drag before stubbing it out on a stone and carelessly tossing it onto the gravel in front of the veranda.

"You take everything far too seriously," she said, her head artistically wreathed in a cloud of smoke. "Maybe one day you'll be able to see that there are things you're not responsible for and that maybe aren't even anything to do with you."

It sounded like an absolution, but it was the least useful thing in the world if she could not tell me what from. Up until then we had avoided talking about Daniel, and even now I didn't ask her if she still felt scared that he might suddenly turn up at her door, or whether she, like most of the others, had accepted that the case was closed, despite all its inconsistencies. The allusion to him seemed all too clear in any case, and while I thought about what I should say in reply, the memory of how she had come out to the river that summer and of how I had watched her and Daniel together down at the water suddenly overwhelmed me. I did not know why it was that picture specifically, but all at once I saw them again, together with Christoph, and remembered the distance I had felt. She had already been pregnant by then and had come to say goodbye, but it was not that. It was something to do with Daniel and with his sadness that day, his melancholy view of his life in the near future. I still had his precise words in my head, the way he had said that he assumed he would be happy, and the thought of the conversation we had had afterwards made me want to tell her about it. Instead I said nothing and returned to my manuscript. She stayed standing where she was for a while, as if she did not want to let me get away that easily, but then went back to her blanket and stretched out again and lit herself another cigarette.

I hadn't foreseen that she would bring the boy the very next day, but even less had I foreseen what the consequences would be. I had thought he would perhaps come out once or twice and that I would be a bit distracted from my work, but no more than that. It must be said that I did not really know how to behave towards him the first time, and I would not have been surprised if it had turned out to be the last. I was down at the river when Judith arrived with him and did not hear them approaching along the gravel bar, and when I turned around and they were standing less than two metres away, I jumped. I did not actually shrink from them, but there was a moment when everything could have gone wrong. I remember Judith's uncertainty, how she hesitated, her hands on his shoulders as though she was undecided as to whether she should push him towards me or keep him at a distance, and how he broke away from her, took a step forward and held out his hand. He was wearing short trousers and a shirt buttoned all the way up and on his head he had a cap with an outsize peak, from under whose shadow he peered up at me and asked if it was true that I was a school-teacher.

It was a moment of embarrassment, and though much has changed since then he still peers at me with that look sometimes. I am not trying to say he chose me, but from the start I enjoyed having him around, and in fact he's with me almost every day now. Judith sometimes brings him before lunch and the three of us spend a while at the river, just sitting there or walking along the bank, and I catch myself holding hands with him and then with her, or she leaves the two of us on our own for hours. Then I go down to the gravel bar with him, the way I did with Daniel and Christoph, and watch him while he collects stones until he finally finds the right one and cannot make up his mind whether he should use it for throwing or put it away and keep it. I have made him a fishing rod and line that he holds tirelessly over the water without ever being disappointed by not catching anything. I have made him a bow and arrow, and when I tell him that there are Indians on the other side, he says that we need to arm ourselves better, we need guns, and I say yes and he is entirely satisfied when I hack him off a branch and tell him that's his shooter and he shoots it wildly in every direction, able to open his mouth and produce half a dozen sounds of gunfire and ricochets and jamming and I don't know what else. We pad together through the undergrowth, or I watch him clamber up a tree, then retrieve him like a cat from the branches when he no longer trusts himself to come down. He randomly drags in things he finds in the forest: a woman's shoe, the remains of a crow, a used condom that has become porous from lying there for so long, or a rusty harmonica, a deflated leather football, a half-rotted straw hat. He loves fire, and when I let him persuade me to light one in the middle of the day he sits in front of it and cannot get enough of staring into the flames. Then every time he wants to know where we would go and what we would do if everything caught fire, and I put an arm around his shoulders, pull him to me and stroke his hair. He watches out for the trains. He dreams of building a raft. He wants to fell trees with me, strip them of their branches, tie the trunks together and then travel with it as far as it will go. He asks me where the river goes, and I tell him, and Judith tells me that he has memorised all the places it passes through. I don't tell him that we would not get far and that we would probably be stopped very soon by a weir, bad weather or a police search party. Among the books in the house I have also found an atlas, and when I leaf through it with him and ask him where he would most like to live, I can tell him as often as I like that that place won't work because there's only water there, but he keeps pointing without fail at a spot in the mid-Pacific or mid-Atlantic, into the deepest blue.

Of course I don't pretend to myself that this can go on for ever. I have already mentioned the hikers, who have started to reappear and who stand unashamedly at the boundary of the property and squint at us. I don't know whether there have been more since the boy started coming out to me, but I know they will have an easy time making up stories if they want to. In fact it would be far easier this time to make up a story that I really wouldn't be able to talk my way out of, a schoolteacher and a child alone out by the river, and to top it all, a boy of unprecedented innocence and helplessness. But it has not reached that point yet. The summer is still holding, even though the calendar says that these are the last days; hardly a breath of autumn but the forest floor between the trees is nevertheless soft with fallen leaves. I like walking on it, and the boy follows me. He stops and stands still in the middle of the forest when I stand still, and looks up, listening, into the treetops that sway with the wind before looking across to meet my gaze and setting off again.

NORBERT GSTREIN was born in 1961 in the Austrian Tyrol, and studied mathematics at Innsbruck and Stanford, California. He is the author of *The English Years*, which won widespread critical acclaim in Germany and was awarded the coveted Alfred Döblin Prize. This was followed in English by *Winters in the South* (2012), and in 2013 he was the winner of the Anton Wildgans Prize for his work.

JULIAN EVANS is a writer, a journalist for French and English publications, and translator from French and German. His translations include works by Michel Déon, André Gide and Jean Hatzfeld from the French, and *My Father's Keeper* by Stephan Lebert from the German.